HARLEM☀MOON
BROADWAY

A Miracle Every Day:
Triumph and Transformation
in the Lives of Single Mothers

The Edge of Heaven

Gumbo: A Celebration of African American Writing
(edited with E. Lynn Harris)

Don't Play in the Sun:
One Woman's Journey
Through the Color Complex

AFTER

A Novel

MARITA GOLDEN

HARLEM MOON
BROADWAY BOOKS
NEW YORK

PUBLISHED BY HARLEM MOON

Copyright © 2006 by Marita Golden

All Rights Reserved

A hardcover edition of this book was originally published in 2006 by Doubleday.

Published in the United States by Harlem Moon, an imprint of The Doubleday Broadway Publishing Group, a division of Random House, Inc., New York.

www.harlemmoon.com

HARLEM MOON, BROADWAY BOOKS, and the HARLEM MOON logo, depicting a moon and a woman, are trademarks of Random House, Inc. The figure in the Harlem Moon logo is inspired by a graphic design by Aaron Douglas (1899–1979).

Book design by Jennifer Ann Daddio

Library of Congress Cataloging-in-Publication Data
Golden, Marita.
    After: a novel / Marita Golden.
       p.   cm.
PS3557.O3593 A69 2006
813'.54—dc22
                    2005044853

ISBN 978-0-7679-1778-0

PRINTED IN THE UNITED STATES OF AMERICA

10 9 8 7 6 5 4 3 2 1

First Paperback Edition

To Joe, always there

ACKNOWLEDGMENTS

The list of people who gave me valuable guidance, suggestions, ideas, and information during the three years of writing and living this book is long, and I am grateful to them all. My agent, Carol Mann, was an early and enthusiastic fan of the idea for this book, and she was, as always, a voice I listened to and heeded. My editor, Janet Hill, nudged me and when necessary pushed me (always gently) in the right direction to tell the best possible story. She is an "old-school" editor who knows that every word counts. I especially owe a huge debt of thanks to Commander Markus Summers for the time he took to read and reread the manuscript, and for the many conversations we had about the story, and about the lives of the men and women who are sworn to protect and serve. Markus imparted to me so much that was valuable not just about a difficult job, but about the nuances and lessons embedded in the lives we all live. Dr. Beverly Anderson helped me to understand the effects of trauma and loss in the lives of police officers, and her comments greatly increased my compassion and empathy for my characters. I thank as well Akintunde Michael Kayode, Leo Bowman, Rodwell Catoe, Sharon McInnis, Chief Brian Jordan, Randolph Perrin, Mark Moore, Ernestine Rashun Williams, Ted

Williams, Steven Sunday, Sonsyrea Tate, Kenyatta Dorey Graves, Cathy Drain, Terry Anderson, Antoinette Lee, Sis Pittman, and Damaris Hill. Thanks to anyone not recognized here but who helped make this possible, and as always my husband, Joe Murray, for being who he is and for believing me into doing so many amazing things.

AFTER

BOOK

1

1

The bullets discharge from the muzzle of Officer Carson Blake's sixteen-round Beretta with the tinny, explosive popping sound of a toy gun. He will not remember exactly how many shots he fires so wildly. Fires with pure intent. Fires, he is sure, to save his life. In the first seconds after the shattering sound of the bullets subsides, he would say, if asked right then, that he had fired every bullet in his gun. Never before has his gun been so large. Never before has it weighed so much. He's dizzy and breathless. His heart beats so fast, he can't believe he is still standing.

When he shoots the man, everything, all of it, unfolds as if in slow motion. He wants to look away. He dares not turn his gaze. The first bullet boring through the man's thick neck riddled with razor bumps, the force twisting his head to the side, as though he is looking with those astonished, horribly open, not yet dead eyes to see where the bullet comes from. The second bullet piercing the skin of the black leather jacket, lodging in the flesh of his shoulder. The third bullet, fired at his groin, bringing him to his knees and then onto his face, sprawled flat out on the parking lot forty feet from the entrance to the Chinese restaurant The House of Chang.

Carson stands staring at the man on the pavement, his body a bloody heap illuminated by the fluorescence of the mall parking lot lights, and sees the cell phone a few feet from the man's hand, and he prays for the ground beneath his feet to shift in a cataclysmic rumble and swallow him whole. *A cell phone*, he thinks, unbelieving. *A cell phone*. Not a gun. He hurls a howl, deep and guttural, into the night. Sinking to his knees, he touches the man, turns him over onto his back, sees the bulbous, bloody wound in his neck, smells the sharp odor of his sodden groin, desperate now to find, to feel, a pulse. There is none. There is only the cell phone. Looking up in desperation, Carson sees a sky unfamiliar and frightening, in which he can fathom not a single star, a vastness that makes him wish for wings.

Carson tries to stand but cannot, and he crawls a few feet away and vomits. When there is no more sickness to spill from his gut, he wipes his mouth and shouts at the dead man, through trembling lips stained with a blistering splash of tears, "What the fuck were you doing? Why didn't you just do what I said?"

There is nothing on this night that hints at disaster. After twelve years on the force, Carson can tell when a shift will be hell on wheels. On those shifts, the dispatcher begins reciting an address and an "incident" (car crash, domestic disturbance, robbery, brawl, accident, murder) even before Carson is belted behind the wheel. Then there are the calm, quiet shifts when hour after hour he's numb with boredom, cruising the nine square miles of his police service area, and after a couple of hours he begins looking for a safe place to park and take a nap.

But he can't get bored. Because bored he won't see the obvious—the missing tags on a beat-up hoopty driven by a carload of young punks looking for trouble and determined to find it. But this night he is bored by 9:45, when he walks into a 7-Eleven near the litter-filled streets of a housing project known as "The Jungle" to buy coffee and a doughnut. Carson ignores the group of high school–age boys hanging out in front of the store at almost ten o'clock on a school night, rapping, jonin', joking, lying. Matches waiting to be struck. *Don't they have homes?* Carson wonders for the thousandth time, then recalls what he has seen in some of the homes these boys live in—rats, roaches, three kids sleeping on the living room floor, toddlers playing near stacks of cellophane-wrapped crack cocaine, no heat in the winter, stifling ovenlike apartments in the summer, overworked mamas, long-gone daddies. Those homes make the parking lot of 7-Eleven seem a step up in the world.

Still, why the hell were they standing outside to talk? *Just hangin'.* He'd read somewhere that this was street corner culture, an integral part of the Black experience. Some urban ritual. But this is Prince George's County. No inner-city street corners here, like in nearby D.C. *But niggahs*, he thinks sullenly, can turn anyplace into a ghetto.

Nearly all the arrests he's made, all his stops, involve boys like the ones he barely looks at as he passes by, feeling them grit on him with a steely stare because he's a police officer. To them he's a cop and he is, in their eyes, the enemy. He's fed up with arresting young Black males—aimless, directionless, often involved in nonviolent crimes that set the stage for all the shit that hits the fan in their young lives. Just last week he was called to the scene of a shooting and saw a kid no more than seventeen, dressed in spanking new jeans, two-hundred-dollar Air Jordans, and a Phat Farm sweatshirt, loaded into the Emergency Services vehicle, *dead*. Shot in the back while standing outside a Popeyes, from the passenger side of a Crown Vic that careened past the spot where he stood munching on a spicy chicken breast and a biscuit while talking to his baby's mama. The car didn't even slow down to make the hit. As Carson watched the EMS vehicle drive away, he wondered how many hits the kid had made. Revenge, payback, and a brutal, bloody synchronicity ruled the lives of too many of the young men he arrested. He saw precious few truly innocent victims. Predators, that's what he calls them, kids like that fourteen-year-old who walked into a convenience store in Oxon Hill and tried to rob it at 5 a.m. and ended up stabbing the Korean owner to death. *What the fuck?* Carson sometimes wonders. *God damn, my people, my people*, envisioning the future of the race in every act and every choice these young men make. He's tried to talk to them, standing in groups like these or in handcuffs in the backseat of his cruiser, but he might as well be speaking Mandarin.

So yeah, he is tough, and he is hard on their Black asses. There but for the grace of God . . . He has a son who in his worst nightmares turns into a wannabe thug giving these young bloods a run for their money. None of it makes sense. On more than one shift he's arrested suburban Black boys from *Leave It to Beaver* homes, hungering to be criminals, proving their street smarts by being stupid enough to land in jail. He's arrested boys with a plasma TV in their basement and their father's BMW SUV and mom's Lexus and their Honda parked in the garage. He'd been a young punk once too, angry, feasting on his own sense of deserved and superfluous rage at a world he couldn't control and that he was sure would never give him room. But bored, this night, Carson doesn't even say a word, just figures his presence, the patrol car, the weapon the boys know is in his holster, will do all the talking for him. He swaggers past the cluster of boys, all of them dressed in baggy jeans and oversize shirts, blue bandannas tied around their cornrowed heads. Carson strides a bit more forcefully than usual, preening to let them know that the convenience store is his turf, not theirs.

Everybody thinks it's postal workers who are the major victims of workplace crime. It's really the immigrants and teenagers and retired giving-my-own-business-a-try salesclerks behind the counters of convenience stores who are the most vulnerable workers in America. It's always open season on them. Every damn day of the week is a "good day to die" for one of them somewhere in the land of the free. By just standing at the magazine rack, thumbing through copies of *Hustler* or *Newsweek*, or shooting the breeze for a half hour with whoever is working, Carson can stop a crime.

Because Carson doesn't tell the boys to move on, to go home, they continue to stand outside, as loud and boisterous as if they were playing video games and sipping forties in their living room instead of standing in a public place. He could get them for congregating beneath the No Loitering sign, but he doesn't.

He and Eric used to debate all the time which was worse, more dangerous: the boredom that makes you lazy, careless, stupid, or the nights of pure adrenaline, responding to priority calls back to back. And don't let it be another officer down. But that's why Carson is out here. Why he's a cop. He loves the rush. The risk. Everything on the line. The pressure. The chance to change somebody's fate, save a life, because he got there in time to catch the burglar, prevent some jerk from giving his wife an ass-whooping and turning her into a corpse. Or maybe he stops a killer on the side of Route 450, pulls him over because the knucklehead is driving a car with broken taillights, expired plates, and when he runs his license through the computer he discovers this is a live one, the kind of scum they build prisons for, and when he searches the car he finds a weapon. And not just any weapon, but one that's loaded and has been used in a murder.

Still, 95 percent boredom. That's Carson's average week. Sometimes his average month. This isn't nearby Washington, where there are weeks when somebody gets killed every night. This is the 'burbs. But still.

On this March night, a night when it is not quite spring, when it's a chilly forty degrees, there's this flat-out wide-faced moon in the sky. A moon so big and awesome it's like a gigantic neon eye or face. A full moon, bursting the seams of the heavens. Milky and liquid and trembling. It's not white but some strange kind of or-angey yellow, like no moon Carson can ever recall seeing in the sky. *The full moon.* That's the only odd thing. The only unexpected thing on this night, when Carson has given a couple of speeding tickets and the radio has been mostly silent.

Carson isn't superstitious. Not like Steve, who keeps a rabbit's foot in his wallet, or Eric, who recited the Twenty-third Psalm, closed his eyes and said it silently in the squad car before he pulled out of the station lot. *"The Lord is my shepherd, I shall not want."* No, Carson figures all that just attracts catastrophe. Why depend on luck instead of yourself? Why close your eyes to pray when what you fear could be closing in? So that moon, which he will tell Bunny about if she's awake when he gets home, that's the only strange thing so far this night. His patrol service area includes everything—the area around Martin Luther King Boulevard, the weathered houses and streets of the working-class neighborhood near the FedEx Field football stadium, and the moneyed commu-nity called Heaven's Gate. It's mostly the area around King Boule-vard that keeps him busy with burglaries, robberies, drug traffic. But this night, one hour before his shift ends at midnight, Car-son congratulates himself. It's been quiet. Maybe too quiet, even for a weeknight. But there is nothing in the quiet that makes him think that the worst will be saved for the last moments of his shift.

Half an hour after leaving the 7-Eleven, he's making one last swing around Enterprise and Lottsford roads, past million-dollar houses and the estates behind the barriers of gated communities. He isn't doing *that* well, but with his salary and the $25-an-hour part-time security work he performs, and Bunny's recent raise, they are a $150,000 household and he lives fifteen minutes away. He doesn't live in Heaven's Gate, the community he's just passed that has been written up in magazines and even the *New York Times* as symbolic of Black suburban progress. He lives in Paradise Glen, and Carson is just as happy in paradise as he figures he'd be in heaven. He knows police officers who drive Jaguars and Benzes, have high-six-figure salaries, and are in debt up to their ears, cops addicted to doing nothing but working and making money the way some are in the grip of booze and women.

Carson spots another squad car parked in the lot of Kingsford Elementary School. When he pulls up beside the cruiser, he immediately sees that it's Wyatt Jordan. The fluorescence of the parking lot lights glows on his massive shaved head. Carson parks beside Wyatt and gets out. He stretches his arms and shoulders as he walks around to the other side of his cruiser. Jordan's thick, rumbling laughter is the only sound besides the occasional car cruising past on Enterprise Road. The conversation, which Carson hears through Jordan's half-open window, has the sound of an easy, illicit dialogue, and he figures Jordan is having phone sex. There are all kinds of rumors about Jordan, that he's hooked on Internet porn sites, and Carson knows he's a player, has seen him in action. He's been busted more than once for stopping by his girlfriend's house for a quickie while on duty, and his wife waited for him to get off his shift one evening and jumped out of her Volkswagen and charged after him with a baseball bat.

"Drama Queen" is Carson's nickname for Jordan. He's got no respect for cops who let their lives become a public mess. He knows Jordan from a distance, and he's fine with that. But hell, he can shoot the breeze for a minute. Jordan ends the call and snaps the cell phone shut.

"Am I interrupting something?" Carson asks, leaning on the side of the cruiser, letting a wide, wily grin spread over his face.

Jordan extends his beefy arm out the car window, a raucous laugh rumbling up from his chest. The two men slap palms and shake hands. "Come on, Blake, ease up—I know what you heard, and it's all true."

"All the hardheads must be working a new shift or stayed home instead of risking running into you," Carson says.

"That's what it looks like. Only real action I had tonight was a domestic disturbance call over near Bowie High School. By the time I got there, the dude didn't wanna press charges."

"Say what?" Carson laughs at the thought of where this story is headed.

"No joke." Jordan opens the door of his cruiser and lifts his bulk out, leaning on the side of the car. He's six-seven, two-seventy-five, and solid as a rock.

"You heard me. Dude was getting a Mike Tyson work-over by his girlfriend. He had a black eye. I did the counseling routine. When I got there and saw what was happening, I figured she kicked his ass over another woman. But she claimed he stole some of her money. In my man's defense, though, she had about three inches on him. He was drunk and kept telling me he called 911 'cause he didn't wanna hit no woman."

"So this was love and money?"

"Yeah, you know, half the calls are rooted in one or the other."

"You going to the cabaret at the Chateau Saturday night?"
Carson asks.

"I'ma get my ticket at the door," Jordan says.

"I ain't gonna tell you what I had to do to get Saturday night
off—I owe Benson big-time," Carson says sheepishly.

"Out with it, tell me . . ."

The two men stand gossiping, trading an easy banter that makes
Carson ponder that this is the first time in a long while that he's
really talked to Wyatt Jordan. Jordan finally looks at his watch and
says, "I better start heading back in. And I hope like hell I don't
run into anything on my way."

Jordan pulls out of the lot and Carson sits in his squad car, sa-
voring the silence, the night, and once again looks at that damned
full moon. He has decided to follow Jordan in when a car with no
lights speeds past on Enterprise Road. He should just let it go, let
it slide. He'd been thinking about his warm bed in the moments
before the car sped by. But he isn't that kind of cop. He doesn't let
much slide. He didn't become a police officer to let shit slide.
There have been several carjackings in the area in the past month,
and Carson wonders if the idiot speeding by with no lights is some
teenage car thief who could cause a fatal accident or some psycho
like the predator who waited outside the home of a doctor a mile
away and shot him outside his house, stole his wallet, and used his
credit cards an hour later, or maybe some kid from D.C., out
joyriding in the county.

Carson pulls out of the parking lot and puts his lights on, ra-
dioing in to the dispatcher, "I'm behind this guy who's speeding,
no lights, and he's not stopping."

"Do you have backup?"

"No."

Carson hears Jordan's voice break into the call: "I'll head back
over there."

Carson's all up in the ass of the car, glued to the vehicle, but the driver won't stop. The black Nissan crosses the intersection and finally the driver abruptly pulls into the near-empty parking lot of a strip mall. By the time the car has stopped and he's parked behind him, Carson's skin is tingling and he's tense, buoyed by the involuntary adrenaline rush that's an invisible body armor, priming him for action.

"Get out of the car, sir," Carson yells, approaching the car, his Beretta pointed at the man behind the steering wheel with his hands in the air.

"Open the door slowly."

The door opens and the driver steps out as Carson moves back. He's twenty-five or twenty-six, Carson guesses, clean-cut, sober-looking, with a serious, proud, unflinching face. He's wearing expensive jeans, a bulky sweater, a leather jacket, and Timberland boots. His hair is braided and he's got a chiseled, tough/soft handsomeness that reminds Carson of the Black male models he's seen on the pages of *GQ*, advertising Hugo Boss suits, or the actors on Bunny's favorite soap opera, *The Young and the Restless*. He's that smooth. And for all his disarming good looks, the man standing before him could be a robber, a murderer, or just an unlucky SOB caught speeding when he thought no cops were around.

"Turn around, face the trunk of the car," Carson orders. "On your knees. Put your hands behind your head." The man drops to the ground and faces the trunk of the car.

"What did I do? Why was I stopped?" he asks, his voice injured, surprised.

"What'd you do? You crazy, man? Fleeing an officer. Driving with no lights."

"What? I wasn't eluding you. I didn't realize my lights weren't on. I mean, I had an argument with my girlfriend and I've been f'd up all evening," he says, turning to look at Carson to make his point.

"Where's your license? Your registration?"

"In my wallet in my back pocket."

Carson begins to approach the kneeling man when he sees him drop his left hand and reach inside his waistband.

The quick, small movement chills the night and freezes Carson's blood.

"Put your hands up," he shouts, a surging infusion of fear flooding his insides, as liquid and warm as blood.

He's no longer a pretty boy but a looming threat. The man is holding an object in his left hand, smooth, hard, shiny as the moon in the sky.

"Put your hands up." Uncertainty balloons inside Carson. The words bruise his throat as he issues them with a force he hopes the man will immediately respect.

"I'm not . . . It's not . . ." the man pleads, again turning his head to face Carson and in one swift move rising from the ground.

Where is Jordan? Carson wonders, another surge of fear sliding down his spine. Pointing the object at Carson, the man steps forward.

"What's in your hand?"

"Look, I said it's . . ." the man insists, taking another step toward Carson, pointing at him with the hand holding the object. The night, the sky, the stars overhead: they all swirl around him, a dreamy encroachment. Carson is alone. In a darkened parking lot. And terribly afraid.

"Drop what you're holding and put your hands behind your head," Carson orders as his finger trembles, a whisper away from the trigger.

"Officer, I said . . ."

It's his fingers and his hands, both of them clutching the Beretta, it's even his body, that pulls the trigger. All he sees is the man's hand and the object pointed at him in the moment he fires his weapon for the first time ever.

Wyatt Jordan pulls into the strip mall parking lot and parks a few feet away from Carson and the body on the ground. Two minutes ago he heard Carson radio in to the dispatcher that there had been a shooting: "Shots fired." Through the radio system that connected Carson to the dispatcher and Wyatt to them both, Wyatt heard Carson's voice, shell-shocked and unraveling. *Damn,* Jordan thought, accelerating toward his destination as he heard Carson's call, wondering who was down and what he would find.

Walking from his squad car to Carson's cruiser, Wyatt Jordan realizes that Carson Blake is no longer a fellow officer he just barely knows. As the first to arrive at the scene, he will be bound to Carson from now on by the kind of knowledge both men can only submit to but never fully understand.

Jordan examines the man on the ground, scans the area around the body for a weapon, sees the cell phone, and then walks over to Carson, slumped in the front seat of his cruiser. The driver-side door of the car is open. Jordan crouches down beside Carson and pries the gun from his moist, steely grip. "What happened, Blake? Are you okay?"

"I thought it was a gun, I swear, I thought it was a gun." The words are breathy and heavy, whispered like a confession. Jordan sees before him a mere remnant of the man he had joked with half an hour ago.

Wyatt Jordan looks away, seeking relief from the face, from the husky sound of Carson's sobs as he weeps into his hands. Jordan lets his eyes scan the circumference of the parking lot and the darkened houses across the street where people are sleeping. Then he turns back to Carson, his large beefy arm enfolding Carson's shoulders, cradling him in a stiff embrace. He doesn't know what else on earth to do.

Emergency Medical Services is the first to rumble into the parking lot of the strip mall and begin examining the body. Soon the lot is ablaze with high-beam-intensity lights from fire trucks, a fluorescent halo hovering over the length and breadth of the search for shell casings and other evidence around the body cordoned off with yellow tape. More than two dozen men and women are swarming around the scene, from Internal Affairs, Homicide, Evidence, the Criminal Investigation Unit; the president of the Fraternal Order of Police and the district commander are there as well. Other officers, hearing what happened on their radios, mill about, curious and concerned, all of them thanking their private gods that on this night they are not Carson Blake.

Carson's sergeant, Melvin Griffin, arrives, and after talking to the crime scene investigators he sees Carson and Wyatt Jordan sitting in the backseat of Jordan's cruiser. He approaches them. At the sight of Griffin, Carson rises slowly from the backseat, and Griffin, a trim, gentle-eyed man of medium brown complexion, whose handlebar mustache and large, mournful eyes make him appear more solemn than he is, reaches for Carson, puts his arm around his shoulder, and says, "Come on, walk with me."

"You okay?" Griffin asks as they walk slowly away from Jordan's cruiser. Because this question seems the most puzzling inquiry he has ever heard in his life, Carson says nothing, although his gratitude for the question is immeasurable. Carson and Melvin Griffin walk away from the hive of activity immediately surrounding the crime scene, to a secluded space in front of the post office, Griffin's arms fatherly, sheltering, on Carson's shoulders.

"Obviously you were in fear for your life?" Griffin asks, standing at Carson's side, not looking at him, but waiting, Carson knows, for the only answer he can give. The answer he will have to give.

"Yes," he mumbles.

"You thought he had a gun." Carson hears not a question but a statement.

"Yes."

"Well, then this looks like a clean shooting to me," Griffin concludes, casting his gaze back to the site they have just walked away from.

"Take care of yourself and make sure you take your ten days. You call your wife?"

"Not yet."

"Call her, son—it's gonna be a long night."

Griffin begins walking back toward the fire trucks and squad cars, the investigators, the officers from Internal Affairs who Carson knows want to talk to him, gently leading Carson back toward that assembly with him.

"No, no, can I just have a few minutes?" Carson asks.

"Take all the time you need," Griffin tells him, and walks away, leaving Carson in the shadowy darkness outside the post office.

He feared for his life. He thought the man had a gun. If he had done the right thing, if he had done the only thing he could do, why did he now wish that he'd been rendered mute so that he could not speak, or blind so that he could not see what that fear and those thoughts had wrought?

No, he had not called Bunny. He wouldn't. He couldn't. He'd have to tell her this face-to-face.

"Be sure to take your ten days," his sergeant had told him. Ten days before he had to make an official statement to anybody about what had happened, about what he had done. Ten days that would turn into weeks. Ten days to get his story straight? Ten days to keep silent, when all he really wants, even now, forty-five minutes after he has killed a young man holding a cell phone and not a gun, is to talk, to explain. But this is Maryland, and the state has legislated ten days of silence for a police officer after a shooting. Ten days to live alone in his own head, the last place he wants to be.

He can't stay in the shadows forever, he knows, so Carson heads back to the others, still feeling the shadows engulfing him no matter how fast he tries to walk. He is still a police officer, and he has to bear witness to what has happened. To what he has done. He tells the story of the stop and the shooting to Margery Pierce, an investigator from the Criminal Investigation Division. She's a red-haired, blue-eyed, frumpy matron Carson has seen at other major crime scenes like this one, and her hand rests on Carson's shoulder as he leans against her van and talks to her, hearing his own voice as though from a great distance, as though it belongs to someone else. When Margery walks away, Lester Stovall from Internal Affairs steps toward Carson, asking first, like Margery, like everyone, if he is okay, and then before Carson can answer says, "Can you tell me what happened?"

Just as Carson is going to answer the question, Matthew Frey, the Fraternal Order of Police lawyer, walks out of the crowd surrounding the scene and puts his hand on Carson's chest like a barrier between Lester and Carson and says to Lester, whom he knows and respects, "You know I get to talk to him first."

Matthew Frey wears a wrinkled trench coat over a white shirt and khakis. He had hurriedly dressed in the bathroom of his Clinton, Maryland, rambler after hanging up from the call from the president of the Fraternal Order of Police. Gently shaking his wife awake, he told her where he was going. He has defended police officers for eighteen years. In his office desk in Largo, he keeps a twenty-inch billy club that his grandfather used when he was on the force in Baltimore. Matthew Frey stands before Carson, trying to gather quickly how much he can handle, if he is an officer who will fall apart because of this night or one who will turn to stone. No matter how long he looks at Carson, he cannot tell for sure.

Carson sees Matthew Frey's longish gray-white hair and his pencil-thin lips and reads in the man's blue eyes that he is perhaps the only person present whose job is to protect him.

Frey walks with Carson to his Volvo, and they sit in the front seats.

"You smoke?" he asks Carson, offering him a cigarette.

"Naw."

"Then I won't. You called your family?"

"I can't bring myself to do that just yet."

"I understand. You okay?"

"Not really." This is the first time Carson has answered the question. The first time he has spoken what he knows unalterably to be the truth.

"When you're ready, I want you to tell me what happened. Take your time. Tell me everything just as it happened, as much as you can recall."

Carson recounts the incident, filling the narrative with all the questions and the doubts that plague him, working through the silences that strangle him and hurtle him back into the moment with the retelling. "I know now that I should've waited for Jordan. He radioed he was on the way. It all happened so fast. So goddamned fast. I lost control. I mean, before I knew it he was reaching into his waistband and had turned around and was on his feet. On his feet, facing me. It couldn't have been more than a few seconds before I lost control of the stop. That's not supposed to happen, I know. But once he was on his feet, facing me, he was holding this object—he wouldn't drop it like I kept telling him to. He kept trying to tell me something, but I wouldn't listen, I couldn't take the chance. He looked like a good kid. He gave me some lip, but he wasn't at all what I was expecting. I was afraid for my life. I thought he had a gun."

Frey listened, knowing that memory is fractured and heightened, made suspect by the lingering effects of trauma. Every time an officer tells him details of a shooting he's been involved in, Frey recalls the conclusion of his favorite writer, Gabriel García Márquez, that life is not what one lives but what one remembers. Carson tells him much more than he needs to know. The days and weeks and months looming ahead of Carson will be even more crucial than this moment, as he helps him to remember the incident in ways that would render what happened inevitable rather than criminal. "You don't have to make a statement when you go back to CID. Get one of the other officers to take you and I'll meet you there. I'll help you fill out the Discharge of Firearms report. You'll be asked what happened. You're not to say anything. Do you understand?

"Yeah."

"Have you ever fired your weapon before?"

"No." Then Carson asks, "What's gonna happen to me?"

"I don't want you to worry about that tonight. I'll protect your rights. Just know that."

Carson has been in CID many times but never like this, with the eyes of the few officers in the building offering him so much compassion, never with those same officers stopping in the hall to pat him on the back, tell him he'll be okay, to ask how he is.

In an office next to the area where roll call is held, Carson is asked by a Colin Barnes if he wants to make a statement. Barnes at two-thirty in the morning wears a cashmere jacket over a cream-colored shirt with a silk navy blue tie and large silver cuff links, stylish as always amid the grimy gray funk, the stale, listless air, the battered furniture and indifferent decor that Carson knows too well and that weigh on him with an awful heaviness at this moment.

Then Barnes reads Carson the Advise of Rights form: *You have the right to remain silent. Anything you say can and will be used against you.* Carson is now a cop who has been Mirandized. He signs the form.

"Don't people know when you say 'Drop what you're holding,' we mean drop what you're holding?" Colin murmurs irritably as he places the form before Carson to sign.

The Discharge of Firearms report asks everything from the type of weapon used in the incident to how much sleep Carson had in the last twenty-four hours. The single eight-line paragraph that Frey tutors him on will be used for a press release that the Office of Communications will send to the media.

Carson agonizes over the brief paragraph, which contains the sketchiest rendering of the event even as it answers the primary who, what, when, where. The only question left unanswered is why. Carson hands Barnes the form studded with erasures, damp with sweat, the cursive script small and tortured.

"You been given a replacement weapon?" Barnes asks.

"No, not yet."

The gun used in the shooting is now evidence. He can't leave CID without a gun. On administrative leave, he is still a police officer. Still expected to protect and serve if he sees a "situation," while gassing up his car or shopping for a new pair of shoes. He's got to have a gun. He could be on some thug's kill list. Maybe he's got enemies he doesn't even know about among all the people he's arrested and helped send to jail. He's responsible for *his* life. The lives of others. And his Beretta gives him all the authority he needs. The one or two times he's left home without his weapon he's felt naked, like a moving target. His Beretta is a strap-on body part. He wants a gun but can't imagine holding it without remembering how he held it moments before the shooting, with focused, unfamiliar horror and dread. If he had to fire his weapon again he is not sure that he could.

Matthew Frey waits with Carson for Derek Stinson, the armorer who provides officers with new weapons. Stinson, a small, monklike man who like Matthew Frey was awakened from sleep, arrives carrying the metal case that is with him at all times. He's an ex-cop who keeps a collection of guns in his St. Mary's County home.

Stinson places the metal case on the same desk that Carson used to sign the Miranda forms and to write the report of the shooting. The four guns lie in the case embedded in foam, with magazines for each gun. Stinson gently lifts the Beretta and a magazine from the hold of the foam and offers them to Carson. Carson holds them in his dry, ashen palms with a reverence that stills the moment. Derek Stinson tells him, "In situations like the one you were in tonight, this is your only friend."

After Carson has put the new Beretta in his holster he tells Stinson, "I'd never fired my weapon at a suspect before. I never wanted to have to do it, but still I wondered what it would be like. Now I'd give anything not to know."

At 5:30 a.m., Carson unlocks the door to his house, weak with the desire to see the faces of his children. It is a desire that fills him like hunger. Like thirst. He walks quietly in the dark to his twin daughters' room, which he painted pink for their birthday. The night-light plugged into the wall socket casts an eerie frosting of muted half-light over the room's darkness. Barbie posters claim nearly all the space on the walls. Stuffed teddy bears, dolls, and Beanie Babies are scattered all over the carpeted floor. Standing in the doorway, Carson is stunned by the cheeriness of the room and it nearly buckles his knees, nearly sends him crashing onto the floor, but he steadies himself and walks to the bed of Roseanne, lying on her side, sucking her thumb reflexively in her sleep, her body curled, snail-like, beneath the sheet. Carson wipes the tiny beads of sweat from her forehead with his fingertips. Leaning closer, he listens to the heavy grunt of her breathing. He closes his eyes and allows that sound, the slightly asthmatic, ragged breathing of his daughter, to drench him like rain.

After a few moments Carson pads softly over to Roslyn's bed. She is sprawled on her back, arms and legs akimbo. A gentle fluttering of her eyes behind her closed lids makes it seem as though she's merely feigning sleep. Roslyn's left leg twitches several times and she turns on her side.

In Juwan's room, the boy sleeps too, a copy of *Treasure Island* tucked beneath his pillow. Carson stares at the face slack with sleep. He looks deeply into the face of a son that he is sure, even before this night, he has already lost.

Carson stands outside Juwan's door and considers the steps he will have to take to enter the room where his wife, Bunny, sleeps. The thought of those steps fills his mind like a forced march. Bunny wakes up at 7:00 a.m. Maybe, just maybe, he will have a reprieve until then. He knows he won't be that lucky but walks back downstairs anyway, slumping into a chair at the breakfast nook in the kitchen. He is more than tired, feels an ache that is primordial and awful in his bones and in his skin. He'd like to make a cup of coffee but doesn't want to make any movements that would signal that he is home. There have been other times in his twelve years on the force when he was hours late because of a fatal accident. Sometimes he had a chance to call. Sometimes he didn't. Bunny knew this was part of The Job. Shit happened. So she would have guessed, Carson convinces himself, that shit happened last night. To someone else.

If he can just be alone for a while. So that he doesn't have to face Bunny, to tell her what he did. Even if alone means having nothing and no one to distract him from the images and the memories of the shooting playing over and over in his head. A videotape that on the ride home he promised that he would only allow to play for fifteen minutes of every hour, a promise he has absolutely no power to keep.

The clock on the kitchen wall ticks in all this silence, too loudly, and when he finally switches on the kitchen light to see that he has been sitting in the breakfast nook for half an hour, Carson hears Bunny coming down the stairs. She stands in the kitchen doorway, bundled in a terry-cloth robe, her hair in rollers.

"I couldn't sleep. I haven't been able to sleep all night," she complains, yawning and walking over to the table.

"What's wrong? Why are you so late?" she asks sleepily. "Why are you sitting down here? Why didn't you come to bed?"

"I know I should've called," he begins.

"I was worried . . . I started to call the station," Bunny whines.

"I'm sorry."

"Carson, sorry just doesn't cut it. You don't seem like yourself. You look strange, Carson, what's wrong?" she asks, sitting down heavily beside him.

He thinks he will tell her calmly, slowly. Instead, the words speak themselves, stumble out. "I'd given him the ticket. The stop was over. I was on my way home."

"Carson?" Bunny asks, saying his name like a question, and to Carson his name sounds as odd as the inquiry he has heard, it seems, a thousand times this night, *Are you okay?*

"It was dark. Hell, I didn't know. How could I? All he had to do was drop what he was holding. Like I told him. Then I would've known."

"Carson, you're scaring me."

"It happened so fast." And that is the truest thing Carson has thought or said this night. "It happened so fast. I killed a man. I stopped him because he was speeding and driving with no head-lights."

"And you killed him?" Bunny whispers, rising so quickly she nearly falls, clutching the collar of her robe tight at her throat and covering her mouth with her hand. Carson stands and walks to Bunny as if he could protect her, save her, from the wrath of what he has done. They cling to each other. Never before have they held each other with love so total and so blind.

They sit down again at the kitchen table and Carson tells Bunny what happened. He can tell the story now without think-ing. "I couldn't believe it. That I'd actually shot him. And he was holding a cell phone, not a gun. That's what was in his hand. God, Bunny, God help me, I don't think I really saw him, *really* saw him, until he was dead." Carson searches Bunny's face for forgiveness but sees only confusion and horror and pity for him.

Bunny hugs Carson and lays her head on his shoulder. "You didn't mean to kill him. I know that. You were afraid for your life."

Afraid for your life. Afraid for your life. Like the forty officers killed all over the country last year while on duty, nine of them during traffic stops. Like Cecil Warren, a D.C. cop shot in the back with his own gun a decade ago, whose story was a case study at the police academy of what not to do. Afraid for your life. Four words that are supposed to provide absolution but provide Car-son with no peace. Four words to explain the inexplicable. The four words that provide a police officer with a moral escape hatch but that can sometimes turn the heinous into the justifiable. The mantra every cop knows by heart, "I was afraid for my life." I was afraid for *my* life, so I took *yours.* Before you could take mine. Carson has never until this moment heard the chilling paradox embedded in the words. The brutal math. If the cell phone had

been a gun, would his anguish be less searing? If he'd killed a kid-
napper, a robber, a murderer, would he still feel consigned to hell?

Was he afraid? Although he has told everyone, Matthew Frey,
Melvin Griffin, the investigators at the scene that he was, he
doesn't remember what he was feeling. He remembers only what
he did. "Even while I was pulling the trigger, Bunny, I was praying it was a dream. And when I saw what I had done I prayed that
he was asleep, or maybe that I was. That if he didn't wake up, then
I would."

2

Maybe it's a dream. Carson allows himself to think the hopeful blasphemy, throwing off the sheets and spread, sitting up, his feet hitting the bedroom floor with a thud that sounds to him, on this morning, totally ominous. He looks around the bedroom, sees everything he knows so well—the deep green and red paisley drapes at the window, the photos of Bunny and the children, his mother, and Bunny's parents atop the mahogany chest of drawers, the twenty-six-inch television on a wide wooden table that faces the bed, the clock radio, the mobile phone, Bunny's nightgown and robe flung over the back of the leather recliner, three pairs of heels huddled in a corner. It's all familiar, and it's all so strange. His uniform is bundled on the floor near the entrance to the bathroom. He tossed it there after stripping it off at six-thirty and diving beneath the spread and the sheets to hold Bunny, to let her hold him a few more minutes before she woke the children, prepared them for school, and left for work.

It was under the sheets as they lay together that Carson said, "I'll tell the children that I'll have to be off from work awhile. I'll tell them what happened."

"Everything?"

"As much as I think they can handle. I'll pick them up from school today."

"Are you sure?" Bunny asked skeptically. "There's still time."

"No, there isn't. It'll be in the papers today, maybe tomorrow. They'll have to know, and they need to find out from me."

He has made that promise, and now, sitting on the side of the bed at eleven o'clock, Carson wonders if maybe what happened was a nightmare. He can't shed this hope, even as it's contradicted by the brooding malaise and queasiness festering inside him.

Nothing would have seemed out of the ordinary to his children this morning. Carson often sleeps through their departure for school. When he's on the midnight shift and sleeps during the day, they've been told to use their "quiet voices" when they come home from school, tiptoeing without much success outside their parents' bedroom door, behind which Carson's body clock struggles to adjust to the rhythm he has to maintain for the three nights of the shift. He's in permanent flux. Four days on the day shift and then three days off. Three evenings on the night shift and three days off. On the day shift, he hits the streets while Bunny and the kids are showering and getting dressed. On the evening shift, he misses dinner. On the midnight shift, he comes home to an empty house at 8:00 a.m.

It would have seemed like any other morning to Juwan and Roseanne and Roslyn. While they dressed for school and bickered over breakfast, Daddy was asleep. How will he tell them? He sits on the side of his bed, a stranger inside his skin. He's on leave with pay from the department. Still a cop. But not able to be a cop. He can't even work his part-time security position. Anything that might require him to use a gun is off-limits. But, he thinks with a bitterness that swells his heart near to bursting, because he's still a cop, he couldn't leave district headquarters without a weapon.

Carson stands up and sees the blinking red light on the answering machine. He'd heard the call as he lay in bed, unable to sleep, unable to rise, an hour ago. It was Matthew Frey calling to ask if he was okay, if he needed anything, telling him that he would have his secretary call him to set up an appointment for next week. Telling him to call him anytime before then if he has questions or just wants to talk. "If you need a mental health professional to talk to, I can provide you with some names. It'll be confidential. No one in the department will have to know," he assures Carson in the slow, melodious baritone that schooled Carson last night on what to do now that he is on the other side of the law.

In the twelve hours since the shooting, he's been seized by the desire to end *once and for all* the guilt he feels, guilt undiminished by the sanctuary he found in his wife's arms. Surely he's damned, but he's not crazy. Not yet. He's not ready to eat his gun after a bad shooting, like Boone, James, and Tremont, their names whispered like a shameful taboo, three police officers in the state of Maryland *that he knows of,* since he joined the force, who took their own lives. Carson stands looking at the answering machine, off-balance, dizzy, longing to conceal and to confess.

On a normal day he'd wash a load of clothes for Bunny, pick up grocery items on the running list on a pad held to the refrigerator by a duck-shaped magnet. But this isn't like any other day, so after Carson has showered and dressed in jeans and a sweatshirt he stands in front of the open refrigerator, enveloped in a cocoon of cool air, sickened by the sight of shelves bulging with food, and in the end makes a cup of instant coffee. The house is too quiet. If this were a normal day he'd have relished the quiet of the neighborhood of prosperous retirees who spend as much time on jazz cruises or volunteering at the nearby schools as they do at home, and the busy two-income professional couples who don't pull into Paradise Glen until six or six-thirty in the evening. But this day he's cloistered by the silence intermittently broken by the sound in his head of bullets discharged from a gun. Imprisoned by a sound that erupts relentlessly, that he cannot stifle or escape.

Even the daytime court shows, which he flips through after settling on the sofa in front of the television in the family room— *Judge Hatchett, Judge Joe Brown, Judge Judy*—don't muffle the intermittent flashbacks. The sight of the hapless adulterers, embezzlers, and con artists standing before the TV judges intensifies the trembling of his hands, the painful galloping of his heartbeat, the hallucinatory image of the mask of awful surprise on the face of the young man he shot.

Carson sees the *Washington Post* tossed by Bunny near the fireplace before she left. He rarely reads newspapers anymore, and even when he does he barely trusts the veracity of what's in them. Yet when he turns, his fingers slick with sweat and shivering with a chill, to page 2 of the Metro section and sees the brief account under "Crime & Justice: Maryland," Carson knows what he's reading is the truth.

OFFICER INVOLVED IN FATAL SHOOTING

A man was fatally wounded last night by a Prince George's County police officer, who stopped the man for speeding and driving with no headlights. The shooting occurred shortly before midnight in the parking lot of the Watkins Glen Mall on Central Avenue and Watkins Park Road. It was not immediately clear last night what prompted the officer to open fire. It could not be learned if any weapons were found at the scene. None of the people involved in the incident were immediately identified.

The article renders the tragic as routine. Carson suddenly realizes he doesn't know the name of the man he killed. He should know at least that. But soon he will know, for tomorrow's paper will identify the dead man, and then he will know more than he can bear. Carson folds the paper and turns up the volume on the television. Maybe that will silence the sound of the gun that keeps going off in his head. The last sound he ever wanted to hear.

It had gotten so that Carson rarely told anybody he didn't know that he was a police officer. When he was out in plain clothes, shopping, at a game, shooting the breeze with a stranger, people were friendly. If it was a woman, maybe she would flirt. But then somehow it came out that Carson was a police officer and instantly silence oozed like poison, filling the suddenly yawning space between them. The relaxed, easygoing banter curdled into a wary hesitance that left the man or woman Carson was talking to bereft of speech, except to ask in a hushed whisper, "You're a police? *For real?*" When he confirmed again that yes, he was in *law enforcement,* people sometimes backed away from him or turned to talk to the person in line behind them. They'd shut their mouths, fold their arms protectively across their chest, look at Carson not only as though because he was a cop he was undoubtedly corrupt and brutal, but as if they were afraid he could see into the tight, tiny chambers of their hearts and glimpse the unpaid traffic tickets, the supplies stolen from the job, the dress shoplifted when they were sixteen, their fantasies of hiring someone to hurt the boss they hate but have to kiss up to in order to keep their job.

In the eyes of those people, every White cop hog-tied and beat

Rodney King, a brutality caught on videotape and shown around the world. Every cop shot Amadou Diallo, unleashing forty-one bullets into the body of that skinny kid from Senegal in the doorway of an apartment in Brooklyn. And to some Black folks, there's a war on Black people, and cops are waging it. Because he killed an unarmed man he'll be considered a foot soldier in that war.

Then there was Bunny accusing him of wearing his uniform all the time. What was he supposed to do? He carried a gun everywhere. He slept with a gun—not in his hands but in his head. *A cop is a cop 24–7,* Carson thinks, feeling the coffee incite a rumbling inside his empty stomach. *A cop* while singing hymns in church on Sunday morning. *A cop* sitting in a restaurant with his family, eyes scanning the place (he can't help it, it's automatic), hoping, *Please, nobody go crazy up in here and start acting a fool.* But just in case, his revolver is strapped to his ankle. *A cop* when stumbling out of some bar in plain clothes, head tight, but not quite wasted, coming upon a robbery, the sight instantly clearing his head; he pulls out his revolver, and when a fellow officer, *in uniform,* arrives, he yells, "I'm on the job. I'm on the job," thrusting his shield into the darkness so *he's* not pegged as the thief. So *he's* not busted or blasted. He's out of uniform, so he's just Black, not Black and blue. Carson goes into the bathroom and pulls off his sweatshirt, wipes his arms and chest and back with a towel, and finds a bottle of aspirin under the sink. He swallows two with a glass of water. *Maybe this will ease the sweats and chills,* he thinks, but without much conviction. What can he take to stop the sound of the gun firing in his head?

It was 1988 when he joined the force. With only a month on the job, Carson was called to break up a fight outside a liquor store. His partner had called in sick that day. Young. Inexperienced. Scared of fucking up, making a bad arrest. Driving to the parking lot of a warehouse-size liquor supermarket that was a magnet for troublemakers and rowdies, Carson had a blast of adrenaline pumping, pushing through his veins, making him feel crazy/invincible and, yeah, still scared. Right off the bat he violated rule number one: wait for backup. But he wanted to prove himself. He's always wanted to prove himself. Surely, he thought, he could handle this.

There was a crowd, but they were just watching the two men go at it. A big burly Incredible Hulk mutha and a wiry short guy, bloody but unstoppable. Carson radioed for backup. But he didn't wait. He couldn't wait. Hell, the guy could get killed. So he jumped out of his cruiser and swung into the crowd. His nightstick broke when he slammed it on the back of the bruiser, who turned around, not even flinching at the sight of Carson in uniform or the sound of him shouting into his hand radio for backup. Carson tried to body slam him, but it was like scaling a mountain. Suddenly Carson was on the ground and the monster was astride him, choking the life out of him, he was sure. The crowd's voice was lurid, wild, jeering, some rooting for Carson, some shouting, "Kick the cop's ass!" Straining to remove the huge greasy hands from his neck, Carson heard the sound of his radio sliding cold and slick across the parking lot into the crowd. The bastard started banging his head against the cement. Once. Twice. Pain blasted across Carson's temples and he was momentarily blind. Then two men from the crowd jumped in, wrestled the guy off Carson just as two police cruisers arrived. The lights and the sirens, loud, disorienting, scattered the crowd. And that wasn't the only asswhooping he'd gotten. He was shot in the arm at the scene of a bank robbery, suffered whiplash when his cruiser crashed into another patrol car chasing a stolen SUV. But he always gave as good as he got. Got even. Got even and then some.

Back then they had partners, and Carson's first partner was a

White guy named Deek Rehnquist. Deek had a slow, country, long-legged gait and the beginnings of a paunch. His buzz crew-cut revealed more of his scalp than was legal. He schooled Carson those first months on everything he needed to know, how to write a comprehensive, readable crime report, the importance of keeping his uniform crisply starched and his appearance neat at all times. It was called "uniform integrity," and sloppiness was a violation. They'd been trained like soldiers at the police academy—obedience, honor, integrity, service. You sucked it up and just forgot shit you couldn't handle.

His uniform wasn't just the gray shirt and light purple pants with a stripe running down the side; it was his gun, pepper spray, his ammo pouch with two magazines that held fifteen bullets each to back up the fifteen in his loaded Beretta, handcuffs, and a baton, all this strapped around his waist. Deek told him how they had to be courteous with the public. "You don't know how many times I've been called a honky bastard or a son of a bitch during a stop. Carson, you just got to let them call you a motherfucker and say 'Yes sir, yes ma'am, but I still have to write you this ticket.'"

Courteous to the public, but among themselves obscenity was the second language—*shit, fuck, damn*, a macho lingua franca they used during roll call, interspersed throughout every conceivable conversation as shield so nothing and nobody could get to the places inside, where the officers might be hurt and so become ineffective. For what else could you say when you were called most often to riot and mayhem and loss, hardly ever to celebrate or rejoice or just hear good news, when you jumped out of your car? Carson learned soon that many cops felt deeply the effects of the accumulation of misery and the unfathomable—like why a father would throw his three-year-old from a twelve-story window to make her stop crying. To keep from feeling, they'd tell dirty jokes standing around a sheared and mangled car cut in half by the force of a dump trunk, bodies still inside, or complain about the questions on the test to become a sergeant while looking at an elderly gentleman slumped in a rocker in front of his TV, the channel turned to *Jeopardy!*, the game show he'd been watching before he blew out his brains with the gun on the floor at his feet because he'd been diagnosed with lung cancer the day before. They took all that home with them, with nowhere to unload it, hide it, make sense of it. Obscenities were the words that seemed most appropriate for the work they did that nobody, not even they, fully understood. Their jobs seemed to confirm that there was no God, and if there was He was surely in cahoots with the devil. They even used to joke about Eric because he didn't curse, asked him if he knew how. Eric just said, "I don't need to." "Yeah, that's right, you pray," they'd jeer like schoolboys before roll call started, and Eric would answer, "That's right, I do." There could be no displays of affection between two male cops, ever, unless one of them had fucked up bad, been shot, or killed the wrong person. Once when Carson hadn't seen Eric in a while and embraced him in the hall, the officers who passed by sneered, "Why don't y'all get a room?"

In the midst of those memories, Carson thinks, *I've done this ass-backwards. Eat first and then take aspirin, that's the rule.* He goes into the kitchen, deciding to eat a bowl of oatmeal, hoping the cereal will absorb the aspirin and the waves of gastric juices his tension has unleashed now roiling against the walls of his stomach. After pouring a cup of water into a saucepan, Carson stands before the stove, waiting for the water to boil.

Deek had talked about the early eighties as if it were Korea, or Vietnam. "Shit, man, sometimes we'd take fifteen, sixteen service calls a shift," he told Carson, shaking his head and letting out a long, smooth whistle of disbelief at the memory. "We were patrolling all the hellholes. The crack dens, the open-air markets. And for all that work, till we got the minimum mandatory sentences it was just a revolving door." Very quickly Carson realized that a partner was like another wife. On Bunny's birthday, his and the kids', on Christmas, on his wedding anniversary, more often than not he was with Deek. Half his shift was just talking, talking to his partner as they cruised the streets, keeping their eyes on the street and everybody *on the street*. When Carson in those early days and months complained of the boredom of some shifts, Deek told him, "Carson, there's gonna be times you'd give up all you own for a slow shift. It's just like the front lines in a war zone: ninety-five percent boredom, five percent terror. I been out here a while now, and that equation ain't never changed, and the incidents that make you earn your pay often creep up on you, come disguised, like a domestic disturbance that's murder when you get there, or a traffic stop where you get more than you bargained for."

After a while it didn't matter to Carson that Deek was White. He was his partner, and that meant that while he wasn't necessarily his friend, he was the person who held Carson's life in his hands. Deek was one of two or three officers he invited to his wedding when he and Bunny married two years after he joined the force. And Carson had more than once gone to hear Deek and his bluegrass band play at a club in Alexandria. When Deek's seventeen-year-old daughter got pregnant and decided to keep the baby, Deek told Carson, "They're talking about gettin' married when they graduate next year. I don't care that the boy is Black— I just wish they could've kept their pants on a while longer."

Still, there were two different cultures on the force. One night a year after he'd joined up, Carson went to the bar at the Fraternal Order of Police Social Club and walked into a room full of White officers who stopped talking when he came through the door.

Cops, some of whom he knew, who didn't take their hostile, questioning eyes off Carson until he backed out of the door he'd come through only moments before.

The FOP Club was where White police officers hung out. Black police officers did their own thing. This was the unspoken rule Carson learned on his own. Carson had signed on in the aftermath of a discrimination suit filed by a group of Black officers. He joined the force despite its reputation for brutality against Blacks, racism, and a scandal in which a group of rogue cops called the Death Squad had turned into vigilantes, meting out their own brand of justice.

Nobody was more surprised than Carson when he became a MP in the army and then joined the force a couple of years after his honorable discharge. He knew the world was gray, but as a police officer Carson could try to make it neat, simple, black-and-white. Order. Discipline. Those were the tenets of his secret religion. The world was all chaos without them. His wasn't just a job. Misunderstood, disrespected, his was a sacred calling.

There was one incident early in his career he'd always remember as a kind of initiation. The day after Easter Monday, two dealers erupted into a shoot-out over a drug deal in a housing project on the Prince George's County side of the county/D.C. line. A twelve-year-old girl riding her bike was killed, caught in the crossfire. Within an hour the department knew who they were looking for. Everybody was working overtime, questioning witnesses and cruising, looking for the suspect.

It was seven o'clock and Carson and Deek got lucky when they passed a Burger King and Carson spotted the suspect. He was leaning against the hood of a car, laughing and talking trash. Carson wondered if he was laughing about the little girl he'd killed earlier that day. Carson was behind the wheel, and as he pulled into the parking lot the suspect broke into a run. Deek radioed for backup and Carson bolted out of the car and gave chase to the kid, who was running like an Olympic champ, heading behind the stores to the back of the mall. Deek was trailing Carson but not close enough. There was the tumultuous screaming sound of several other squad cars closing in. The suspect tripped and fell in front of a dumpster. On the ground, he held his ankle in pain, squealing like a pig. Carson's flashlight speckled the darkness with a slice of illumination that landed on the kid's face. He was maybe sixteen at the mos.. His dark-skinned, childish face was twisted by belligerence and rage. Deek finally caught up and was all over the kid, searching him and cuffing him, rising from the ground with a gun and a palmful of tiny cellophane packets of crack.

Several squad cars screeched to a halt, closing off the entrance to the alley. Carson heard more footsteps and turned to see Vince Proctor running toward them. The first time Carson saw Vince Proctor, he thought he was White. The slicked-back straight hair, the tiny pencil-thin mustache, the blue veins bulging through the skin of his neck, the gray eyes as hard as flints. A Black man with a complexion that was ghostly white. Some cops loved him. Some cops hated his guts. Back then, when Carson was a rookie, he didn't know why. To him Vince Proctor walked like a man who had everything he needed *with him, on him. All the time.* He was a kick-ass who preferred the uniform to undercover and who saved the life of one officer trapped in a burning car and another who had a gun pointed at his head in a hostage situation. On the ground, the kid was yelling about the cuffs being too tight and his ankle being broken.

"Niggah, if you don't shut up I'll give you a real reason to scream," Proctor shouted.

"Fuck you, muthafuckah," the kid spat back at Proctor.

"This ain't no rap video, you stupid ass," Proctor yelled as he began kicking the kid in the head, the ribs, the groin, the back, his thick muscular arms outstretched, as if he were performing a dance movement, with each kick. The kid's moans strangled the warm April air. Deek, his eyes huge and still, held the gun and the crack and silently watched Vince Proctor.

"Fuck *you*, muthafuckah," Proctor taunted the kid. A dim halogen bulb hanging from the roof of the back of the pizza parlor above the dumpster revealed everything. The boy's face, blood-soaked and unrecognizable. Proctor's foot on the kid's stomach as though to hold him in place. The grim, determined look on Proctor's face, and his presence making Carson feel smaller and the moment bigger than anything he'd ever been a part of before. "Blake, you want a piece a this?" Proctor asked. His answer would tell Proctor and Deek and the circle of half a dozen other cops gathered a few feet away, who saw and who pretended not to see, who Carson was. What he was made of. A little girl riding her bike had been killed so this scum at their feet could sell drugs.

The kid's moans sickened Carson. But Proctor and Deek were watching him, sizing him up. Carson's first kick was halfhearted. The second and the third, he just closed his eyes, blocking out the kid's face, trying not to see the face of the girl he'd killed, a thick veil of blood staining her cheeks, dripping into her eyes as she lay at the foot of her three-speed bicycle a few feet from the elementary school playground where the bullet found her and roared through her skull. The fourth and fifth kick, Carson was a machine. Then there was Proctor's hand on his shoulder and his voice saying, "I think he's got the point." Carson opened his eyes and turned to face Proctor, who winked at him, and Carson knew the lesson was through. Carson and Proctor and Deek hauled the kid off the ground and led him out of the alley. Carson never mentioned what he and Proctor had done that evening. Deek never said anything to him about it at all. Yet he knew that he'd left a part of himself on the ground that night, mixed in with the trash and dirt overflowing from the dumpster.

Pouring the oatmeal into a bowl, Carson sprinkles sugar, pours milk, and smears a pat of butter over the lumpy mass and sinks into a chair at the kitchen table. All he wants to do is eat. He tries to think about the oatmeal, moist and soft, filling his mouth. He tries to imagine it traveling down his throat, into his stomach, but all he can do is think about everything he's done on The Job. He profiled, all officers did. For self-protection. If he saw a car loaded with young Black males, he started wondering. If it's a beat-up hoopty they're driving, did they use it in a crime? If it's an expensive ride, how can they afford it? He might radio in to see if it's been reported stolen. What are they doing in the car? Are they moving to the beat of the rap blasting from the car stereo or stuffing drugs under the seat? Are they driving too fast? Too slow? But you weren't supposed to stop them without backup. Not a carload. Driving while Black. Yeah. Driving while dangerous. Driving while armed. Driving while looking for trouble. There wasn't one civilian he knew who could do his job for one shift. The vigilance, the paranoia it required. All to keep the peace. Carson sits at the table in the kitchen and stares at the oatmeal, grateful that these memories of the past have smothered the visions of last night.

The traffic stop is the most dangerous stop of all. You never know who's behind the wheel, an honor roll student or somebody wanted by the FBI. You never know. So every night's a war. That's why you take control from the start. Let them know who's in charge. Every complaint against Carson (and there had been half a dozen) had been investigated. Every time he was cleared. A prostitute resisting arrest charged him with brutality because she hit her head when he wrestled her into his cruiser. He got a complaint because he told a woman he was ticketing for reckless driving to stop crying like a baby. Bogus, cynical, time-wasting shit that Internal Affairs had to investigate as if he were Rambo. Sure, there were times when he went overboard. The body slam. The choke hold. Cuffs extra tight. You can't deal with some people until you get their attention. Until they're subdued. Until they've calmed down. Capitol Heights, Oxon Hill—that's not Mayberry. Some people deserve a beating. That's all they understand.

Lifting a spoonful of oatmeal to his lips, Carson wills himself to think of something good to blot out everything else. And he remembers that he wanted to be a hero. A hero like Eric.

Carson decided early on to do as much as he could to draw a line in the sand between The Job and the rest of his life. He saw the wreckage The Job wrought in the lives of veteran officers— the divorces, the alcoholism, the gambling, men so hardened and broken by years on the street that they could be classified only as collateral damage. He didn't have many friends on the force and didn't want many. Carson was afraid that the dysfunction he saw in some of the cops he respected most would rub off on him. The crazy shift changes, every four days switching to day or evening or night shift, the generalized and specific stresses of The Job, and so much more made it easy for Carson to maintain workplace friendships that never spilled over into the rest of his life. Then Eric Bradshaw was assigned to the district.

Often a group of officers on the same shift met in the parking lot before the shift began, to decide where to have dinner together. Eric had a different kind of conversation during those dinners. He wanted to talk about more than wives and children, who beat the Wizards, or gossip about other cops. He'd read books Carson had never heard of—*They Came Before Columbus*, about Africans journeying to the shores of America hundreds of years

before White men, *Stolen Legacy*, *Africa's Gift to America*, books
about Marcus Garvey, Carl Jung, and a novel called *Siddhartha*.

What Eric had read on their pages had endowed him with a
quiet wisdom that Carson came to envy. Carson borrowed *Stolen
Legacy*, and although the language and the allusions were arcane,
unfamiliar, and challenging, referencing Greek, Roman, and
African history his community college education had left uncov-
ered, Carson persevered and spent weeks talking with Eric about
the significance of George G. M. James's conclusions about the
true sources of Western civilization and the story of Africa.

Soon Carson and Eric started talking every day, going to computer shows, and double dating with Bunny and Eric's girlfriend,
Jennifer, having dinner on the wharf at Hogates or going to hear
jazz at a club over in Baltimore.

Carson saw evidence of Eric's deeply rooted religious faith in
the mourning brown eyes that stared at the world with a prophet's
steely concern that could be neither shaken nor surprised. For
Eric, The Job was his ministry, and he joked that God was his bul-
letproof vest. Eric kept it quiet that he was a deacon in his church,
that he had a divinity degree from Howard, although he wasn't ordained so he couldn't preach. He wore all this lightly, perfecting a
kind of spiritual masking so as not to disrupt the requirements of
The Job for everyone to fit in, to wear the uniform as though
dressed for battle.

Mostly it was a quiet righteousness, a calm, an openness that informed anyone who looked at Eric that God called and he answered. Carson had seen him bow his head, whisper a prayer in
the locker room before he hit the streets. Eric was known to break
up gang fights with words, pull young bloods aside, eighteen-,
nineteen-year-olds who had predicted the time and place and year
of their own deaths, who had bragged they wouldn't live to reach

twenty-one. Aside, off to the corner of the rec center and playground, Eric held the rangy, angry, anguished body, looked into
the resisting face, and defused the suicidal impulse. Everyone,
other cops, the young bloods come to rumble, even Carson, stood
a few feet away. Watched the young gangster's body stance melt as
Eric looked him dead in the eye and said . . . what? Offered what?
Life? Love? God? On his beat they said Eric could part the waters.

"I couldn't do this without my faith," he told Carson. "Seeing
people at their most vulnerable, when they're raging or stoned or
have just committed some act that proves there's evil in the world.
I have to believe I'm in this, that we're in this to do more than just
use handcuffs," he said with the melodious, slow, thoughtful
rhythm of the preacher he could easily be.

"You sound like the administrators, the brass, the ones who
haven't been on the streets in years, the sociologists," Carson said,
shaking his head. "I've got faith too. Faith in me. In my training.
My instincts. I couldn't do the job without *that*."

"I'm not judging you, Carson. But I know that without my
faith I'd be a psycho like Proctor or I'd be a drunk like Cooper—
that's all I know. There's a group of us meeting for Bible study, before the shift, at Robinson's place."

"You're shittin' me."

"Naw, naw, man. You oughta join us."

"You all just pray for me, okay?"

Then Eric was gone. Three years ago. He stopped to help a
woman on the side of 495 change a flat tire. It was 10:15 p.m.,
during a heavy rain. A drunk driver careened off the road and
plowed into Eric, off duty, stooped and bent over, his back to the
road as he changed the tire and the Korean woman stood near the
trunk saying a prayer of thanks for the action of the Good Samar-
itan. The Jeep smashed Eric into a sodden mess of broken flesh and
cracked bones. Eric, gone. Just like that. There was grief at Car-

son's house, where his children had to come to terms with the first death of someone they knew, and at the district, where cops headed for their shifts in a daze.

Carson was unmoored and sinking for months. Even now, he still misses Eric. Still talks to him in his thoughts every day. But since last night, that sporadic conversation with the ghost of his best friend has stalled. Carson had no idea how he would resurrect it. Eric was the only person who knew of *his* crimes, transgressions committed in the wanton haze of youth. When he told Eric the things he had done, Eric shrugged and said, "When you joined the army and then the police force, you made a decision to be born again. The ability to keep creating life anew, over and over, to rise from the ashes of our sins—that's God's true gift to us."

After Eric's death, Carson felt literally broken. He hadn't just lost his best friend. He now had to live without the only person in his life who understood The Job, and who knew who he had once been and forgave him. If he passed a motorist in distress, with a flat tire or a dead battery, it would all come back to him, what Eric's last moments must have been like on that rainy night. And he'd wonder why he wasn't there to save him. Soon, what he had been able for years to let go of began to build up, and he could feel the weight of the accumulated calamities he'd witnessed congeal in his bones. Driving down Route 193 at night, he'd spot roadkill, a dead raccoon or once a deer, and when he looked out his window closely the dead carcasses looked back at him with eyes on a human face. He and Eric had been stop valves for each other. Now he was alone. An archive of misery filled and rent his soul, always with him. It was with him in the mall parking lot.

After breakfast, Carson calls the school and informs the secretary in the main office that he'll pick up Juwan, Roslyn, and Roseanne at three o'clock. He spends the hours before leaving home by rummaging through the debris of his mind for words that will accomplish the impending task. When he leaves the house he has no idea what he will say and wonders if the words will hijack the moment, come out spastic and floundering, much like the emotions he feels. But how can he calmly tell his children what he has done? He doesn't want to tell them inside the house. It was enough to tell Bunny in the kitchen. Where in the house would Juwan and Roslyn and Roseanne ever feel safe again if their home was the place he told them he killed a man? He has told the story once inside the walls of the house he and Bunny have turned into what feels to Carson like the only home he has ever had. He won't do it again.

"If Daddy is picking us up, then he's got a surprise for us," Roslyn tells her shy older brother and her sister as they walk together to their father's car, parked across the street from the school.

"But let's act like we don't suspect a thing, okay?" she orders Juwan and Roseanne.

"Hi, Daddy," Roslyn says as she hugs Carson, settling into the front seat beside him, her knowing, confident smile breaking Carson's heart. The car is flooded with childish energy, hot and intense. In the backseat Roseanne and Juwan throw their backpacks on the floor and greet him as well.

"Can we go to McDonald's, Daddy?" Roslyn asks, settling back in her seat after locking her seat belt. That would be a perfect way to stall, to use up time, to delay, Carson thinks, pulling up behind a school bus exiting the parking lot. But not now.

"Some other day, okay?"

"Okay."

Where will he take them, he wonders, driving away from the school and heading who knows where. Carson drives past the in-progress housing developments along Church Road, cranes and bulldozers hollowing out acres of trees and foliage to make way for what a sign says will be Harmony Estates. He's oblivious to the snickering and laughter of Roseanne and Juwan in the backseat. Beside him Roslyn is moving her head to a tune on the radio, her high-pitched, quavering voice singing along with a now-dead young singer named Aaliyah, who, Carson vaguely recalls, married a much older singer when she was fifteen. Didn't he hear something about that singer, R. Kelly, being sued for taking videos of himself having sex with another underage girl? Aaliyah is sultry and bristling with a throaty sensuality, singing about rocking the boat, working the middle and changing positions. Eyes closed, fingers snapping, Roslyn is transported, and Carson wonders if his daughter knows she is singing about sex.

The children are not impatient, not asking where they are going, not until Carson has driven past Wal-Mart and Ruby Tuesday's and the BaySox Baseball Stadium where he and Bunny take them to see Minor League games in the summer, and they seem to have been riding in circles. Not until the children recognize the streets passed ten or fifteen minutes earlier do they begin to fidget with concern.

Carson is unaware of the uneasiness in the car, of Roslyn's turning to look at Juwan and Roseanne, her brown eyes big and bulging with uncertainty. It is finally Roseanne, so quiet but as strong-willed as her sister, who asks, "Daddy, where are we going?"

The question jolts Carson back to the present, and he turns and drives into the parking lot of a mall that's all restaurants and a twelve-theater cinema. "This is the surprise, I told you," Roslyn shouts triumphantly, "I told you." They all begin to clap.

Carson parks several rows from the entrance to the theater, in a corner of the parking lot, and the children smile at him expectantly as he unbuckles his seat belt. They unbuckle their belts and Roslyn reaches for the door.

"No, we're not going to the movies. Not today."

"But . . ." Roslyn begins, the sight of the sorrow in her father's eyes plunging her into silence.

Carson will not remember exactly how he tells them when Bunny asks later that evening. Just as he can't remember exactly how many bullets he fired (he thinks it is four or five, although he clearly saw three and that's how many shell casings Evidence found), he won't recall all of the words partly because in the end there were so few words. So few words to talk about the end of the world as he has known it. The end of someone's life.

Carson drinks in the faces of his children. There's no escape from Juwan's gaze, the lashes as thick and lush as fur. Not once he turns those eyes on you. Carson studies the shapely head and the frail, almost feminine face of his twelve-year-old son that lives behind a veil of something secret and unreachable. As if at any moment, with the slightest pressure, the boy will break. The girls are olive-skinned like Bunny, their hair a mass of tiny twists, their toothy grins and dimpled, open faces gazing at him with so much trust. As a cop he is all too aware of the world's darkness.

He wanted more than anything to keep that darkness from his door. From his wife and his children. He had thought if the darkness ever entered, it would surely not be because of him.

"You know how on my job I carry a gun?" he asks. "Well, last night I was in a situation that required me to use it. I had to shoot a man. And he's dead."

"Like Uncle Eric?" Roseanne asks.

"Yeah, like Uncle Eric."

"Did he shoot you, Daddy?" Roseanne asks meekly.

"Does it look like he was shot?" Roslyn says harshly.

"Don't talk to your sister like that."

"But Daddy, what a stupid question. He shot him because he was a bad man," Roslyn pronounces, glaring at Roseanne.

"Maybe Daddy was hurt where we can't see," Juwan says firmly.

There were none of the questions he had expected or feared, questions they would have not known how to ask: Was he carrying a gun? Did he threaten you? Was shooting your only option?

"I have to be off my job for a while. It's a serious thing when a police officer fires his weapon. Even when the person isn't killed. So they have to do some things relating to the case. And then when they're through I can go back and be a police officer again."

Carson is astonished at the precision and confidence he's mustered. It's all false. His hands are shaking slightly and he's sweating again, all signs of the hellish state that has descended upon him, which he hopes his children don't see.

"Were you scared, Daddy?" Roslyn asks, gazing at Carson with that unflinching stare.

"Yeah, yeah, I was scared."

"I'd be scared too," Roseanne says, rising from her seat and laying her head on Carson's shoulder.

He would remember but he would not tell Bunny that Roslyn asked, as she watched her sister comfort him, "Daddy, why are you crying? Are you still afraid?"

3

The immense gun. The man's quizzical expression. The object he holds in his hand. The thunderclap of bullets. Carson wakes, clutching his chest, convinced it's his own blood, streaming from his chest, that's filling the bedroom with a reeking, heavy odor.

"Calm down, calm down. Breathe. Hold on to me," Bunny whispers in Carson's ear, her arms bracing him against her body. She comforts. She submits when Carson frees himself from her embrace only to push her beneath him, his tongue hungering for hers, his hands roughly shoving her gown above her thighs, his sex a shattering blow inside her. And when he is done, he still clings to her, Bunny on her side, curled tight to hide her wounds, Carson gripping her around the waist, skin to skin, body to body.

In the morning when he is alone in the house, Carson remembers what he dreamed. And what he did. How he used his wife as a sexual punching bag. All to forget. But he didn't forget. In the morning paper, filled with accounts of the prelude to war in Iraq, yesterday's brief synopsis has become "Officer Shoots Unarmed Man" on the front page of the Metro section. The twelve-paragraph story reveals the name of the man he shot, Paul Houston, a twenty-five-year-old third-grade teacher in southeast Washington, who was a graduate of Morehouse College and the School of Education at Columbia University. The article quoted one neighbor of the family who said, "He was a young man who had everything to live for. He was setting an example of the good things it was possible for a young man to do with his life."

Carson is identified as the officer who shot and fatally wounded Paul Houston in an incident under investigation. There it is. Everything. *In black-and-white*, the time Carson called in to the dispatcher, saying he was in pursuit of someone driving with no lights and speeding, the name of the mall where he faced Paul Houston in the parking lot. The fact that Houston was unarmed was stated several times in the story. There was no mention of the cell phone.

He didn't shoot a gangbanger, a drug dealer, or a suspect who had preyed on others and so in the eyes of most cops had cheapened the value of his own life, Carson thinks as he folds the paper.

Moments later he calls Matthew Frey.

"Did you see the article?"

"I did. But I don't want you to worry about this. Eventually I'm gonna get a call from the state's attorney and they'll invite you to testify before the grand jury. Carson, I'm not recommending this. You wouldn't have immunity and I can't be in the room with you. You have a Fifth Amendment right against self-incrimination, and I don't want you to violate that."

"But I have nothing to hide," Carson shouts into the phone.

"That's not the point."

"I was afraid for my life. Why can't I testify before the grand jury and make my case?"

"There'll be a prosecutor whose job it is to make his case, and from what I know of the evidence so far and because of your state of mind, I don't want you to testify."

"If I could just tell someone my side. What happened."

Frey hears the panic in Carson's voice and tells him, "Carson, it'll be weeks and maybe months before the grand jury meets and decides anything, whether you testify or not. We need to take one step at a time. After the grand jury makes a decision we'll know what to do next. I'm confident you'll come out of this all right, Carson. I know it doesn't seem now like that's possible, but I've been defending honorable men like you caught in terrible situations for more than twenty years. Right now, Carson, the next best person after me for you to talk to is a mental health professional."

"I don't need that now. I need to know I won't go to prison for this. Can you tell me that?"

"Carson, you know I can't make that kind of statement."

Now Frey knows what he could not fathom the night of the shooting. Carson Blake is crumbling. He hears this in the gruff insistence that he needs no help and in the prickly, panicked argument over Carson's testimony. Frey waits a full minute before he speaks again, hoping Carson will dive into that blank space with a courageous reconsideration of Frey's advice that he seek help. When he does not, Frey says, "When you're ready to talk to someone, Carson, let me know. I'll call you in a few days."

When he hangs up the phone, Carson remembers Bunny's warning this morning when she sat on the side of the bed before leaving for work. "Carson, you can't go through this alone. We can't go through this alone. I'm here for you, you know that, but we need help with this. Carson, this is a place we've never been before."

"I'll think about it, Bunny, that's all I can say," he mumbled, rolling over, responding to her plea with the sight of his back.

How could he seek counseling for post-traumatic stress disorder? Carson wonders, staring at the phone. Other officers would think he was crazy. He was sure then to lose his job, already in jeopardy. He'd never needed help before. Why couldn't Bunny's love be enough? It had been enough before.

He almost gave her a ticket. That's how they met. A Saturday night, and Carson was parked off a stretch of Annapolis Road. There was a club called Ecstasy not far from the VFW headquarters, and every weekend he racked up a pile of tickets, stopping speeders headed to the club. Parked in a strip mall, Carson saw a blue Corolla roar past, going almost seventy-five in a fifty-five-mile zone. He turned on his lights and followed the car as it crossed the intersection on a yellow light and then pulled over to the side of the road. When Carson scanned the interior of the car he saw five women, all in their early twenties. The car vibrated with nervous giggling and reeked of perfume, cigarettes, chewing gum, and marijuana. The sight of so many young women jolted and excited him. Bunny was behind the wheel. His flashlight illuminated her face, and he liked what he saw. She was wearing more makeup than he preferred on a woman, the mascara thick and hard on her lashes, but she was nervously, coyly licking her lips, and that turned Carson on. She was twenty-one, no more than twenty-two, he guessed, with a mature face that did not hide her youth. Bunny was staring dead at him. Carson liked that as much as the way she looked, as much as wondering how it would feel to kiss her. The other girls were looking away from him, out the window, sitting up straight; the one in the front with Bunny turned down the sound of Michael Jackson. But Bunny was looking straight at Carson.

He told her how fast she was going and that there were a lot of drunks out behind the wheel on a Saturday night.

"I've got no excuse, officer. We're on our way to Ecstasy to meet some friends. It's Saturday night. I know I was wrong."

"The club'll be there," Carson scolded her gently. To scare her he asked for her license and walked slowly back to his cruiser, where he called in to headquarters over the mike and asked for a check on her. He had no intention of writing a ticket or checking the car for drugs. He just wanted to delay her, send her a message. And so he dragged the stop out so he could look at her a little longer. Carson copied her address on a piece of paper and put it in his shirt pocket. Then he walked slowly back to the car.

Leaning through the driver-side window he said, "I'm just gonna warn you this time. But I'll probably be out here when you're on your way home. I don't want to stop you again."

Bunny smiled at Carson broadly, and he said, "Have a good night, ladies."

On his day off a week later, Carson knocked on Bunny's door.

"Hello, my name is Carson Blake," he began, figuring that the woman who opened the door must be Bunny's mother. Her suspicious, uncharitable gaze was so penetrating, Carson feared she knew about the sex dreams her daughter had inspired. He was a cop, and this squat, brown-skinned little woman who opened the door had him squirming. "I'm a friend of Belinda's." The lie relaxed him.

"Bunny," she called, stepping back, and to Carson's surprise and relief, moving from the entrance and ushering him into the hallway of the small, tight house. She didn't invite Carson to sit down on the plastic-covered furniture in the living room. The house smelled of cigarette smoke and fried chicken. Carson knew even then that he was standing in the home of the woman he would marry, and he wondered who smoked, the woman staring at him (he could not bring himself to think mother-in-law) or "Bunny." Carson liked the nickname. Carson heard someone coming down the stairs, and then there she was, in tight cutoff jeans and a halter top. Her hair was in rollers. But to Carson she looked beautiful. There was a moment, a brief flicker of surprise that bloomed in her eyes and that she quickly blinked away because her mother was looking from Carson to Bunny, back and forth, trying to figure out what was going on and who he was.

"Hi," Carson said softly.

"Hi."

"I know this is unexpected, but . . ."

"Come on, let's go outside."

"Outside?" her mother asked.

"Yeah, outside," Bunny cooed, sweeping past her mother and opening the front door.

The front porch was small, but there were two wrought-iron chairs on it. Flowered cushions shielded them from the chair's heat on the eighty-five-degree day. Carson sat down beside Bunny. Never before had he met a woman this young so comfortable in her body. She was an inch or two taller than Carson. But he forgave her for that.

"I wanted to make sure that you got home all right."

"I did."

Bunny crossed her legs. Her olive-toned skin was burnished by a slight tan. A mole lay just above her lip. She said nothing about how he had just shown up at her door; she just sat beside Carson as if they already knew everything of importance about each other.

"Did you have a good time at the club?"

"It was all right." She shrugged. "It's never as good as you think it will be."

"You go there every week?"

"Not *every week*." She laughed as though the idea was ridiculous.

"I didn't see your boyfriend in the car."

"That's right, you didn't," she told him, her eyes wide with a slow, sly assessment of him that silenced them both. Then she asked, "How long you been a police officer?"

"Two years."

"You like it?"

"Yeah, yeah, I do. Especially sometimes on Saturday nights," he joked, surprised at the subtlety of the humor. This didn't sound like Carson, but he liked what he heard.

"You always do stuff like this? I mean, track girls down?" Bunny placed her foot on the edge of her chair, hugged her knee, and stared at Carson the way she had looked at him on the night he stopped her.

"Believe me, this is the first time I've done something like this. This is blowin' *my* mind, but you're a hell of a woman."

Bunny stared at Carson, trying to decide, he knew, if he was a deranged serial murderer who puts on a cop uniform on Saturday nights or really a dude with a serious jones for her.

"You know my name, but I don't know yours," she said.

"Carson. Carson Blake. And I owe you an apology. And you don't owe me a thing." He hoped this new strategy would get him off the hook and speed things up. Shading her eyes from the glare of the sun with her long, red-nailed fingers, Bunny gave Carson one last look that took in everything about him that she could see and everything she suspected and said, "I'm hungry. You wanna take me to get something to eat?"

"Sure, this is my day off."

"Wait till I change my clothes."

Bunny came out of the house wearing a navy blue batik sleeveless dress that flowed lovingly over every curve of her body and big dark sunglasses. Her auburn hair was pulled back in a bun. Her mother looked out the window as Carson and Bunny walked away.

"What would you have done if I wasn't at home?" Bunny asked after she had buckled her seat belt.

"Kept coming back until you were."

Bunny laughed, the sound throaty and unrestrained. She re-moved her sunglasses and stared at Carson again. It was as though it finally hit her what she had done and she was holding this thought in her mind, measuring it to gauge the full weight of why she was sitting in his car beside him.

Bunny put her sunglasses back on and stared straight ahead, and Carson reached over and touched her hand. Without looking at him she entwined her fingers in his. Over lunch at Rips, sur-rounded by the slightly darkened rustic decor, she asked, "So you never did this before?"

"That's the second time you asked me that."

"I know."

"Why'd you come with me? I know even now you must be a little . . ."

"No, I'm not scared," she insisted. "Not anymore. I came be-cause I wanted to. You don't frighten me. I got in your car because I knew I'd be safe."

"That must be some feeling. It's one I'm not familiar with."

"A woman can tell."

"A man can too."

"What do you mean?"

"You're not the only one risking something here. Knocking on your door was harder than the hardest thing I've done on my job."

Carson sat outside Bunny's house for a full ten minutes, won-dering what he'd say. He sat in his car so long, a group of boys rid-ing bikes in front of the house next door huddled together and began whispering and pointing at him.

Now Bunny was sitting across from him in a booth at Rips. Listening to him. Since the night he almost gave her a ticket Car-son had tried to plot out what he'd do, what he'd say, if he were lucky enough to get inside her house. Nothing about his complex, haunting desire inspired him to think that what was happening would happen so easily, so fast.

"Did you always want to be a policeman?"

"No, I never thought about being a cop before I became one. I joined the army after high school. It made me feel like I was part of an effort much bigger and more important than me. I was stationed in Frankfurt, Germany, did two tours, and when I got back stateside I went to Prince George's Community College for two years, then decided to join the police force. I wanted to get that feeling back again."

"I've never been overseas, but I heard those German women love Black men," Bunny said while reaching for a bread stick from the basket on the table, then shifted her gaze to a penetrating study of the bread stick she held between her fingers.

"Yeah, some of them do."

"Did they like *you*?"

"Some of them did."

"Did you like them?"

"I liked quite a few. But it was never serious. I always felt they had an ulterior motive, like wanting to get to the States."

The women Carson had been involved with had often been older divorced women with children. Bunny's hazel eyes, now gazing at him, were a crystal ball in which he could see the real meaning of those relationships, how he had been just marking time. Stalling. Waiting for this. Waiting for her.

"Are you ever afraid on your job?"

"Sure," he told her with an easy shrug.

"Have you ever fired your weapon?"

"Not yet. I hope I never do. It's not like the cop shows on TV. They make more arrests in one day than we make in a month. When they shoot someone, they're back on the streets the next day. In real life we get put on leave that can last days, weeks, some-times as long as a year."

"What do you like about it?" Bunny asked each question with no hesitation, cradling her chin in her palm. Carson felt as if he'd never been looked at or listened to until now.

"Catching a bad guy, saving somebody's life.

"My first assignment was in my old neighborhood. So I knew everybody and I had to arrest some guys who'd been my friends. That's probably the hardest thing I've done so far.

"The first time you see a corpse it's a shock. Nothing prepares you for it. All that time I was in the army I was never on a battle-field. But my first week on the force a guy got shot in a drug deal that went bad. Shot in the face. I was just out of the academy, but I had to look at the body, get over the horror I felt, and knock on doors in the neighborhood to see who knew anything, who might have seen what happened. I learned pretty quick how to stand a few feet from a corpse and talk about sports or some TV show, how to laugh at another officer's joke, all so as not to lose it or fall apart because I'd just seen someone's brains splattered all over a kitchen wall or heard a four-year-old girl tell me or another offi-cer that her daddy had raped her.

"I've seen my own death in my mind. I've imagined it. Because I've seen other people die, up close, in a way I couldn't explain away. I found a sixteen-year-old girl murdered and buried in a shallow grave behind a high school. Most of the time it's quiet, but when all hell breaks loose, my own death flips through my mind. I can't help it. I'm not anticipating it, just acknowledging that any-thing, *anything,* could happen."

"Then you probably value life more than most people."

"I try to. I really do. Most people wouldn't think a cop would say that. They think we've all seen so much that's ugly, that's bad, that life gets cheap. There are a few officers on the force with me now—I call them the walking dead—they're like zombies, shell-shocked and callous. Bad apples. I never want to be that way. I'd quit before I got like that."

Carson decided then and there that Bunny was the most beautiful girl he'd ever met. Hers was a muted yet eccentric beauty expressed in the details of her face, wide, olive-toned, featuring her pug nose, the mole above her lip, and the gap between her two front teeth, the generosity and frequency of her smile. In the weeks following this first date, Carson would come to love just looking at Bunny, dressed in an outfit that rippled with colors that seemed Asian or African or some melding of both, her jewelry always some ancient-looking precious stone—topaz, amber, or jade—dangling earrings, made of the same natural stones, that when she laughed peeked out from the shadows of her long auburn hair. She loved rings, silver mostly, and wore one on nearly every finger. She'd turned herself into a work of art, woke up every morning and saw herself as a canvas.

The stories she told Carson that day about herself were blessedly normal. She was a Big Sister to a fifteen-year-old girl named Chantal who wanted to be a veterinarian. Bunny had graduated a month earlier from Marymount College in Arlington, Virginia, where she studied commercial art. During the summers she landed internships with local firms and had been hired by a small design firm in Georgetown as a junior designer, a job she would start in a week.

"Everything in the world is designed," she told Carson. The firm she would join created the logos and signs for the Arthur M. Sackler Gallery at the Smithsonian. "And I mean everything, from the rooms in the gallery, to posters, the brochures, maps, napkins in the cafeteria. Carson, everything you touch, from a bar of soap to toothpaste, has been designed. Nothing in the world that we live in is random. It's either been designed by us or by God. I'm pretty good at details, and I have a steady hand. I feel sometimes like the work I do, as much as I love it, is theoretical, mostly a concept. But I like it because it's functional and it can be beautiful at the same time. But what you do is so real. It's so essential," she told him, emphasizing the word *essential* as her fork grazed the flesh of her salmon steak. The word felt to Carson like an unexpected kiss on his lips.

"So you're an artist?" he asked, famished to know everything about her. Now.

"Well, yes and no."

"You have to show me some of your work," Carson said, nudging his way into her future, into days beyond this one.

"I will."

When they talked about their childhoods, Bunny told him she was an only child.

"That's how I always felt," Carson said, "although I've got a younger brother. But it toughened me up. Made me hungry for what I grew up missing, taught me that in the end you've got to depend on yourself to make it."

"I don't believe that," she shot back quickly, pleading her case with eyes he was now convinced could see everything he was and hoped to be. "We need each other, Carson—pitiful and cruel as we are, we're all we've got. I'll never believe we're supposed to go it alone."

Her words were like the flash of a comet, inexplicable and grand across the dark firmament of the past that Carson carried always with him and used as a weapon and a balm. That night he would dream of Bunny saying those words and wake up the next morning remembering the relief he felt at how bravely she punctured his cynicism.

Soon they were a couple, Carson going with Bunny to backyard barbecues and picnics and clubs on the Saturday nights he had off. Until then, he had taken all the overtime he could get and put in extra hours on the weekend at a security gig at one of the malls. The women before Bunny had to take his schedule or leave it. Between the overtime and the part-time job, Carson doubled his salary and had a fat chunk saved. He was just making the money and squirreling it away. Now he knew he'd been saving that money to start a life with Bunny.

There was no rush, because this was for keeps, he thought in those first weeks. Still, there was so much more of Bunny, so much more than he had imagined as he watched her walk toward him, coming out of the ladies' room as he stood in line to buy popcorn at the movies, or away from him, her hips undulating in the tight jeans she sometimes wore, as she walked to her front door when Carson took her home. So much more of her than he had thought from holding her on the dance floor at Ecstasy, his hands roaming the geography of her back and her hips as he throbbed bloated and impatient against her groin, as she laughed in his ear and ran her tongue across his lips. There was so much more of her when she was finally in his bed and he suckled her heavy, bulbous breasts, the dark brown nipples tense and veined with desire. Her thighs were more muscular than he thought, and they imprisoned him as she rocked beneath him, her moans not garbled but articulate and clear, chiseling an ancient language on the walls of his room. And there was so much more of her than Carson thought as he kissed her abdomen, the mixture of sweat and perfume, the biting smell of her, blistering his tongue. She shifted her body so that Carson was staring at her pussy as her fingers played with his ears and her hands massaged his head. He didn't hesitate to kiss her there. Bunny was thrusting and tensing with moans she muffled with her own hand.

And after Carson made love to her and then fucked her and made love again, and their bodies were twisted and joined in an embrace Carson swore to make last forever, they talked, because what they had just done didn't shut Carson down like when he'd just made it with the wrong girl.

Carson asked Bunny about her mother, who still assessed him warily when he came to the house, whose approval he could not seem to win, who set him shuddering with undeserved generalized guilt the way his stepfather, Jimmy Blake, used to do. Bunny lay propped up on several pillows, clutching the sheets above her breasts. Her hair was rumpled, framing her face in a seductive, delicate architecture.

"My mom's got a problem. It's called my dad. They divorced when I was ten and my father remarried. My mom won't move on, won't let go of him or what they went through."

"So when she looks at me she sees him?"

"Sort of. I mean, she just doesn't trust men."

"Tell me about it." Carson sighed, placing his hand beneath the sheets, embedding it between Bunny's thighs.

"Maybe you ought to find her a boyfriend."

"She can never meet anybody good enough for her. And when they get serious she breaks it off."

"Damn, so you mean she *wants* to be miserable, unhappy, and alone?"

"This *is* my mom we're talking about," Bunny said, punching him on the shoulder. "But yeah, sometimes it seems that way."

Carson wanted to ask Bunny what her mother had said to her about him, but he didn't want her to confirm the disdain he saw so often in Doris's eyes and he didn't want her to lie.

By the fall Carson was ready to ask Bunny to marry him. He had quit the weekend security gig to spend more time with her, easily, gratefully letting the job go. Bunny passed the ninety-day test. In ninety days, Carson was convinced, you discovered everything you needed to know about a woman. In ninety days you usually discovered why you'd stay. Or what would one day make you say good-bye.

Still, Carson kept waiting for Bunny to tell him she couldn't handle the demands of The Job, how much it took out of him. How little it left, some nights, for her. But she never said those words.

A week after Thanksgiving Carson met Bunny's father. Eddie Palmer owned a Ford dealership in Queens, New York, and was staying at a hotel one weekend while attending a dealers' conference. When he opened the door of his suite, Eddie grabbed Bunny and hugged her, lifting her a few feet off the floor and twirling her gently in his arms. Bunny had told Carson that she talked to her father every day.

When he released Bunny, Eddie offered Carson an energetic, nearly combative handshake. He had the practiced, slick enthusiasm of a deal maker. His hair was combed back from his face and was so black Carson wondered if it was dyed, and he imagined the man preening before the mirror, applying a coat of some heavy pomade. Eddie was dressed in khakis, a sleeveless undershirt, and suspenders and leather house shoes.

"Come on in, you two, come on in," he boomed. "Make yourselves at home." The suite was cozy and Eddie had finished a room service dinner, plates and trays and metal covers stacked on top of the mahogany dinner table. Carson and Bunny sat at the table and Eddie lifted the trays and dishes and placed them on the floor outside his room. He went into the kitchenette and brought out a bottle of red wine and a couple of glasses and several beers.

"Beer or wine?" he asked Carson.

"Beer."

Bunny opened the bottle of wine and poured her glass half full. Then Eddie sat down and shoved a beer and a glass toward Carson and opened a beer for himself. Carson sipped his beer and listened quietly as Bunny and Eddie talked family, Bunny's job, Eddie's convention, and Doris. Bunny had his pug nose, and Carson sensed in Eddie a purposeful confidence that bathed him in a sudden, welcome warmth. He had passed that on to Bunny. *He's probably a hell of a salesman*, Carson thought, watching Eddie sipping beer and eating pistachio nuts. Bunny wandered over to the sofa and turned on the television so that, Carson knew, he and Eddie could talk.

"So you're in law enforcement?"

"Yes, sir."

"Eddie."

"Yes, Eddie."

"A law 'n' order man," he said with a wink, opening his fat palm and releasing a fistful of pistachio shells onto a saucer.

"Well . . ."

"Oh, don't explain. Anybody who's got something to protect believes in law and order. You know, I never had a run-in with the law in my life. Never once, not even a ticket. I give the boys in blue their props."

"It's tough. Sometimes people see me in the uniform and just assume, well, you know . . ."

"Yeah, that you're a kick-ass. Our people got to grow up." Eddie wiped his hands on a napkin and looked over at Bunny, now cuddled on the sofa, shoes off, laughing at a rerun of *Living Single*. Eddie got up and sat beside Carson in the chair Bunny had left vacant.

"Bunny talks about you all the time. She told me how you met. Did Bunny ever tell you how I met her mother? I bumped into her as she was coming out of the telephone company after paying her monthly bill, and ended up following her for six blocks until she gave me her phone number." He laughed and shook his head at the memory. Then, with a knowing smirk that occupied not just his face but his whole body, he asked, "What was your plan? Arrest her if she didn't go out with you?" Eddie turned on a megawatt smile.

"Daddy," Bunny scolded him from the sofa.

"Aw, he can take it. You go on and watch TV. I'm talking to your man. This is between him and me."

Your man. Carson liked the sound of that.

"Honestly, I didn't have a plan. I was just hoping she'd give me a break and maybe a chance."

"Looks like she did. I don't know where you two are headed. I don't know if you even know. Even though her mama and me been divorced a while now and I'm remarried, it's important for you to know that I didn't go AWOL. You know what I mean, don't you?" Eddie looked at Carson steadily, his gaze holding its breath. "I pay my taxes, my bills, and I paid child support."

He was telling Carson that he was no statistic. No deadbeat dad. No trifling Black man who dropped his seed and didn't stick around to watch it grow.

"I know exactly what you mean."

"That's my baby girl. She'll always be that. They always make it seem like the mama's love is the deepest. The most important. But I'm more proud of staying in Bunny's life than anything else I ever did. I wasn't just a monthly paycheck. I was a father. And believe me, Doris didn't always make that an easy thing to do. I want you to handle my daughter with care. She says she loves you, so that means she's yours. But I gave her life, so she'll always be mine."

Eddie Palmer moved closer to Carson as he said all this, each word propelling his chair forward. He had given Carson an assignment, not a warning. He was the kind of man who could've whispered in Carson's ear, even as Bunny sat unsuspecting across the room, "Get out of my daughter's life," and said it with a blinding smile that dared Carson not to do as he'd been told.

"Do we have your blessing?" Carson asked.

"I'm not religious. I'm a businessman, Carson. I don't know the first thing about you. But I trust Bunny's judgment, and she wants me to trust you with her. All I'm saying is, I will."

Now he is entrusted with Bunny. Entrusted with his children. He has done more than let them down. He has revealed why he did not deserve them in the first place.

When he's in the shower like now, a week after the shooting, he can almost block out the sound of the cell phone ringing in his ears. Standing in the shower stall beneath the pounding watery baptism, Carson hears only a faint echo, a brief musical staccato. He turns his head to allow the onslaught of water to pour into his ears and drown out the pandemonium only he can hear. The water masks the ringing momentarily. But he knows the sound is still there beneath the steady pulse of the water. It's the imaginary ringing of Paul Houston's cell phone, the ringing he didn't hear that night. Did the phone ring? Was it on vibrate? Is that why he reached for the phone?

There are times when he can muffle the sound by focusing all his thoughts on a task. Like now, as he dresses, devoting all his senses to a discovery of the jeans and sweatshirt, socks, and slippers, all to deny the sound of the cell phone the oxygen of his attention. The durable strength of the jeans, their weight and surprising thickness, remind him that he bought them nearly a decade ago. Stepping into the pants ceremoniously, he allows himself to feel them slide snugly against his legs. Durable. Reassuring. Real. Not like the sound of the cell phone, which he doesn't trust even as he filters every conversation through its harrowing reverberation.

He's about to sit down and eat a breakfast of eggs and ham when the phone rings.

"May I speak to Officer Carson Blake?"

"Who's calling?"

"My name is Randy Albright. I'm a reporter for . . ."

"You know I can't talk to you."

"I'm calling because I'm doing a follow-up story on the shooting you were involved in."

"Why don't you leave me alone? I don't even have to talk to my commanding officer now. Why the fuck would I talk to you?"

"To give your side of the story," he says as though offering Carson the deal of a lifetime. "I got a call from a community group out in the county that's staging a protest against police brutality at the county executive's office today. Yours is the fifth fatal shooting of a suspect by the county police since December, and . . ."

Carson hangs up the phone. *Fuck it,* he thinks, *I'm not gonna let some asshole ruin my breakfast.* But the eggs and ham taste like paste and land heavily in his resisting stomach. Halfway through the meal, the spasm in his abdomen forces him up from the table only moments before he expels the ham, the toast, jelly, and coffee in a seizure of retching, exploding them all over the kitchen floor and table. The sight of the food, still undigested, and the acrid odor of gastric juices sickens him even more as he slumps against the kitchen counter. And he can hear it again, the phantom cell phone, its ringing. If it's not the sound of the phone, what fills his mind is the image of him going to prison. A former cop in jail. What inmates would try to do to him. What he would have to do to survive. His wife and children visiting him, incarcerated at the facility over in Jessup, talking to him via phone, the only connection allowed through inches of Plexiglas.

It takes the rest of the morning to recover from the call and the botched attempt to eat. The reporter has reminded him that he's now a prisoner of the bureaucratic hell of the police department. Even after the grand jury decides whether or not to indict him for the shooting, there is the Internal Affairs investigation. His case will be one of the thousands IAD investigates every year, everything from complaints of police officer rudeness to brutality to charges of wrongful death. And the protesters? *Let them march,* Carson thinks bitterly, *let them shout, let them give interviews for the six o'clock news.* None of them could do his job or live the life he's got now, not for one single day.

In the afternoon Carson goes outside to retrieve the mail. His neighbor Earl Mattheson is walking down his driveway. The day is chilly, too cold for casual banter, Carson thinks as he plots a quick retreat back into his house after getting his mail. Earl waves politely, and Carson feels immediately the wariness in his glance. There are the odd days when he and Earl will talk for a while, clutching hands full of junk mail, bills, and magazines. When Earl discovered that Carson was a police officer he told Carson he had wanted to be a fireman when he was in high school but as he got older realized he wanted money more than he wanted to be a hero, so he went into accounting. Carson and Bunny have been to dinner a couple of times with Earl and his wife, Sheila, a flamboyant, buxom woman who's made a small fortune selling cosmetics out of her home. They're good neighbors, friendly but not intrusive. Carson enjoys Earl's gruff but warm greeting when he sees Carson drive up to his house some mornings after a late shift. Earl, behind the wheel of his BMW, will pull close to Carson's cruiser and lean out the window and ask, "Man, when you gonna stop all this crime out here?" jocular and teasing.

"I can't do it all by myself," Carson would say through a grin, throwing his hands in the air in mock confusion as both men laughed.

Today Carson just wants to get the mail and go back inside his house. He's got an armful of magazines, *Essence, Jet, Popular Science, Woodworking,* and a stack of bills when Earl turns around clutching three envelopes and walking toward Carson, saying, "I been reading about you in the paper."

"Yeah, everybody has." Carson is intentionally rude, pretending intense interest in the envelopes and magazines, riffling through them to avoid looking at Earl.

"In the paper it said that young man you shot didn't have a gun."

This is just like Earl, Carson thinks, *blunt as a hammer.* Carson turns to look at his neighbor standing before him, his body trim, his stance rigid, arms behind his back. As usual Earl is impeccably dressed, today in brown slacks and a white turtleneck sweater. He's a tall man, coal black. His mustache is flecked with gray and behind his bifocal glasses his small eyes squint impatiently, looking at him, Carson thinks today, as though he's seeing him for the very first time.

"That's right. He didn't," Carson says defensively.

"But you thought . . . ?"

"Obviously, Earl, I thought he was armed."

Bringing his arms from behind his back and folding them across his chest in a grand, sweeping gesture, Earl tells Carson, "A friend of mine knows the family real well. Says he was a good kid."

Before Carson can say anything Earl goes on, "You know, I never understood how you all decide to shoot to kill." He's drawn out the last words, articulated them slowly, carefully—*shoot to kill*—so that they hang like an incontrovertible judgment between them.

"Earl, trust me, you have to be there, in the moment," Carson says, forcing a reasonableness he does not feel.

"But if he had no gun . . . I don't understand. How was he a threat to you?" Earl shifts his weight from his left leg to his right and is clearly prepared, Carson sees, to stand outside for as long as it takes to interrogate him about the worst moment of his life.

"It's a tragedy, Earl, that's what it is."

"Maybe it's a tragedy for you. But it's over for that young man."

Carson turns away and walks up his driveway, the weight of Earl's disdain nearly grinding him into the blacktop with each step. Earl stands proud and censorious at the base of Carson's lawn, watching him, Carson thinks, as though he is a formerly tame animal who has committed an unprecedented act of violence. Earl watches him, Carson thinks as he closes the front door as though he is deciding whether he should be destroyed for his own good.

He doesn't make a move until he's sure Bunny is asleep. Then he risks waking her with a kiss on the cheek and the lingering of his fingers on her arm resting on the comforter. He turns away from the sight of his wife, for if he looks at her too long he will lose his nerve. Sliding off the bed, he decides to leave his pajamas on. Why get dressed? What difference would that make? Walking out of the bedroom into the hallway, he's chilled by the vacant quietude of the 3:00 a.m. darkness. So still. Outside, morning shrouded in tones of night. His house plunged as well into listless gloom. He pads quickly past the rooms of his children, forcing himself not to think of their faces in the aftermath. But what good is he to them now? How can he teach his children to be honorable, honest? Rest assured in the orbit of his wife's love? Juwan locked each evening in his room, shunning him. Roslyn and Roseanne strangely hesitant to kiss him good night like before. And Bunny's lies enrage him, that Juwan's simply studying for the standardized tests, that the girls are worried about him, not afraid of him. No, he's seen it: more fear of him in their eyes than he saw in the eyes of Paul Houston. He's seen it, or has he imagined it? But imagining makes it real.

In the garage he turns on the light and gets in his car, out of habit, behind the steering wheel. Leaving them behind feels harder, more impossible than what he is about to do. He has written no note. He could not imagine any words that he could use to explain. Or say good-bye. He feels selfish and generous. Selfish because it's all about him, what's in his head, the dreams, the sounds, the face, relentless, constant, more reliable now than his heartbeat. It's about what everyone knows about him now. Even if they haven't read the papers, seen the TV news reports, he is marked. Indelible. Transparent. Only the blind could not see what he has done, who he has become.

He's been planning, deciding to commit the final act while the world as he knew it has already crumbled at his feet, while he walks through the skeletal remains of what he has done. This is generous, because everyone he leaves behind can go on, free of the agonizing sight of his meltdown.

In his hands the Beretta is merely an extension of his fingers, his arm. He's carried a gun so long, worn one every day for twelve years, that it feels perfectly normal. As an officer of the law he carries an instrument of death, annihilation, as a matter of course. He never talked about it with anyone, not even Eric, how easy it is for them as cops to blow their brains out. End it all. Anywhere. Anytime. In their cruiser. On the toilet in the bathroom. No need to buy pills, rope, rifle through the kitchen drawer for the sharpest blade. Everything they need is always on them. Within reach. Strapped on their ankle. In their holster. In a lockbox in the basement. Under the driver's seat of the cruiser. Always there. Friend. Protector. Crutch. Answer. Question. Even now.

There is a savage certainty about placing the gun in his mouth, the metal cool and passive against his tongue. He closes his eyes and feels a tense and terrible strain of tears against his lids, tears that well up in his throat. There is no replay of his life behind his trembling lids, as he had expected. There is only, immediately, the face of the woman he loves, the children whose lives he made. And in this moment, stripped, he is sure of hope, and even of love; it is their faces and no others, not Paul Houston's, not his own, that he sees. Tears glut his throat and he coughs, loudly, harshly, expelling the gun from his mouth. It slides onto the floor of the car.

At four-thirty Bunny frantically opens the door to the garage and sees Carson behind the steering wheel of his car. Running from the bedroom, barefoot, she refuses to think what she fears. When she opens the passenger-side door, she stops breathing at the sight of the gun on the floor. But Carson is asleep, snoring gently. She eases into the car beside him, places her hand on her chest to still her heart. She closes her eyes, leans back in the seat, and reaches for her husband's hand, and she holds it until dawn.

4

Carrie Petersen's office looks nothing like Carson expected. A cocker spaniel sleeps on the floor beside her desk in the basement office of her Columbia, Maryland, home. Among the rows of framed photos on her walls are articles about police officers killed in the line of duty and decorated for acts of valor. She has a wide, flat face that seems some mixture of Caucasian and Indian or Asian, and she wears a short brown pageboy. Despite the spike of crow's-feet in the corners of her eyes, her age is indeterminate. She's a former cop turned private therapist, with a client base that includes many police officers and emergency service workers. She's plump in a black pantsuit, patient as a suburban Buddha as she sits waiting for Carson to answer her question.

"How has it been for you since the night of the shooting?"

No one has asked him this question. He's been offered sympathy, pity, judgment. But until today he has not been asked this question: *How has it been for you?* This inquiry is so stunning and unexpected, Carson lets the words roll across the floor of his mind like marbles at play. He still feels like shit, still hears the echo of the imaginary cell phone as a backdrop to every waking thought.

It was the touch of Bunny's fingers on his that woke him,

stranded and shamed in his car beside the wife who now knew the unforgivable about him. There was only their hands entwined and the sound of their breathing for the longest time, his heavy, deep, hers shallow and stunned. Then, sitting in the car in the garage with him, letting her hand in his signal everything that was possible for him and for them, the Beretta retrieved stealthily from the car floor and hidden in the pocket of her robe, Bunny told him, "I won't let you do this to us. Carson, I'm going to get the name of a therapist from Matthew Frey, and you have to go. If you don't . . ."

"If I don't what?"

"I won't be a witness to this."

"Bunny, come on . . ." he pleaded, turning in his seat to look at her, replenished by her presence, ready to forget the gun if he could forget nothing else. "You know . . ." he began, but she flinched, drew away from him, her back a thud against the passenger side door.

"Don't touch me."

"What?"

"Don't touch me until you're ready to fight for what we have, fight for our future. Fight for our life."

"I wouldn't have . . ."

"Stop lying," she screamed, moving even farther away from him. "I could've woke up a widow. My children, orphans."

"Bunny, I just feel . . ."

"I know what you feel. Don't you think I see it?" she shouted.

Leaning back in his seat, he told her firmly, "I can figure this out by myself. I just need some time."

"Like you figured it out after Eric died?"

"Eric's been dead three years."

"And for you it's like it was yesterday. You keep it all to yourself, but I know what you feel. I know how you feel it. I'm your *wife*, Carson." It was a bitter, urgent harangue delivered in a voice he had never heard, a voice at once edgy and resolute. "We don't have time—we've only got our life, and ten minutes ago you wanted to destroy it."

"Just give me a few days, a week, to think about it."

Bunny opened the door and slid out of the car, then took a last look at him, saying, "You've run out of time."

"How has it been for you since the shooting?" Carrie Petersen asks again.

"I can't sleep. The shooting's like a tape stuck on Play in my mind all the time."

"Can you tell me about the shooting, frame by frame as it unfolded, as you saw it in your mind's eye?"

"If he just hadn't touched that damn phone," Carson says, gazing at his hands, taut, gripping his knees as if to stall the possibility of flight. He hasn't had to tell the story of the shooting in a while, although he's relived it every moment of every day. He doesn't know where to begin, but when he finally speaks the words come torrential and fevered. "He'd been speeding with no lights. By the time I caught up with him, by the time he stopped, I was all revved up. You know how it is. You used to be out there. You're in the cruiser, chasing someone, with no idea who's in the car. Your body just goes on overload. Everything you feel, whether it's suspicion or anger or impatience or just 'What the fuck is going on?' you feel it so intensely. So by the time he pulled into the strip mall parking lot, I'm wired . . . He did everything I told him to do at first. But then he starts talking to me like I'm his homey, about his girlfriend and an argument they had and how he was so fucked up about the argument he didn't even know he was driving with no lights and he didn't stop because he didn't think I was following him . . . And I don't want to hear this—I want to go home. I want to ticket him and let him go. And then while he's on the ground with his hands behind his head, he reaches in his waistband for something and then before I can do anything he's up on his feet. Up on his feet, facing me. I told him to drop whatever it was, and he's moving toward me. Pointing the object at me. I'm yelling at him and he's yelling at me and I don't know how the fuck this has happened. By all rights I coulda shot him the minute he reached in his waistband. But now he's standing up! He's facing me! And it's like he made one step too many. He moved his arm one time too many and I shot him . . . And it was all in slow motion . . . So slow, God, it was so slow. I thought surely maybe the bullets could turn around and reenter my gun when I saw him fall back from the force of the first bullet. Time stopped, everything stopped even as it was going forward. Even as the other bullets were being fired. I was suspended and frozen and firing all at the same time. Everything was so big—him, his body as he fell, my gun, my hands. And when I saw the cell phone, God damn, when I saw that he'd had a cell phone I would've changed places with him. I would've changed places with him." Carson wipes the tears that have puddled on the bridge of his nose.

"What was going through your mind?"

"Scared. Confused. I could feel every muscle in my body contract." He pauses. Wiping his eyes with the back of his hand, he says, "I hadn't even had a chance to search him. *I would've changed places with him.*"

Carson hides his face in his hands, a damp and humid refuge. Carrie walks over to Carson, touches him gently on the shoulder, and offers him a box of tissues.

"When your wife called me to make an appointment, she told me about the night in the garage."

"I was depressed. I wasn't going to kill myself. I love my family—I'd never hurt them like that."

"Wait a minute," Carrie explodes dismissively. "You had a gun in your mouth—tell me, what did you think you were going to do?"

When Carson refuses to answer, she asks, "Does your wife know everything you're feeling?"

"She knows about the nightmares. I can't talk to her about anything else. I don't want her to know. I've put her through enough."

"When your wife called me she was frantic. Don't you think your death would've put her through even more?"

"I swear, I *didn't* want to die."

"Why do you think you were in your car with your gun?"

"I couldn't get the cell phone to stop ringing in my head. I couldn't eat. I kept seeing his face. What kind of father can I be? Can Bunny love me despite what I've done? I could go to prison for this. I . . . didn't know what else to do."

"So you didn't want to die, you just wanted the pain to stop."

"Yeah, that's right."

"Carson, you survived the shooting and even the night in your garage. But you won't survive the aftermath of either if you don't change. You're a closed system, a database of one. This is a cancer inside you, and you've got to talk about this or it'll destroy you." Carrie Petersen pauses and watches Carson for the effect of her words. "All your nevers have come true," she says gently, softening her voice. "Most police officers *never* fire their weapon. You have. The shooting is a part of who you are. I know you want to deny that, but it has to be a part of you that you accept, face up to, and own—that's the only way you'll be able to move on. I'm here to help you make a new meaning for your life that includes that night, a meaning that you can live with and grow from."

Carson leaves Carrie Petersen's office drained. The pit of his stomach feels hollowed out, and it rumbles noisily. The session has disturbed and dislodged an affliction. Sitting in his car outside Carrie Petersen's before he drives off, Carson knows this momentary emptiness has merely shifted the malady that tortures him.

On his way back home, he takes an absurdly circuitous route to avoid passing the strip mall where the shooting happened. The barbershop he frequents is in that mall. He needs a haircut, misses the oratorical preening, and jiving, the raucous debate that simmers and boils over in the always-crowded shop. But Carson fears that his entry on a payday Friday would halt all conversation. The regulars and the barbers all know he's a cop. He's held forth in their midst about crime in the county and what it takes to do his job. Carson is sure that some of them, the ones who've seen his name in the newspaper or the twenty-second report on TV, feel he should be arrested.

The county is in the throes of a development frenzy. So he figures he will never have to go to *that* mall for anything ever again. The strip malls, the stores, most of which are megasize cathedrals to commerce, are addictive and necessary. Even the new churches resemble warehouses: One Fundamentalist denomination simply bought a decaying, largely empty mall, built an auditorium to seat ten thousand, and renamed the mall, which still featured a busy office supply store and a health food emporium, Kingdom Hall. Carson grew up in the county and feels oppressed and slightly alienated by the rolling expansiveness of the economic and commercial growth that has sparked both prosperity and crime. Prince George's County seems to him now a bedroom community that's all function and commerce, with little that's quirky, beautiful, or surprising.

He promised Bunny he'd pick up her clothes at the dry cleaner's on his way home and then get several rolls of film. Carson slides the pink receipt across the counter and avoids looking at

the pudgy, bespectacled Korean youth who greets him with a
cheery, heavily accented "Hi, how you today?"

Carson nods and stares at the clock on the wall and the poster
touting the environmental and health benefits of the chemical-free
solvent used by the cleaners. He's been coming here for years. Yet
today he stands before the young man, who is handing him several of his shirts and Bunny's silk blouse and two pairs of her slacks,
all nerves and prickly with a sudden desire to flee. He takes the
plastic-covered clothing, hands the young man a twenty-dollar
bill, and without waiting for change turns to leave, bumping into
a woman carrying an armful of shirts. A flicker of annoyance burns
in her eyes, and is it his imagination or is there recognition in her
glance as well? But Carson has never seen this tall, square-jawed
woman before. Recognition, yes, that is what he sees, he's sure of
it. Not of him but of what he's done, the eyes seeing not just his
face but the depth of him, the quagmire roiling inside.

At home Carson goes to the basement and sits at his workbench, sees the small tools hung from the Peg-Board nailed to the
wall and his larger tools—the sanding block, various clamps and
drills, saws, stacked on three shelves. He leans on the cool white
surface of his drawing board. He started making cabinets and
wooden objects after Eric's death. Falling apart, he wanted to work
with his hands, to build objects that would ground and steady him.
Wood beckoned. Working with wood, his hands, and a single, simple vision of an object, he made a keepsake box for Roseanne, a
slender three-legged table with a glass top for Bunny to place a
small sculpture from Zimbabwe on, a bookcase for Juwan, a table
for no reason at all. He was working on his largest project yet in
the days before the shooting, a cabinet in Swedish yellow ash.
Woodworking is involved, intricate, straightforward, and in some
ways simple. There is the deceptively subtle beauty of the cherrywood keepsake box that left Roseanne bereft of speech when he

gave it to her for her birthday. Her hands rubbed the box as though a genie were inside, and then she said, "Oh, I love you, Daddy."

Wood is alive, and, Carson is convinced, it has a soul. When the work is going well, the tools are an extension of himself, making it possible for the wood to speak its mind, to become what it wants to be. The bookcase he had planned to make for Juwan was going to be a simple shelf, but over the weeks of work the cherrywood called out for union with the fragrant scent and tones of juniper wood and demanded a small drawer and high sides. He had thought his son was worthy of a shelf to place his books on. But the act of creation unleashed the possibility for a holder of the boy's dreams. Carson sits at the workbench, remembering when it was good down here, a stream of shavings curling from the plane in his hands and drifting onto the floor, forming a carpet around his feet. The swish and slide as he rocks to the motion of the work. There is the smell of the wood, which he often gets freshly cut from a dealer in Crofton, never buying from the big hardware chains. He works here in this corner of the basement, content, surrounded by the smells of the wood itself. What he produces is never what he planned. And with the tools, the small knives and the behemoth drills, Carson rounds edges, sands, traces with fingers that read the wood like a book, the grain, heart, and texture of wood, finding so often its real beauty in what seems at first to be its imperfections. Carson looks at the frame of the cabinet, the sight of it swelling his heart. The cabinet is six feet high and one of the doors leans against the wall. He walks slowly over to the door, reaches out to touch it, feels the grain against his palm, like the handshake of a friend, and leans on the wood, his forehead resting on his arm.

This is how Bunny finds him, and he doesn't stir when he hears her come down the stairs and walk over to him.

"How was your session?" she asks.

"Just the beginning," he tells her, standing upright and burying his face in her hair, holding her tight around the waist.

When Carson sees Carrie Petersen a week later, she says to him during the session, "Tell me the finest moment for you as an officer."

"I saved a kid from drowning. I was a minute or two from the house when the dispatcher got the call. I beat Emergency Services. It was a birthday party, and when I got to the house I found all these adults standing around holding their heads, crying, clutching each other, comforting a roomful of kids. There were balloons strung over the patio and a clown, a huge cake, stacks of presents the little girl hadn't even unwrapped. She was lying on the side of the pool, no sign of life, nothing. I performed CPR on her. I remember she was wearing a lime green bathing suit and her hair was all frizzy and damp. She was as limp as a rag doll. She looked about the same age as my girls, and I kept wondering what I'd do if I couldn't save her. The mother was crying, wailing like the little girl was already dead, and the man who I guess was the father was holding her, telling her to calm down, that everything would be all right. I couldn't believe how much water was coming out of the girl's mouth, while I worked on her, with her eyes still closed, even as she began jerking into consciousness. And then she started choking and coughing and opened her eyes and stared at me as though waking from a nightmare. Then she screamed. It's weird. That scream, which sounded so horrible, told us she was alive.

"EMS got there right at the moment she started screaming. The girl's name was Tammy, and she wrote me a letter a couple of weeks later, thanking me for saving her life. I went by her house one day just to check on her and found her outside riding her bike. I gave her a charm bracelet my girls had helped me pick out for her. Saving that kid's life took me, what, thirty seconds, a minute? Just like with the shooting, I thought those moments would never end. But I can't think of anything I've done that made me feel more valuable. Now I'm pretty sure I'll never feel that way again."

5

Cleaning and cooking help Bunny to forget. For a while anyway. *My house, this at least is one thing I can make right*, she thinks, hurriedly pulling her nightgown over her head and changing into underpants, a sweatshirt, and a pair of baggy jeans in the bathroom.

Bunny knows the trick is to keep moving. To start and not stop. That way she won't have time to think about anything. She sorts clothes in the laundry room and fills the front-loading washer. In the kitchen, from beneath the sink she grabs a plastic bucket, fills it with hot water and floor cleaner, lifts it from the sink, places it on the floor, and drops an old hand towel in the warm foamy water as she sinks to her knees. The water saturates the cloth and Bunny wrings it out, begins scrubbing the ivory-colored squares of linoleum. On her hands and knees she won't miss any dirt, and the exertion gives her back muscles a good workout. While the floor dries, she dusts in the living room and cleans the leather sofa and recliner with a creamy liquid conditioner, scrubbing vigorously, using her arms and hands in a way that she feels is purifying, as sweat congeals in her armpits, warms the surface of her skin, cleansing her of the fog that refuses to break its hold on her spirit. Bunny cleans the toilets in the guest and basement bathrooms.

Carson got out of bed at seven, put on his jogging suit, and told her he was going for a run, that he'd get breakfast at Bob Evans and then take his car for an oil change and tune-up. Alone in the house, Bunny cleans in a frenzy for another hour. In the living room, a collection of Black figurines, some no larger than an inch or two, populate a small world inside a ceiling-high, delicately carved wooden armoire with glass windows. Black angels in billowing robes blowing trumpets; a toddler on a tricycle, a mutt at her side barking in delight; a white-haired elderly couple staring with frozen love into each other's eyes; an African princess draped in gold and kente cloth; three children stuffed into an armchair, all reading the same book. Bunny has collected the figures over the years; some Carson gave her as gifts.

Bunny goes upstairs to tackle the master bedroom, where mourning and defeat hang like a stale stench in the air. It's a psychic runoff accumulated during the hours Carson spends in the room alone, sleeping, watching television, drinking beer, in self-imposed hibernation and retreat.

Having cleaned every object and surface in the house, Bunny returns to the kitchen, retrieving a leg of lamb from the middle shelf of the refrigerator, unwrapping it, rinsing the meat, and placing it in a roasting pan. While slicing the pods of garlic to embed in the slits she's made in the thick flesh, Bunny cuts her index finger and draws blood. The wound, when she inspects it closely, is not deep; it's a gash piercing the top of her finger. Still, there is blood, ruby, thick, and there is pain. All she has to do is apply pressure. If she looks on the top shelf over the stove she'll find the bandages she needs to stop the flow of blood.

She bandages the finger as the tears dammed up behind her eyes all morning, the pressure from which has given her a headache, finally begin to flow. Utterly exhausted, Bunny covers the leg of lamb in plastic wrap and places it in the refrigerator. She wants to cry. Again. All day. But none of the tears she has shed since the shooting have changed anything, and more tears will only make her headache worse. She stands in the middle of the living room, assessing her now-spotless house, seeing in her mind the rooms upstairs, the kitchen, the air heavy with the lingering scent of the polishes and cleansers. A good morning's work, she thinks, biting her lip and sinking onto the sofa to weep again.

They have never had a secret like the suicide attempt, a confidence that they both know must be permanently suppressed. She cannot tell her best friend, Pam, dares not speak of it to her mother, can never tell her children. If she had shifted in her half sleep that night and assumed that Carson was in the bathroom when her leg sprawled over the cool, vacant sheet, what would have happened? What would he have done? Bitterness is a bruise on her heart. Love feels like a pretense and a masquerade. She never imagined Carson would kill in the line of duty. Until now, she'd always assumed their marriage was strong enough to see them through anything. It never occurred to her that Carson would think of throwing it all away. They are conjoined in a web of secrecy even with Carrie Petersen, who, bound by doctor/client privilege, could not reveal anything Carson told her to the department. Carson dared not even risk telling Melvin Griffin, his sergeant, that he'd thought of taking his life or that he had sought therapeutic help. The revelation of either could derail his return to work.

Bunny wonders if there will ever come a time when they laugh again. The way they used to laugh about how they met. And the fact that yes, she *was* waiting for him the day he showed up at her house. She's extremely intuitive, can feel and sense things and, unlike most people she knows, isn't afraid to trust what she feels. She trusts what she feels more, in fact, than what she thinks. It's like when she's working on a design project. Carson has asked her so many times how she decides what colors to use and what shapes a logo demands. She doesn't know. She just keeps at it until the colors and shapes take hold of her. She tries to tell him that the worst thing to do is to think her way through a design. She has to stumble into whatever symmetry and beauty the project has to offer. *Stumble and feel.*

It was that way with Carson on the Saturday night that he stopped her and almost gave her a ticket. And she recalls it as though it happened not then but now, is happening now. *He is not particularly handsome,* she thinks as she sees his face illuminated in the glow of the flashlight beaming on her face. He's got freckles across the bridge of his nose. It is a flat, wide, square face. His complexion is a shade, just a whisper, darker than hers. But she doesn't fall for the face. It's never the looks with her. It's a man's energy. And that night Bunny feels *it.* While Carson is gently scolding her for speeding, while she is looking at him dead on, directly, right in the eye, Bunny feels some soulful, high-frequency current pass between them. And she knows that Carson feels it too. Once or twice before she has felt this sexual/psychological voltage pass between her and a man, but never like this. Never like this.

When they marry of course she wants to know, and she does not want to know, everything about what Carson calls The Job. She's not just a wife. She's a cop's wife. And that means that every time that Carson comes home from his shift Bunny counts it as a reprieve. He doesn't like to talk about the streets, what he sees and what he does during his shift, but he doesn't have to tell her. It's all revealed in the tension she feels in his shoulders, his neck, his whole body, especially on those nights when Carson comes in and after a shower she gives him a massage. His body tells her every-thing he won't. She's a cop's wife and a member of a tribe. There are Bring Your Own Bottle cop cabarets and dances and parties and weddings. And most of the cops that Bunny comes to know over the years are like everybody else and yet absolutely unique in their perspective on things. They have to be. There is the sense that they are different. Not like everyone else. Their jobs are in a special category marked life or death.

She should have seen this coming, she thinks. But how could she have seen what she still can't believe? That Carson would kill an innocent man. Someone who was no threat to him. It was al-ways his life she had feared for. They had been so lucky. Carson was just like most cops on the street, men and women who never once fired their weapons. Now he was someone else. Now he oc-cupied a separate space, a parallel world, a hell of his own making where he had crossed a border and saw no way back to who or what he used to be.

Because she has cried and feels wretched but oddly chaste, Bunny allows herself to feel, full blown, the tremble of fear that swallows her up when she thinks of what Carson has done. She feels the fear even as she imagines her own version of the chilling, unalterable moment and what Carson must have felt, and she wonders what the man he killed thought, watching the bullets turn him into a target. Bunny has never been afraid of Carson. She is not afraid of him now. But if this could happen . . . The shudder passes and Bunny vows never to think this way again. But she doesn't choose all her thoughts.

If he had just gotten off the streets, taken the test for sergeant like Eric—but Carson shunned the idea of becoming part of the force's bureaucracy. Whenever Bunny mentioned Carson's joining the police department's administration as a way to get off the streets, he'd tell her, "I'm no paper pusher. I'd go nuts in an office, some supervisor breathing down my neck. This way I do my shift and I'm done."

Bunny showers and changes clothes and goes back to the kitchen, where she places the lamb in the oven. By noon it will be ready and she and Carson can have an early dinner for two, she thinks, and maybe she can coax him into taking her to a movie. As she begins to think of what she will prepare to accompany the leg of lamb, the doorbell rings.

Through the peephole at the front door Bunny sees her mother and takes a deep breath, feels the familiar agitation that Doris's presence so often inspires.

"I didn't know you were coming," Bunny gently complains, ushering her mother into the house.

"Since when do I have to call my own daughter? Why can't I just stop by?" Doris asks, her voice stilted with mock hurt.

Doris's black velour running suit is more stylish than practical, set off by large hoop earrings and a gold chain, and nails polished a startling deep red. Doris casually and quickly removes her light-weight jacket and follows Bunny into the kitchen.

"I just wish you'd called. You know how things are now," Bunny says as Doris fills the teapot with water and puts it on the stove.

"You don't mind if I have a cup of tea, do you?"

"Mama, come on, not today," Bunny says with a sigh.

"Well, you always make me feel like I'm invading your home, not visiting."

"You know that's not true."

"It's how I feel, whether you want me to feel that way or not," Doris says, leaning against the counter as she waits for the water to boil.

Bunny reaches for several potatoes from the basket on the counter and begins peeling them.

"Where're you coming from?"

"I had lunch with some of the members of my bridge club," Doris says. "And where are my grandchildren?" she asks eagerly.

"The girls are spending the weekend with a friend, and Juwan is on a Boy Scout camping trip."

"And Carson?" Doris asks pointedly.

"He's out."

Steam blasts from the teapot nozzle. Doris turns off the burner and pours hot water into the Orioles mug Bunny has placed on the counter with a tea bag inside.

Bunny has never forgotten Doris's dire response when she told her that Carson had asked her to marry him. "I've heard all kinds of things about those police officers. A girl like you could do so much better."

A girl like you. A girl with her father's soft, straight hair and olive-toned skin, which had people wondering sometimes if she was Hispanic. Whose mother combed and brushed her hair as though the act was a sacrament, and told Bunny repeatedly, "Thank God you got your daddy's hair and didn't get mine."

When Bunny told Doris about the shooting, Doris said, "Well, I'm sorry to hear that. Real sorry." That was all she said, but underneath those words Bunny heard the unspoken "I told you so."

"How is Carson?" Doris asks, stirring her tea.

"I finally convinced him to seek some help. He's seeing a therapist," Bunny says, placing the knife and the potatoes on the counter.

"Good." Doris beams with what appears to be sincere approval. "Who is it?"

"Mom, it's no one you'd know. She's in private practice." This revelation feels momentous to Bunny, unused to sharing details of her married life with her mother. Still, it falls far short of telling

Doris that Carson had thought of taking his own life. Bunny would never tell her mother about that.

"And I don't want you telling any of your friends he's in therapy, either, Mom."

"I wouldn't. But is he ashamed of needing help?"

"It's not that. It's just that it could change the way his fellow officers look at him, the way they feel about him, if they knew."

"Lord God, that makes no sense. Why did this have to happen?" Doris asks, taking a sip from the mug of steaming tea. "I feel for that family."

"We all do, Mama," Bunny tells her, peeling potatoes once again as a mound of skins litters the counter. She realizes that she has peeled more potatoes than she needs, but she'll make potato pancakes with the leftover mashed potatoes.

"Umph, umph, umph," Doris mutters. "It sure is a tragedy all around. But you can't help but wonder. I mean, you never hear of this kind of thing happening to White people. It's always one of us gets shot like this. Seems like our lives are so cheap."

"Are you saying Carson did this on purpose?" Bunny asks as she scoops the potato peelings into a plastic garbage bag.

"Of course not," Doris shoots back defensively, her face bunched in horror at the question. "But why is it always us? And it doesn't make it any easier that Carson is Black and that young man was too. In fact, it makes it worse."

"He's not a killer." Bunny announces this with a firm voice bristling with conviction as she turns from the sink to look at her mother. Doris casts her own gaze away from the withering condemnation she sees on her daughter's face and takes another sip of tea.

Praying silently that her mother will find it impossible to forge ahead in this line of rumination, Bunny runs cold water over the

potatoes, now in an aluminum bowl. She puts them in the refrigerator, washes her hands, and removes her apron before grudg-
ingly sitting down across from Doris.

"Bunny, just hear me out," Doris pleads, placing her warm
palm on Bunny's folded hands. "It just seems that something happens when they put on that uniform. I told you about Jacob, that
boy in my choir at church. Stopped for going through a red light.
Sure, he was wrong, and he admitted that to the officer, but by the
time the stop was through he'd been handcuffed and slammed on
the ground, and my gracious, he's a big boy too. You met him at
my church picnic two summers ago. He's almost six feet tall and
plays on the basketball team at his high school, and he ended up
with a broken arm. His parents filed a complaint with the citizens'
review board. Didn't make a bit of difference. Sure, they investigated, but what happens? After a year, a whole year, they got a letter from Internal Affairs telling them that the police officer had
used reasonable force. Reasonable force—I never heard of anything so outrageous. We're the majority in what used to be a
county that was a hotbed for the Klan, and damn near every time
you read about somebody getting shot by the police, it's one of us.
Now tell me, why is that? Bunny, I'm not the only one asking that
question. You know you've asked it too. When you married Carson I prayed he'd never be mixed up in anything like this."

"Where's your sympathy for Carson? For us?"

"Oh, honey, I don't mean to sound harsh. But you got to ad-
mit, it looks terrible. At the beauty parlor the other day some of
the women, wives and mothers, were so concerned, saying the
same things. You remember that case with Bobby Washington."

"Oh, Mama, have you lost your mind? That was over twenty
years ago."

"But people still remember it."

Bobby Washington was a fifteen-year-old sophomore at DuVal

High who, on the night that he and two other boys were picked up for stealing a car, shot and killed two White officers ten minutes after being taken into a room for interrogation. The case struck all the racial nerves of the county, pitting Blacks, who believed Bobby Washington's account of being beaten at the hands of the two cops, against Whites, who saw a crazed, violent Black youth who had murdered two veteran officers. Bunny was a sophomore at DuVal who knew the abiding fear that many of her friends, especially the boys, had of county police officers. She also had heard stories about Bobby Washington, the skinny, waiflike boy who, according to her classmates, tortured animals, beat up his own brothers, and was hauled out of the cafeteria one lunch hour after calling the principal a peanut-head motherfucker to his face.

Community activists marched to keep Bobby from getting the death penalty. He was given a life sentence. And when he had rehabilitated himself in prison, after serving seventeen years, getting his GED and a degree from a respected correspondence school, and writing articles on the need for prison reform published in progressive journals, there was agitation for his release. A Black federal appeals court judge released Bobby from prison. He married, got a job as a paralegal, and then inexplicably robbed a bank and was killed on the scene when he aimed his gun at an officer.

Bunny had believed Bobby's story during the trial, that he feared for his life at the hands of the police officers who were brutalizing him. But she and Carson had discussed Bobby Washington many times. "Sure, maybe they were roughing him up," Carson would say. "But do you know how mad dog he had to be to shoot two officers? Not one, Bunny, but two?" And Bunny thought about the widows of the officers, who each time Bobby Washington came up for parole had testified about what had happened to them because of what he had done. When she read accounts in the newspaper of their tearful pleas before the parole board to keep

Bobby Washington in jail, Bunny saw in them the woman that she could easily one day be.

"You've never been on our side. You've never believed in Carson."

"Bunny, I'm just speaking the truth. You know I am."

"The truth isn't so simple to me anymore. No matter what you say, it's just not black-and-white."

The twins were seven. Carson and Bunny heard the nervous but shuttered whispers coming up from the basement when they came in from a quick run to Blockbuster to rent videos. "Let me hold it," Roslyn peevishly insisted, words that made Carson and Bunny exchange a worried glance and head to the basement. Standing on the bottom step, clinging to Carson's shoulder, Bunny saw the girls huddled in the center of the basement standing over his workbench, enthralled by an object neither Bunny nor Carson could see. But Bunny knew what it was. The burning in her stomach, the leaden silence of the basement, told her the twins had found Carson's second gun. The girls were so intent, so absorbed, they had not heard Bunny and Carson's footsteps over their labored, puzzled breathing.

"Roslyn, Roseanne!" Carson called out to them harshly, their names a verbal blow designed to scare them into moving away from the object neither parent could see but both dreadfully envisioned. When Roslyn jerked around to face her parents, Carson's second Beretta lay in her small, trembling palms like an offering.

Bunny gripped Carson's arm, holding him back from rushing over to the girls. "Carson, you'll frighten them," she whispered, straining not to scream.

But they were already frightened. Roseanne stood beside her sister with her arms enveloping her body, staring at the floor, rocking back and forth. The weight of the gun seemed to have paralyzed Roslyn as she stood, her small body teetering on the edge of crumbling. Finally her first whimper cracked the silence. "Daddy. Daddy, help . . ." Carson and Bunny took breathless, hushed, tiny steps toward the girls. Then in a voice lulling and firm, soft but insistent, Carson talked the gun out of Roslyn's hands.

These are Bunny's brooding, insistent thoughts as she watches Carson undress. She's in bed, a hardback copy of Maya Angelou's *I Know Why the Caged Bird Sings* on her lap. Bunny rereads the book once a year but has found the memoir suddenly as impenetrable as the newspapers and magazines she's abandoned since the night of the shooting. Nothing can compete with the current narrative of her life. Evenings when she would normally read, she watches television, an unaccustomed habit, reveling in the surrender of her will to laugh tracks and commercials and the inexhaustible supply of channels, faces, and situations, grateful that she can erase a tragic ending or an outcome she rejects simply by pushing a button on the remote.

But on every channel there is news of the war in Iraq, now official since the invasion and despite ten million people all over the world marching in protest. George W. Bush has his war, with body counts and death tolls making it real, despite the television rendition that presents it as a sophisticated video game. Over dinner the children had asked about the war and she and Carson struggled to explain why the war was wrong, unjustified, why the president wanted to wage a war over oil and water and vanity and belligerence and pride. "But my teacher told us Saddam Hussein is a bad man, that he wants to kill us with nuclear weapons," Roseanne told them.

So much violence, so much crime, Bunny thinks as she grazes the channels some nights now and sees, in addition to footage of bombs falling in Baghdad, which she feels landing in her soul, an endless procession of dramas that begin always with a dead body discovered, a murder within the first thirty seconds, autopsies, investigations, serial killers, rapists, crime scene investigations, lawyers, judges, law and order and guilt and innocence and blood, always blood.

But tonight she would read. That's what she thought, anyway, but she sat thumbing disinterestedly through the now-familiar text when the flashback to the incident with the girls and the gun sprang from her unconscious.

Carson sits on his side of the bed with his back to her. He's bending over, and although she can't see his hands, Bunny knows from his movements that he's unstrapping his Beretta from his ankle.

"Why do you still wear that?" she asks in an urgent whisper.

"You know why. I'm duty bound to carry it at all times," Carson says, turning abruptly to face her.

"Don't you think . . . ?"

"No, I *don't* think what you think."

"We can't even name what you were going to do. We can't even say the word."

"We won't have to if you just let it go. If you'd forget it."

"How can I?"

"I told you, I wouldn't have killed myself."

Bunny crosses her arms in front of her chest, purses her lips, and looks away from Carson.

"You didn't fire that gun, but it feels like you did," she says, aiming the words not at him but at the ceiling. Still, they hit their mark. "I don't know why I feel this way, but I do. It's as if a part of me feels widowed, betrayed by what I saw sitting in the car with you that night. I'm grieving, but I don't know what for. Maybe I'm as scared of saying what we've lost as I am of saying out loud what you almost did."

"Do you think I like wearing it? But if I don't and I'm in public and there's an incident, Bunny, I'm still a cop. My reflexes will kick in. I'd take action and I'd be ineffective. No way I'll go down like Madison over in the second district. Didn't like wearing his weapon when he was off duty. Gets carjacked one night in front of an ATM, locked in the trunk of his own car, driven from District Heights over to Oxon Hill by some kids out stoned and joyriding. Officers caught the kids, saw them speeding and going through red lights. One of the kids, a fourteen-year-old, had a gun—that's how they forced Madison into the trunk. He hasn't lived that down yet."

He's lying again. The weapon weighs on his lower leg like a tumor. He can hear it ticking like a time bomb in the glove compartment of his car. The gun is part of the pretense that he's still capable, competent, the ultimate symbol of the facade required to remain in good standing, even on administrative leave. He's told Bunny that his reflexes would kick in. He can't tell her there are probably thugs gunning for him. That he can't risk not wearing his weapon. He's arrested too many drug dealers, been aggressive in arresting thugs who'd relish the chance for payback if they found him parked alone somewhere, anywhere, day or night. But he's absolutely certain he'd freeze, think twice, delay, if he had to use his gun now. The Beretta is a fig leaf that barely covers the truth nobody in the department can know.

He watches Bunny refusing to look at him, closing the book in her lap, and reaching to turn off the halogen lamp on her nightstand. "Bunny, please, don't make me wish I'd pulled the trigger that night. I can't lose you too."

6

Carson worries about his children now more than he ever did before. Worries because he fears one day there must come some cosmic payback. Paul Houston was a son too. When he thinks of his son, Juwan, he thinks of the word *soft*. But there is another word that rumbles in his mind, noisily, too often, especially now that Juwan, at twelve, stands on the brink of adolescence. It is a word that fills Carson's mind like a mushroom cloud when he watches Juwan walk, his hands and wrists poised slightly outward, his hips rolling gently with a reflexive tilt that imbues him with a rhythm that to Carson is not male, not female, but gay. He holds on to the hope that there is time for Juwan to learn to walk, to sit the way other boys do. To be like other boys are. Will he have to explain his son? What will he say when other officers make jokes about queers, fags, jokes he has made, easily, unthinking, not caring or wondering if any of the officers in earshot "went that way"? Will he stand up for Juwan? Neither he nor Bunny has ever said the word. Bunny rejects it as a label; he resists it as a fate. For his son. Will his son be whispered and joked about? Assumed, even by the most liberal and understanding, to not be quite one of God's children?

And yet there is the boy's art, for which he is already winning prizes, citations at school and in the classes he takes on Saturdays at the Y. Juwan's room is almost clinically neat, the stacks of comic books, Japanese Anime, the video games (James Bond, Final Four, Need for Speed) and CDs in alphabetical order. One wall in his room is filled with his drawings—pencil drawings of Roslyn and Roseanne, the details so precise they resemble photographs, the head of Earl Mattheson's golden retriever, a vase filled with yellow roses, all done by a hand so steady and mature that when Carson looks at them his pride momentarily extinguishes any remnant of concern about the boy, and swells his heart.

The art is a gift, a bridge he walks across into an imperfect manner of loving his son. The pictures make him almost forget, make it possible for him to sometimes pretend that what he is sure of can be changed. At twelve, Juwan is quiet, a nearly pensive boy given to solitary pursuits—stamp collecting, drawing, writing poetry—endeavors that he pursues for long hours behind his bedroom door. Activities that offer Carson no way, he feels, to enter into and shape his son's world. Juwan's friends are other precocious, nerdy boys in the sixth-grade Gifted and Talented program. And he is beautiful. There is no other word to describe him—the slender elegance of his frame, already as tall as Carson, the symmetry of his face, and his startling gray eyes that stun and mesmerize.

He is an affectionate boy, spontaneously reaching for Carson's hand to hold when he takes the children to the movies or when they all go out to dinner. It is not the clammy clutching of his daughters' hands, tense with the need for reassurance, that he feels when Juwan entwines his fingers through his, but rather an affirmative joining of his son's tenderness with his callused flesh.

Sitting outside the house, parked and waiting for Juwan, Carson sees the boy walk down the sloping driveway. Like the obsessive thoughts about the shooting, his anguish about his son rises, unbidden, automatic, impossible to control, and, he knows in his heart even as it grips him, irrational and unfair.

Why does he always have to be so damned neat? Carson wonders, assessing the tight, tapered jeans and the spotlessly white T-shirt Juwan wears. He sits thinking this even as he recalls with disdain the baggy, crotch-riding beltless jeans he's seen on boys in the neighborhood. When Juwan slides into the car beside him, Carson hisses through clenched teeth, "When are you gonna stop walking like that?"

"Like what?"

"Like a girl."

"I don't walk like a girl. I walk like me."

"I've told you over and over to stop carrying yourself that way."

"That's the way I walk, Dad," Juwan insists, his voice a tinny screech. "I can't help it."

"That walk's gonna get you in trouble if it hasn't already."

"How come you criticize everything I do?"

"For your own good."

"That's not how it feels." Juwan reaches for the car door, angry, his eyes damp, his sniffles filling the car like muffled explosions.

Before he can open the door, Carson abruptly pulls off.

"Cut the crying game and take your hand off the door."

They drive the two miles to the Beltway in silence, Juwan huddling protectively against the car door, sulking and morose.

"I know I'm hard on you. But that's the way dads are. Mine was a bulldog. But he cared."

"But I'm not walking the way I do on purpose, Dad. I can't help it. It's me. A couple of boys at school call me gay, but what do they mean? I'm not gay. I'm me. The kids call anybody who's not like them gay."

"Juwan, I don't want you to be hurt."

"But *you* hurt me, Dad. You do. Lots of times."

"I want what's best," Carson mumbles, stunned by the accusation.

"You want me to be different than I am. Is that what's best, Dad?"

Carson yearned for a son, to give himself a second chance to be a boy, a loved boy, and to be the father he never had. And he is not just a father. Juwan is not just a son. He is a Black father. Juwan is a Black boy. So there is more to this than love, more than legacies and hope for the future and carrying on his name. There is teaching his son to walk tall through the quagmires he will see and those that are camouflaged, all set, all waiting for him because he is Black.

His son will be profiled, suspected, guilty until proven innocent. How to prepare his son for this world? A world that expects so little of a Black man and lies in wait for him to prove that the skepticism is justified. The girls are like Bunny, able when necessary to slap some sense into the world. He's seen both girls, even Roseanne, put their small hands on their narrow hips and face down other girls and boys on the playground, has seen them bristle with a sense of impatience at classmates who unlike them don't make all A's. He does not worry about his girls. It is the boy, his son, for whom he fears.

When Juwan was born it was days before Carson felt confident enough to hold him, terrified that resting the small body against his chest would reveal not all his strength but the fault line that is his trembling longitude and latitude. He was a quiet baby, his face a mirror of Carson's. Carson's mother, Alma, said, "No court of law could ever say this baby doesn't belong to you." Bunny breast-fed Juwan and before Carson left to hit the streets, he'd sit and watch her, her breasts swollen with milk, the veins flat and wide, translucent beneath her skin, shuddering as Juwan suckled. Those breasts tumbled from her nursing bra in a rush as she prepared to nurse, and Carson watched his wife and son, all three of them silently enchanted, bound by a spell.

In bed with Bunny, Carson held those breasts, kissed them, and suckled them too, the thin sticky fluid binding him to his wife, the mother of his child. Carson wanted to master everything, and he'd feed and bathe and change diapers, washing the pale brown rear end and the nub between Juwan's fat thighs as he wriggled, his lips stretched into a smile, his eyes brimming with amazement at the sight of Carson, his father.

"If we do nothing else together, we have done an amazing thing," Bunny whispered one afternoon as they sat together in the nursery. Juwan was asleep, his fists balled, his breathing a thin, whispering song. Carson had painted the room powder blue. Clouds were pasted to the ceiling and the wall trimmed with teddy bears, lollipops, and ducks. The shades were drawn against the mid-April sun. On that day, as on others since Juwan's birth, Carson dreaded the impending departure for his shift, rent by a new fear that the streets might swallow him up, take him away from his son.

"I want to do this right, Bunny."

"You will. *We* will."

"I want to give him the childhood I never had."

"Carson, he deserves a childhood of his own, one that belongs to him."

"I know, but I can't help it."

"Don't keep fighting with Jimmy Blake. You've already done that. Don't do it in the name of our child."

Juwan's baptism brought Bunny's dad, Eddie Palmer, and his wife, Madeline, down from New York. Carson was no church-goer. Bunny attended a Baptist church in District Heights once or twice a month. Bunny used to tease Carson about hell and damnation and he'd remind her that he had already been there.

Carson hadn't been in a church in so long that the day of Juwan's baptism was like entering an alternate dimension of time and space. But he was back. Back in the sanctuary Alma made Carson and his brother, Richard, attend with her every Sunday until he turned sixteen, old enough in her eyes to make his own choice. Back in the hold of stained-glass windows that never felt like they offered shelter or mercy. The mottled windows of every church Carson ever attended struck him as a kind of spiritual graffiti. The service that day, long, fervent, passionate, rekindled in him memories of his past church-attending days. Days when he prayed for his stepfather, Jimmy Blake, to accept him. For Jimmy Blake to love him. Not to care that Jimmy Blake didn't love him. Not to care that he didn't accept him. To know who his father really was. *Our Father, who art . . .*

When Carson and the family were finally called forth, however, to face the congregation, to name his son Juwan Aaron Blake, he stepped forward eagerly. Even when he was sprinkled with water, Juwan hardly batted an eye. *Now,* he thought that day, looking at the boy, *I have even more to live for. Even more to lose.* But by the time Juwan turned five, Carson knew the boy was different. And his *difference* struck Carson as a purposeful act of betrayal. Juwan was not only hopelessly awkward and clumsy at sports but brutally uninterested in the ball games he tried to teach him in the backyard. Carson's anger at the boy's indifference thrived in the muddy swamp of his own inability to forget that for him there was no father tossing him a softball on a spring day, or gripping his hands in his as they both held the bat and he taught Carson to swing. Jimmy Blake never did those things with him.

When Juwan was younger and Bunny baked Christmas cookies with the children, Juwan excelled, his face gleeful and satisfied, obsessed as he squeezed icing from the tube to decorate ginger- bread men, giving them eyes (with lashes) and lips and creamy frosting smiles. He gazed in studied, grown-up assessment of his creation. Roslyn and Roseanne, dough and icing smudged, made of the effort a game that ended with them mashing cookie dough in their ears and hair. Bunny ordered the girls out of the kitchen and tied an apron around Juwan and cleaned up the kitchen with his help. Where is the grit, the toughness he assumes a son of his should have? When Juwan was younger he preferred Roslyn and Roseanne's dolls and play stoves to the trucks and toy soldiers Car- son bought him. When Carson tried to talk to Bunny about his concerns, he got nowhere.

"He's sensitive, that's all. He's bright and excels in school. Any other father would be proud of him," Bunny said with a shrug one evening two years ago, when Juwan was ten.

"I am proud, but he needs more than sensitivity to make it in this world."

"You want to kill his beauty. Juwan has a special nature. So he's not macho—that's not the only way to be male. Do you want him posturing and acting out like a little thug? Like that nonsense you see in the videos? Thank goodness Juwan so far is a Black boy in his *own* way."

"You make me sound like a caveman."

"Well, Carson, that's how you sound. He's a sweet kid. And you bully him."

"I don't want my son to be a sissy."

"Sissy? Carson, nobody uses that word anymore."

"Well, I'm using it. And you know what I mean. Anybody who hears it knows what it means."

His son is soft, and in the world as Carson knows it, being soft gets you ignored, stepped on, or killed. The children of cops have so much to prove, to rebel against. Has he been a father or has he been a warden? If he doesn't prepare him for the world, if he doesn't prepare him for the worst things that can happen, then who will? A mother's love isn't enough. There's got to be a father's expectations, always a little out of reach, so that the boy has something to strive for.

The waiting for the grand jury decision has made him a father again. He's almost used to it, for the waiting suspends him in a zone between the night of the shooting and whatever is to come. *Whatever.* A few years back, the word was favored teenage slang. *Whatever.* A defiant shrug. An indifferent pout in the face of destiny. Carson feels like that some days, but he can't too eagerly embrace *Whatever* as a belief. He's worked too hard. Come too far. *Whatever* doesn't give him a fighting chance to seal his own fate. He no longer calls Matthew Frey every couple of days, asking if the grand jury has been convened. He can wait. He has to. The children are now on summer vacation, and he thinks of other things. *When he can.* Because he's at home during the day, he and Bunny decided to allow the twins to forgo summer day camp. They ride their bikes around the neighborhood and spend afternoons in the oak tree–shaded wading pool of the family who lives behind them. Evenings, they continue a marathon game of Monopoly that's been going on for two weeks, neither girl agreeing to call an end to it.

Carson works in the basement in the mornings, and has gotten interest from a specialty furniture shop in Annapolis about carrying some of his smaller pieces, this after he decided he could begin parting with some of the tables and chests he'd made, which have begun to inhabit the basement like lost strangers waiting to find their way home. He's taking Juwan with him this day to discuss a commission for an armoire that one of Bunny's coworkers wants him to make.

Bunny has been promoted to creative director of design at Image, Inc., where she still designs but is charged mostly with overseeing design projects. And the small firm was written up in *Business Week* for landing the contract for the redesign of a major cell phone company's products and promotion. She is absorbed in her work, and content. They don't talk anymore about the shooting or the night in the garage. That's how they survive. That's how they get along.

They are on 495, cars speeding past, the quiet between father and son feeling ancient and so like a strange healing. Carson aches for closeness with the boy, for the sound of his voice, and tells him, "I'm seeing someone about what happened, the shooting."

"A psychiatrist?" The bluntness of the question surprises him, but Juwan instinctively rejects euphemisms or anything he suspects is a lie.

"She's not a psychiatrist. She's a therapist."

"How often do you see her?"

"Once a week."

"Oh." Juwan looks out the window at the four-lane highway, the interstate, the cars whizzing past. Although Carson is driving the speed limit, the implications of what he has told his son propel him faster, he feels, than the speed of sound.

"I hear you sometimes at night when you dream."

His son, his boy, has heard him sobbing, the guttural, brutal sound of him retching over the stool in the bathroom. *Which dreams has he heard?* Carson wonders, staring straight ahead, not daring to look at Juwan. Straight ahead at the highway, just like his son.

In the dream there is only Paul Houston's face, frozen, framed forever in the moment when he knows the bullet whirling toward him will call his body home. When he knows he cannot outrun the bullet or stop it. A face

gone gray and ghostly, filled with the essence of its own demise, a still-life,
dire mask.

"That's why I'm seeing her. Because of the dreams. Because of
everything I feel about shooting that man."

"How long will you have to see her?"

"I don't know."

Carson hopes nothing in his voice hints at how he resents the
sessions, how they gnaw at his image of the man, the father, the
husband, the police officer he worked so hard to create—in control, master of his own private universe. That hallucination shot
to hell in ten seconds. But he continues to see Carrie Petersen, to
find the respite he fears will ultimately elude him, and he sees her
to save his marriage and family. Every session begins with the rec-
ollection of what has brought him there. He killed an innocent
man, and he thought of killing himself. He measures progress by
how easily he can, on any given day, banish thoughts of self-
destruction. But why go on? Is life worth living, even with Bunny,
if the price of the ticket is the dreams?

Carson allowed himself to see in his son's silence a reprieve
from judgment. How would he feel, Carson wonders now, if he
knew *his* father had killed a man? The knowledge would surely alter everything between them. He'd know what his father was ultimately capable of. He'd know more than any son should know
about his father or ever have to forgive.

"Do you have to take any drugs?" Juwan asks, shifting in his
seat to look at Carson.

"Drugs?"

"You know, like they advertise on TV for when you're depressed."

"Sometimes. To help me sleep. To calm my nerves."

"You won't get addicted, will you?"

It's a risk, no doubt about it, he thinks, and then tells Juwan, "I wouldn't let that happen."

"Do you miss going to work?"

"Uh-huh."

"Some of the kids at school teased me when it first happened, said you were a killer. I didn't know what to say back to them."

"Why didn't you tell me?"

"It would worry you and I didn't want to make things worse. Dad?"

"Yeah?"

"If you can't sleep at night, you could ask me and I'd sit with you and we could watch TV."

"I couldn't wake you up for that, Juwan."

"When you have bad dreams I can't sleep. I have bad dreams of my own."

"About what?"

Juwan looks out the window, his face impassive, mute.

"Juwan, tell me—you don't have to protect me. I'm supposed to protect you."

"Dreams about you going to jail for what you did."

The admission occupies the car, heavy and stifling.

"Juwan, I don't know what's going to happen. I only know I love you and your mother and your sisters. That's not everything, but it's a lot. Try to make it enough to let go of *your* bad dreams."

"Okay. Dad?"

"What?"

"Maybe you could use it to let go of yours too."

"I'll try, Juwan. I promise, I'll try."

7

Jimmy Blake, the man he thought for most of his childhood was his father, was a swaggering, blustering force who inhabited the house he grew up in like a shadowy, dark, rumbling threat of disaster. A meat cutter for Safeway, he spent his days in the cold room, lifting heavy sides of beef and pork and turning the fleshy tonnage into chops and sirloins and roasts. The job had given him arthritis in his hands, and the top of his right index finger was cut off one day while he was slicing a side of beef on a heavy-bladed machine. The deformed nub fascinated Carson, and what enthralled him even more was Jimmy Blake's indifference to that finger, how he used it to deftly pluck a card from the deck during games of tonk, or pointed it at him, hollering, "You better watch it, boy," the finger thrust like a malevolent, curse-filled wand.

Carson knew something was wrong from the way he looked. How different he was from his brother, Richard, who was a full shade darker than him. Carson was a "dirty yellow," with a raw, reddish cast beneath his skin, like the remnants of a hidden, unhealed wound. Richard was the same color as Jimmy Blake, the color they call "pretty brown," the tone of expensive furniture and elegant picture frames. His mother, Alma, was *almost* as light as

Carson, but his color marked him, set him apart. He knew it was his color that Jimmy Blake hated. Because it was not like his. Why else would his eyes always skim the surface of Carson's face, looking at him furtively, as though to look at the boy closely risked turning Jimmy into stone? Jimmy looked at Carson as though when doing so there was nothing to see, as though his glance had passed over a vacant space. When Carson looked at himself in the mirror, which he did throughout his childhood, obsessively, holed up in the bathroom for hours, earning Richard's wrath, he wished for a cream that could make him darker. A cream would be so much faster and more permanent than the sun.

He was five when he asked his mother for the first time why he was light and Richard was brown. When she caressed Carson with her eyes, she took refuge in his face, and in his skin, as she stared at him and hugged him in response. The embrace, Carson learned over the years as he asked the question repeatedly, was meant to stifle his stubborn, famished curiosity. When Alma did answer, she said, "God gives families a rainbow of ways to be. We've got all the colors in us." But it wasn't just Carson's color. Richard was taller than he was, long-limbed like Jimmy Blake. Carson was built thick and compact, like the squat remains of a once-majestic oak. With Richard he shared his mother's wide, heart-shaped face. He resembled his mother but looked nothing at all like Jimmy Blake.

That was why, Carson was sure, Jimmy never touched him. Why he denied Carson even the brusque, roughhousing, affectionate wrestling matches he clearly relished with Richard. Richard pummeled and punched Jimmy Blake as Jimmy squealed in fake agony, begged breathlessly for a time-out, then surprised Richard with a slam onto the carpeted floor that he cushioned with his own body, on Sundays when he and Richard and Jimmy watched football in the living room and Alma was in the kitchen frying chicken, baking biscuits, and cooking greens. Richard climbed onto Jimmy's lap and settled there. Carson would climb into that space too, but Jimmy Blake barked, "Git offa me, boy. I can't hold both of you at the same time." Carson's tears only hardened Jimmy's gaze (he did not think that possible), and so he wordlessly slid back onto the carpeted floor to play with Roscoe, the family cocker spaniel, grateful for the musty, slathering wetness of his tongue on his cheek, his back turned in self-defense against his father and brother.

On Saturday nights when Jimmy Blake came home late from evenings spent without Alma, he noisily entered the bedroom Carson and Richard shared. His entrance always woke Carson, but he pretended to be asleep. There was Jimmy Blake's shadow on the wall, his weary grunting as he sat on the edge of Richard's bed and straightened the rumpled blankets. Peeking over his shoulder, stealthily holding his breath, Carson watched Jimmy lift Richard from the edge of the mattress and gently place him in the middle of the bed and tuck him beneath the comforter. He saw Jimmy Blake kiss Richard on the cheek. Carson quickly turned his face to the wall as his father stepped away from Richard's bed. With just a few steps he stood over Carson, the smell of the liquor a stink in the small room, watching Carson sleep for what were some of the longest minutes of the boy's life. In the darkness Jimmy Blake's gaze was a scalpel slicing into unanesthetized flesh.

Cousins at family picnics, at Thanksgiving and Christmas, when no adults were around, teased Carson, telling him he was adopted. Richard took his brother's side, attacked the offenders, twisting their arms behind them, forcing them to recant. As Carson grew older he stopped asking his mother to tell him who his father was. His parents' arguments about him, about the absent touch, the lingering awful gaze, seeped under his bedroom door at night. Alma asking Jimmy to let Carson know he cared, Jimmy in his blustery, hostile, defensive voice yelling, "I ain't got to do nuthin', woman, but die and pay taxes." Arguments that earned Carson no reprieve from his exclusion. Yet, unwittingly, over the years he became Jimmy Blake's son, matching his hardness with a steely indifference. He had lived so long without the man's touch that if he were to find himself within its confines, Carson was sure that he would break.

By high school, Carson figured school was just a place to kill time while waiting to be old enough to actually have a *life*. He didn't drop out, because he'd seen what happened to friends who did—congregating like homesteaders on the neighborhood basketball court all day, sipping forties, talking trash, scaring the little kids for no reason, holing up in their mama's house sleeping till two in the afternoon, watching game shows and soaps till they hit the streets after dark, cruising with their boys, looking for easy money, a high, a little trouble, a girl for the night, a quick fix to erase how stupid they felt for dropping out. Black *and* no diploma. No, he wasn't a genius, but he wasn't that dumb. Because Jimmy Blake had so convinced him that he was nothing, Carson desperately wanted to be somebody one day. But he wasn't smart like straight-A honor roll Richard, for whom everything, *everything*, seemed so easy. Their father's love. Good grades. Getting accepted at Stanford.

One evening at dinner, Jimmy told Richard, "Boy, if I'd had your opportunities back in the day, you better believe I wouldna been no meat cutter. Your generation, y'all got the breaks. And I want you to take advantage. Take advantage of everything. The world done split wide open for y'all."

Richard was talking about being a doctor, a goal that Jimmy had adopted as his own, vicariously, bragging to friends as if Richard had already opened his practice.

"So what *you* got planned?" Jimmy asked, throwing the question at Carson the way he haphazardly tossed Roscoe the bones he brought home from work.

"I don't know." Carson shrugged. He was sixteen but felt in the rumbling onerous wake of the question like a three-year-old asked to explain the theory of relativity.

"Don't know," Jimmy grunted. "That's just the kind a niggah the White man likes, one that *don't know*."

"Jimmy, come on, please don't use that kind of language," Alma said, coming to Carson's defense.

"Naw, Alma, you always saying I don't give him enough attention. Well, I'm giving him attention. That's the problem. Y'all Black women don't want a Black man to tell it like it is. To tell a Black boy, or anybody for that matter, what he needs to hear." He turned back to Carson. "So you ain't thought about nothing you wanna be, nothing you wanna do?"

Carson had thought about lots of things, *astronaut, engineer, fireman, policeman*, but he would never tell Jimmy Blake what he had dreamed. Alma's hand gently rubbed Carson's back. He wanted to push her hand away. Richard sat slowly chewing his roast beef behind a smirk as he looked from Carson to Jimmy.

"No, *Dad*." Carson emphasized the word with a bitter, ruthless sarcasm. "I ain't figured out yet what I want to do."

Jimmy Blake's eyes traveled, slow and thoughtful, around the table, the disgusted twist of his lips confirming Carson's exquisite isolation.

"Well, you better think of something fast. Or else you gonna be playing catch-up all your life."

The house became a place for him to sleep and eat. If school weighed on him like prison, the house repelled Carson. He actually preferred school, and hanging out at the mall, or on the court, or at the rec center (places where he had come to spend most of his waking hours), anywhere but in that house. One night he came home late. It was a school night, and he had gone straight from school to the rec center with his boys Damion and Keith, and they played pool and then Carson hung out at Keith's, listening to tapes and shooting the breeze and talking to girls on the phone. He didn't call home to let anyone know where he was; he didn't want anyone to know.

On the streets, that was where Carson felt like *himself*. Although he was dreadfully unsure who that was, at least on the streets he escaped the wanton disregard of Jimmy and what he felt was the nagging incompetence of his mother's love, the inability of that love to neutralize what Jimmy Blake inflicted. Jimmy Blake had once threatened to throw him out of the house if he kept breaking curfew. Carson just laughed at the threat. What difference would it make?

When Keith dropped him off at home, the light was on in the kitchen. Jimmy Blake was up waiting for him, he knew. Keith, skinny, so dark-skinned that he was almost blue-black, sat in the car with Carson outside the house for several minutes and asked skeptically, "You sure you wanna go inside?"

"Hell, that's my house too. I live there."

Jimmy was waiting to argue, to badger. That in fact was the only time that they talked. The only reason that they talked was to initiate warfare, to skirmish, to confirm the distance between them. Getting out of the car, Carson whispered, "Fuck it," his all-purpose curse, the phrase that was mantra and talisman. He entered the house through the back door, which would mean he would have to pass Jimmy. Carson wanted to fuck with him, to walk right past him. To let him know that he didn't care.

Carson casually strode into the house like it was six o'clock instead of almost midnight. The medicinal, bracing smell of liquor hung like humidity in the kitchen. When Carson closed the door, he turned and looked at Jimmy sitting at the kitchen table. Clutch-

ing the doorknob, his body was braced for battle. A slight adrenaline surge tingled in his muscles. The arguments had become almost intimate, almost a show of affection. They were the way the
man and the boy loved each other, for the conflicts were regular,
passionate, and deeply felt.

Jimmy sat at the kitchen table, staring at a bottle of scotch and
a shot glass. His alcoholism was the family secret. No binges or
falling out for Jimmy Blake. He could sleep it off and get to work
on time. But the house was filled with his liquor bottles underneath the sink, in the unofficial liquor cabinet.

"Sit down," he said, extending his arm, pointing with his missing fingertip to a chair across from him. Carson didn't move, wondering, *What kind of trick is this? I don't have to do what you say. I can
just walk past you. Go to the fridge and get the plate I know Mom has
left for me*, he thought.

Jimmy Blake's face was ravaged. Mostly Carson looked at him
in passing, on the sly, rarely face-to-face, afraid Jimmy could read
his mind, intuit his despair and mistrust and resentment. The broad
nose and cheeks and small eyes had contracted and sat in the middle of his face like a fist. Wrinkles as thick as veins huddled around
the brown eyes staring at Carson.

"Since you so much of a grown-up, staying out all hours,
maybe I ought to offer you a drink." Jimmy saluted Carson with
the bottle.

In response to his silence Jimmy filled his glass and then leaned
over the kitchen counter and reached for a juice glass, set it on the
table, filled it halfway, and pushed it toward Carson.

One night Carson and Keith had gotten older dudes to buy
scotch and Boone's Farm and forties for them. He had tasted
Keith's dad's Wild Turkey when the old man wasn't around, and
he and Keith and Damion had Keith's house to themselves. Carson had been drunk. Pissing-sick-throwing-up drunk. Head-tight-

hangover drunk. And he couldn't see what the big deal was. He didn't feel braver, just stupid. Out of control. And growing up in that house taught Carson that if he could help it, he never wanted to feel out of control. But because he'd been drunk, he knew that much at least about Jimmy Blake. And what he knew gave him no comfort at all.

Carson pushed the glass back toward Jimmy, saying, "No thanks."

"Oh, go on," he said, sliding it back across the Formica table-top. Jimmy Blake had never offered Carson anything this insis-tently before. Carson sat staring at the glass of scotch, the clear brownish tint, which he knew had a bitter, almost astringent taste. Like some liquid designed to scourge or heal. He'd heard alcohol called liquid courage. But Jimmy battered him emotionally even when he was sober. Drunk, he was bitter, morose, mostly silent. Surprising himself, Carson reached for the glass and swallowed the liquid in a gulp. Slamming the glass on the table and pushing it back toward Jimmy Blake, he asked:

"Why you hate me?"

Carson had not planned to ask the question. Had not planned to say anything at all. But he felt so assaulted that he thought, *Fuck it, I can say anything. Ask anything.*

Jimmy drained his glass and stared at Carson through eyes that were cloudy, screened by a milky film. Eyes off-kilter and trem-bling. But Carson sensed that through that haze he was in focus, and that Jimmy Blake had never before seen him so clearly.

"Boy, if you only *knew*," he said with a shake of his head, the words thick, heavy.

"Knew *what?*"

"How little I hate you. How your being in this house proves that whatever I feel for you, it sure ain't hate." His drunken gaze probed Carson unsteadily.

"You're not my father, are you?" Carson had not planned this question either, and he was stunned by how it fell through his lips so slow and easy, after all the years it had bubbled, undigested and acidic, inside him. He knew the answer. But how would he survive if he heard Jimmy Blake say it out loud?

"Your mama wanted to protect you. All these years. But I've thought for a long time now you been old enough to know the truth." He shifted in the chair, turned his body and crossed his legs, hunched his shoulders, pushed the liquor away from him, to the center of the table. Jimmy Blake was stalling. Carson couldn't believe it. Did he fear what he was about to say as much as Carson did?

In those drunken eyes he saw sadness, sympathy, pity. It wasn't all for him.

"Naw, I ain't your daddy."

The words, finally, released and relieved him. He owed Jimmy Blake nothing. No respect. No love. He was free. *But whose child am I?* Carson wondered. He always thought that once he knew the truth that he would want to know who his father was. But Jimmy Blake was more father than he could stand.

"Naw, you ain't mine," he said again, this time shivering mightily, almost as if he could not believe it himself. "For me, there wadn't never nobody else. But your mama, she went off an . . ." he began. *Who?* Carson wondered, blotting out the accusation. The question was as natural as breathing. But he didn't want to know the answer. And, silently, he prayed, *Don't tell me.* If he was a father worth having, Carson reasoned, he'd know who he was. But he could not help but wonder, *Who?*

Behind the storm of these thoughts he vaguely heard Jimmy Blake talking about Alma and the man who was Carson's father. But what Carson heard over and over, what became the only sound in the world, were the words "Naw, you ain't mine." Words that crashed like a ceiling onto his shoulders. He'd thought the truth was a lifeboat. Now he knew it was a sinking ship.

He couldn't tell anyone what he suspected. How could he tell anyone what he now knew?

Alma's love was a shield protecting Carson from the father who seemed not to love him at all. Memory, Carson had concluded even on that night in the kitchen, is the place where nothing good ever happens.

Carson left Jimmy Blake sitting at the kitchen table, babbling family secrets in a hushed whisper. In the room Carson shared with Richard, he undressed in the dark and then, beneath the covers all that night long, wondered why he was crying. Were the tears for Jimmy Blake's wounded pride or his own sense of betrayal? On no other night had he felt himself so completely Jimmy Blake's son.

Two days after that night, when Alma came to Carson, found him cleaning out the garage, she slumped down on the steps leading into the house, hugged her body and rocked herself gently, her eyes closed.

"What is it?" Carson asked, knowing why she sought him out.

"Jimmy told me about the other night," she said, her eyes shuttered and downcast.

"I always knew. It's no big deal."

"Carson . . ."

"He told me everything. Now what do you want to say?"

"I'm ashamed. I have been for years."

"So what else is new?"

His bitterness raised her eyes, and she reminded Carson, "I gave you life."

"I wish you hadn't."

Alma marshaled the marrow of what was required to walk over

to Carson and calmly, quickly slap him. As fast as it came, he could have grabbed her arm. Ducked. Run. But he didn't.

"You think because Jimmy told you he's not your father he told you everything. He told you who you're not. I'm the one who can tell you who you are." She shuffled back to the stairs and sat down. She sat in silence so long, Carson turned his back and began going through the boxes as Jimmy had told him to do, searching for rusted tools and junk he planned to throw away. Carson had almost forgotten she was there when her words summoned and startled him. "Some men love you like a hurricane. What they give you sinks down below the root of all your feelings. Your father, Eli Bailey, loved me like that." Carson turned to look at his mother, her eyes wide, bright with the heat of remembrance.

"I'd been married to Jimmy a year and a half and thought all the life of feelings and passion was gone. Dead and buried. Something I'd never have again. Jimmy's love brought me to shore and kept me tied there. Eli released me, took me out in the deepest water. We almost made it to the horizon. Nobody tells you how long it takes to learn to love somebody, that you got to give up almost everything you want, every dream you ever had, to *be* married, to *stay* married, to *make* a marriage. How humble and grateful you've got to be for love plainspoken and honest. How it doesn't come to you wrapped in shiny paper and ribbons that take your breath away. I did a terrible thing to Jimmy Blake when I fell in love with Eli. But back then I thought because Jimmy had made me feel like my life was over, that was a crime I had the right to avenge."

The words came like a blast, rooting Carson where he stood surrounded by the lawn mower, several sawhorses, the barbecue grill, and water hoses. He wanted her to stop. It was too much. Too soon. Too late. Alma stood up wearily, as though her words,

her confession, aged rather than freed her. But she was not finished. She had just started, and the words that she would speak, the
promise and the threat of them, plunged Carson into obedient,
breathless silence.

"Loving Eli made me feel like I wasn't just fighting for my life
but that I could get it back. When I met Eli I was a married
woman. I still wasn't ready to give nothing up. I was parched and
dry inside. Jimmy's love had turned me into a desert. But I was determined to find a way to bloom. I started hating everything about
Jimmy, everything that I had once respected. His steadiness, his
job, this house that he wanted to buy for us to raise a family in. Eli
and I weren't even together that long. Six, seven months. It
doesn't take long for a storm to rise and drench and soak you and
set you shivering. In six, seven months I met your father and left
Jimmy, went to live with my mother. Eli lived in a boardinghouse
across the street from my mother. Oh, it was a scandal. But I didn't
care. You know, your father would wash my hair? He'd touch me
even when we weren't behind closed doors. Just reach for my
hand like it was a precious thing. He'd kiss me in public, for everybody to see. And we'd talk like talking was medicine. I'd never told
anybody so much about what I felt or what I wanted."

Alma stopped as though astonished at the rhapsodic tone of her
words, but then forged ahead. "I know that may not sound like
much to you, Carson. But those things, those little things, they
save a woman's life. I'd walked away from my husband and I hadn't
looked back. Eli was working construction, making good money,
but he didn't want to work for anybody, wanted to work for himself. Then he said he was gonna go to Brooklyn and get settled, set
up a contracting business, and he'd send for me. I waited but he
never called. The phone number he gave me was disconnected. I
took the Greyhound bus to New York and found the address was
a vacant lot. I didn't want to go back to Jimmy, but he begged me,

said he needed me like I'd needed Eli. When I found out I was pregnant, Jimmy and I both knew it was Eli's child, but he swore he'd love you like his own. I think he did. Until you were born. He didn't forgive me until Richard was born. A couple of years later Eli came back to D.C. and got in touch with me through my mother. Said he knew about you. Said he was sorry, but what he did was for the best. All he asked was to just see you sometimes. He didn't want to disrupt our family, but he did want to see you."

Walking toward Carson, Alma said with a wistful gentleness, "When you were little, sometimes I'd take you places where he could see you. I'd tell him what park I was taking you to play. Once we sat in the waiting room at Union Station and he sat across from us, just looking at you. When you graduated from elementary school and junior high school he was in the auditorium." Her palm cupped her son's cheek, and her voice offered Carson not just her love but the love of the father he never knew.

Carson strained to remember a stranger's eyes on him at a school Christmas pageant or as he squirmed in his seat on stage in the sixth grade. "He lives in Brookland, in D.C. He's a subway conductor for Metro. You look just like him. I can give you his address. His phone number."

"Don't you think it's a little late for that?"

"No. No I don't," she insisted.

"Did you ever forgive him?"

"If I hadn't he never would've laid eyes on you."

Alma thought she had given her son a gift. But all Carson heard and remembered was that his father, a man named Eli Bailey, had run out on his mother. Abandoned her. Deserted her. And him. Why would he exchange Jimmy Blake for a father like that?

The next day Alma gave Carson a slip of paper with his father's name and address and phone number on it. It was years before he used it. It was years before he refuted the sense of himself as nobody's child. Not the child of the father he did not know. Not Jimmy Blake's. Not the son of the mother who could not shield him from the abandonment of one, the rejection of the other.

Jimmy Blake died of liver problems while Carson was in the army. Now Alma goes on cruises to Alaska, the Bahamas, is a member of a bridge club, and works as a part-time receptionist in a doctor's office. Jimmy Blake is dead. But Carson still hears the words "Naw, you ain't mine" every time he enters his mother's house.

He has not intended to reveal so much. Talk so long. Each word seeding a harvest of other words and memories rendered as much with his body as with his tongue. A tongue untied, spilling forth a babble of whispers and secrets. And by the time Carson tells Carrie Petersen that Jimmy Blake is dead, he is hoarse, unaccustomed to the strain of such relentless revelation.

She listens to him as she always does, her eyes focused on him, gentle eyes that he still feels unable to meet steadily for very long. She sits, legs crossed, an ankle-length black skirt billowing, filling the chair, her hands folded in her lap. Carson had asked at the end of one session how she could stand hearing the stories her clients told.

"I choose to hear them and to listen," she assured him. "They are difficult stories to hear, but they aren't all terrible. People reveal to me moments of rebirth and redemption as well as struggle and loss."

"Who listens to you when you need to talk?" he pressed her.

"A good friend and fellow therapist who is a mentor to me. When my mother died last year I talked to him quite a lot."

"You asked me why I became a police officer," he says now. "I don't know why I told you all that. I'm surprised I remember so much. Especially so much I wanted to forget."

"There's actually very little that we forget, Carson. There's a lot, however, that we deny, or bury." Carrie rises from her chair and goes to a small refrigerator on the floor in the corner of the office and retrieves a bottle of water for Carson.

"This is hard, you know," he tells her, taking the bottle and opening it, then drinking the water, which saps so much more than just his thirst.

"What?"

"This."

"It's supposed to be."

"I've never looked at my life. Not like this. It feels like punishment."

"Not every officer could have submitted himself to this. Give yourself credit for that. Can you tell me the worst thing you think your stepfather did to you?"

Carson sets the empty bottle of water on the floor beside his chair. He closes his eyes. Carrie Petersen allows him to choose silence in response to some of her questions. Lets him pass on the occasional inquiry. They have sat for half an hour in this room, Carrie patiently waiting for Carson to blink.

Opening his eyes, he tells her, "He drove me to the streets."

"What do you mean?"

"When I found out for sure that he wasn't my father. When I finally knew for sure, I couldn't stand living in that house. I didn't feel I owed him or my mother anything. I'd been spending a lot of time at the rec center and at Keith's and Damion's houses, but after that night I remember the only place I wanted to be was in the streets. We'd haunt the dark, empty roads and streets of Bowie, Lanham, Capital Heights, in Keith's Crown Vic, on the weekends and now and then even on school nights. I'd lie and tell my mom I was studying at the library with Keith. We spent the evening smoking herb. Or we'd stand outside a liquor store and ask somebody to buy us a six-pack of beer or maybe some cheap wine. Park on some strip mall lot and watch the stores closing down. Then one night we wanted to go to a club and between us we had a dollar. Damion said, 'Gimme five minutes,' and before me and Keith could say a word he was out of the car, striding up to an elderly White man putting a bag of groceries in the backseat of his van. It was maybe nine or ten o'clock. Damion walked up to the man, stood behind him, and we saw him put his hand in his jacket like he had a gun. It took less than a minute before he was walking back to the car. When Damion did that we crossed a border that each one of us, for different reasons, was ready to cross. The first time I did it I got seventy-eight dollars and twenty-three cents from a woman who, when I looked at her closely, reminded me of my mother."

"How'd you feel when you robbed people?"

"In control."

"Of what?"

Carson has never dared to think about why he became a thief, not even when he confessed the transgression to Eric, yet he says with absolute certainty, "My life. I felt in control of my life. It only lasted a few minutes, the time it took to strong-arm them and take their wallet. But the look on their faces. That look always eventually shot my high. Watching them fumble in their pockets, sweat, plead with me not to do anything to hurt them, all that cut right through the alcohol or the weed. But for those first brief moments when those people looked at me, when I caught them by surprise, they saw me. I had their attention."

"The way you could never get the attention of Jimmy Blake?"

"It wasn't about him. I was drunk. High. Stupid. Young."

"Yes, but you were also everything your stepfather said you'd end up being."

"It wasn't about him," Carson insists, refuting his conclusion that Jimmy Blake inspired his crime spree, so angry that the specter of Jimmy Blake looms over this moment, that he feels as though there is an apocalyptic tremor shattering his vision of his world.

"I think you know it was about him, Carson."

"I could take him on. I didn't need those people to stand in for him. He was a punk. A bully."

"Weren't you?" she asks, leaning forward, sliding a few inches closer to Carson when he turns in retreat from her gaze. Carson looks at his watch, hoping the session is over, and Carrie tells him, "You're my last client of the day—we can go longer if we have to. How long did all this go on?"

"A couple months. We musta done thirteen, fourteen robberies, all three of us together like that. Each of us taking a turn." Carson reveals this reluctantly, fully aware that he cannot untell the story he has begun. "Usually it was women, old people, White people, who we figured would be scared of us without us having to use a weapon. We'd toss the credit cards and spend the money. It even got in the papers. We did so many that I guess the cops figured all the reports pointed to a pattern, a serial robber or a gang. I guess that's what we were. A gang. They wanted to warn the public. It wasn't even about the money after a while. We couldn't stop doing it. I knew we'd get caught, and part of me didn't care. Because I was usually stoned when we did it, I'd wake up the next morning and I'd feel dead. And I could only vaguely recall why I felt so bad."

"How did you manage at home and with your parents?"

"I stayed in my room behind a locked door, looking at the things I collected from the people I robbed. A wallet, a driver's license, store receipts. I didn't want to be around my mother at all. I felt so guilty. And I was sure that Jimmy knew I was involved, that when he looked at me he could see what I'd done. It was my senior year. One night over dinner Jimmy started talking about the robberies, saying what he'd do if somebody tried to rob him, how he'd beat the crap out of them. 'Don't you think a man or woman's got a right to defend themselves, Carson?' he asked me.

"He damn near gave a sermon, telling me that whoever was robbing those people wasn't just stealing money but their peace of mind. Told me the victims would have flashbacks, would be afraid to go out of their houses or go to the store. 'I'm just giving you something to think about, that's all. You been staying out awful late recently. You sure you ain't got something you want to tell me, your mama? The police?' he asked me. My mother was sitting at the dinner table between us and she kept looking at me and looking at him. Each time she looked at me after looking at him there was more surprise and more questions in her eyes. I wondered if he'd been in my room, looking through my drawers. Maybe he found those things I'd kept. I figured he'd call the police. I was sure it was just a matter of time. I got up from the table. I couldn't stand them staring at me like that. Both of them. Jimmy stood up and bounded over to me and held me in place so I couldn't move. I was struggling to break free of his grip. The next thing I knew we were on the floor and my fingers were around his neck. My mother's scream made me try to choke him even harder. Then I felt his steak knife against my groin. It drew blood. And I'll never forget, there wasn't an ounce of fear in his eyes. But I was scared. Of what I was pretty sure by then he suspected. That knife cut through the fog I'd been living in. I'd been bleeding inside for a long time anyway.

"After that night I stopped robbing people, and so did Keith and Damion. We never got caught, but I never felt like I got away with anything. I never forgot the things I'd done. And before today I never told anyone but my friend Eric."

"But Jimmy Blake got you off the streets. You owe him that much. You said when you robbed those people you felt in control.

You said the night of the shooting you wanted to take control of the stop. You couldn't control what your mother did. Who your father was. What Jimmy Blake denied you. You've been trying to control things for a long time, haven't you? Isn't that why you joined the force? So you could take control, be in control, and so nobody could ever hurt you?"

Carson sits awash in a split second of living death and resurrection, this moment and every moment he's lived suddenly clear through the fog of denial and shame. He sits across from Carrie, wondering why he's not on the floor howling. Her words have sparked a cataclysm that rumbles and roils in his stomach and his groin and that breaks the seal on his heart.

"Yeah," he whispers, gruffly, the word lodged like a pebble in his throat, offered up so unwillingly that Carrie Petersen has to read his lips.

"I always figured one day I'd have to pay for all the bad things I did. I'm paying now. That man I killed was doing good things with his life. He's dead. I was a thief. I was illegitimate and hated the man who gave me his name. I'm a murderer and I'm alive. Tell me what sense that makes?"

They talk mostly when they meet about where they find rare moments of balance: for Carson, working with his hands; for Matthew Frey, writing a novel based on several cases he's handled. When Carson comes to see him, Frey ushers him into his office, watches Carson sit in the chair across from him, and leans back in his swivel chair, his shock of prematurely white hair thick and tousled, wearing what Carson now knows is his uniform—white tieless shirt and khakis—and asks him, "How's work?" When Carson first told Matthew that he built furniture in his spare time, Matthew urged him to develop the hobby into a livelihood, suggested he take pictures of his pieces and put them in an album, urged him to get business cards, have an open house one weekend afternoon to display his furniture for invited friends and potential clients. And he has jovially monitored Carson's progress, his willingness to turn a hobby into a business.

"I get lost down there sometimes," Carson tells him this day. "Lose track of time, and even though I often have a blueprint for a cabinet, or a shelf, there'll always come this moment when all those lines dissolve and I'm sawing and cutting and shaving from pure instinct."

"I finished the chapter I told you about last time," Frey announces, raising his arms and threading his fingers behind his head. "And the motive was totally different from what I thought it was."

He's written five novels, which various literary agents have rejected, and talks about the novel he's writing now as a kind of mental Olympics that keeps him up until 2:00 a.m. some nights.

"You said you were going to a writers' conference in Tennessee?"

"Oh yeah, I was the only man in the class. I'm convinced, women are the superior species." Frey laughs. "The workshop leader liked what I'd written and we've been in touch by e-mail. She said to get back to her when I'm finished."

"Good luck," Carson tells him.

"I wanted to see you today to let you know that the grand jury will be impaneled next week. I wanted to talk to you about this even though you won't testify."

He's been waiting for months for this to happen, and now that it has, Carson is unsure what he feels. "I still don't understand why I can't tell them what happened."

"You can't tell them what happened because I can't be in the room with you during your testimony. You'd be asked why you didn't wait for backup, what the procedures are for a stop like the one that night, why you pulled your weapon on Paul Houston."

Those are the questions he has asked himself two, three thousand times a day. They are the questions he'll be asked if there is a trial, the questions Internal Affairs will ask. The questions for which, despite the routine prep he undergoes with Matthew for the inevitable Internal Affairs inquiry, he still feels he has no answers. "What do you think will happen?"

"I'm not going to promise or predict," Matthew tells him with a shrug, as though insulted by the inquiry.

"I could be indicted on murder, manslaughter, voluntary manslaughter, right?"

"Murder would be highly unlikely. If there was an indictment, it would most likely be involuntary manslaughter. Let's go over again the basics of what happened that night. You knew backup was on the way, correct?" Matthew isn't even looking at Carson, his eyes are cast out the window, staring at a small plane thousands of feet in the air yet passing his window with an eerie illusion of closeness.

"Yes." Matthew has told him not to elaborate on yes or no unless asked.

"The movement of his hand reaching into his groin, that's what made you afraid for your life?"

"Yes."

"He kept walking toward you and even though you told him, ordered him to drop what he was holding and to halt, the movement of his arm toward you seemed an aggressive move—is that how you interpreted it?"

"Yes."

Matthew turns from the window to look at Carson, who says, "I feel like you're putting words in my mouth."

"I'm trying to save your career. Carson, all stories are true. It's true that Paul Houston could not have shot you with his cell phone. It is true that you thought his cell phone was a gun. It's true that even with only a cell phone in his hand he could have posed a threat to you. It's true that you knew that."

"If all stories are true, how is there ever justice?"

Matthew rises from his chair and goes to the window, looks out at the sky briefly, and then turns to Carson and sits on the sill, bracing himself on either side with his hands. "If there was real justice in the world, this incident would never have happened at all. The men and women on the grand jury are concerned about public safety, and they know how difficult your job is. And your job is to protect them in an imperfect world where you are outnumbered by the bad guys, an imperfect world that offers few easy answers."

"You ever defend anyone else who tried to end it all?" Carson asks.

"You mean commit suicide?"

"Yeah," Carson says.

"Actually, no. Part of my job, as I define it, is to keep that from happening," Frey tells him, gazing openly and expectantly at Carson.

"Would you tell me if you had?"

"No, I wouldn't." Frey smiles grimly and asks, "How's it going with Carrie? She's worked with a couple of other officers I've represented."

"She's good."

"You heard from any other officers?"

"Naw." Carson shrugs, feigning indifference.

"That's not unusual."

"I ran into Wyatt Jordan, my backup that night, at a gas station last week. I didn't know what to say to him. He didn't know what to say to me."

Gassing up their cars, the two men had stuttered out greetings that seemed too much and too little. Wyatt asked, "How you holding up? Some of us were talking about you the other day, wondering how the case was going." Carson stood before Wyatt, flush suddenly with the weighty memory of Wyatt's arm on his shoulder, wondering if he had told the other officers what he saw on Carson's face when he arrived on the scene. Had he told them about the pool of vomit a few feet away from the body of Paul Houston?

Wyatt was off duty, his muscles bristling and shimmering in a sleeveless T-shirt, wearing Bermuda shorts and sandals and wrap-around sunglasses that obscured half his face. Wyatt's wife was sitting in the car in a backless sundress. A cooler was in the backseat.

"You on vacation?" Carson asked.

"Yeah, we're headed to Ocean City."

"I wanted to call you, but I didn't know what to say. Carson, that night's been with me too. I realized now how I got no time for bullshit. A couple days later I talked to my wife about going to marriage counseling. I'm trying to make it right with her. I know you been thinking about heavy shit, man, heavier than my drama, but I been thinking too."

"Was I supposed to feel good because my shit turned his life around?" Carson asks Frey.

"He was offering what he could, and he was honest."

"I'd do the same, I guess. I thought administrative leave was like some paid vacation. Who could complain about getting paid to do nothing? Out of harm's way. I never figured I'd feel so powerless, knowing so many people were holding my life in their hands."

8

It's more difficult than he expected it to be, to tell Bunny how he feels when the grand jury votes not to indict him.

"I thought you'd be in a better mood once you were cleared," Bunny says as they sit on the backyard deck the evening after Matthew Frey calls to tell him the news. He sits on the deck many evenings now, playing checkers with Roslyn or sitting alone watching the sky shift and change as the mystical retrenchment of sunlight gives way to the slow creep of darkness.

"It's hard to feel a sense of victory. There's the Internal Affairs investigation. And there could still be a wrongful death suit."

"Carson, let's not think about that now."

"I don't know what else to think about."

Bunny takes a sip from a glass of lemonade and places it carefully on the wicker table between them. "Maybe about leaving the force." The words are a pronouncement, one that she makes with ease, but to Carson they are a slap in the face.

"Why would I do that?"

"Why wouldn't you?" Bunny asks, turning in her chair to gaze resolutely at Carson.

"Because it's not just my job. It's my career."

"And it's a career we've all paid a high price for."

"I thought you wanted me to be in a good mood?" He attempts to laugh off Bunny's inquisition. "How long have you been thinking about this?"

"A long time." Bunny folds her arms across her chest and crosses her legs, turning her body into a wall of resistance.

"Everything that's happened gives you, gives us, a chance to look at our choices, our past."

"Don't bullshit me. Don't play psychologist. You mean my choices, my past."

"Maybe I do. But Carson, everything that was yours was mine. All of it. You know that."

"And now you want me to bail?"

"Now I want you to consider where you, where we as a family go from here."

"You're making me feel like I *was* indicted. In eight more years I can retire if I want to."

"That might be too late," she tells him with a certainty that makes him shiver even as the humid evening pulses around them.

"Too late for what?"

"To put this all behind you."

"I'll never be able to do that."

"Not if you remain on the force."

"It's not just my job, Bunny—it's my life you're talking about."

"You deserve a new one, Carson. I always thought somebody would shoot you. That's the nightmare I've lived with for twelve years. And you know what? This feels almost as bad. What would you go back to? What would you go back for? We can end this all and we can end it now. You've got your woodworking."

"No, I've got a career that I've worked hard to build. Cops bounce back after an incident like this."

"Lots of them don't," she tells him, the words dire, precise, haunting.

"And of course that's the category you put me in," he shoots back, belligerent and loud.

He sits waiting for Bunny's denial, her quick assurance that what he fears, her tallying of the odds against him, is wrong. She's his wife. If anybody believes in him, surely it's her. But Bunny says nothing, and she won't take her eyes off him. Carson stands up and goes into the house and grabs his car keys. He's got to go somewhere. Anywhere that he can breathe.

When they were first married, when he was on the evening shift, Carson usually came home to find Bunny in bed, propped up on pillows, looking at TV. "Hey," she'd say, offering up the word sleepily, lazily, in a kind of half whisper that filled the room like the sound of worship. Some nights he arrived home wired. Some nights that were slow he was still tired, because doing nothing was more exhausting than answering eight or nine calls, and she'd reach for Carson and hold him, to confirm he was really there. That he'd made it home. Alive. Some nights they just held each other when he got into bed and they'd fall asleep like that. Sex was so many things between them back then. It was play and deadly serious. Still, there were times when Carson shut down. Shut down and couldn't talk, wouldn't talk, didn't talk. Times when a darkness partitioned him from himself and Bunny and everyone else. This darkness had been with him always. Nobody could ever defeat it. Bunny called it a funk. It was not as deep as clinical depression, but it was more than the blues. And when it occupied Carson, sex became a language, a cure, a bridge, and the sex they had when he was in that dark place was a reckless campaign to feel alive. And the lunging and thrusting and biting and humping said what neither of them could. In the throes of that feeling Carson didn't think of Bunny as his wife; that was part of the cure, that she allowed him to be a stranger and she became a stranger too. This was not the way they had coupled to make Juwan or the girls. No, then he loved her like she was already carrying his child. The darkness lifted and he was filled with, and he filled Bunny with, light.

He knew everything about Bunny. She had no secrets. The abortion at nineteen. How she loves her dad more than she loves her mother, and the guilt and bewilderment this causes. The cousin who fondled her when she was nine. Carson accepted everything, every secret, like a tithe or a tribute.

But there were the evenings when he came in from the streets and he didn't shower and he'd lie down beside his wife. Carson kissed Bunny gently on her cheeks so even though she was asleep his lips penetrated her and she would know that he was home, then he left the bedroom and slept on the floor in the living room. The darkness hung, pendulous and uneasy. He dreamed of everything he convinced himself that he had forgotten. His skin held him like the bars of a cell. There was freedom and incarceration those nights on the floor. He was blue and black and shivering with disbelief at what he had made of his life. Made of himself. *If Jimmy Blake could see me now.*

Bunny woke to find him on the floor and could never understand. How could she? It was years before he understood himself. Understood his need to be separate, to replenish the loneliness, the aloneness, bred into him. Sneaking out of the bedroom he shared with Richard and sleeping on the ratty, sweat-soaked sofa bed in the basement. Leaving the beds of countless lovers to sleep occasionally without them on their living room floors. Countering love with this nocturnal declaration of independence.

"Did I do something wrong?" Bunny asked the first time, padding into the room barefoot, wrapped in the chenille spread. She sank onto the floor, hugging herself protectively. It was 6:00

a.m. and Carson wondered what she must have felt when she turned over in sleep, when her arm reached out to find his side of the mattress cold and empty, bereft even of his shadow.

"Naw, baby, you didn't do anything wrong."

"Did I snore?" she asked with a laugh, obviously thinking there was a rational, reasonable excuse for what he'd done, willing to take the blame.

"Uh–uh."

"Then why?" The question ached with childlike petulance, a mewing innocence molded in steel.

"It's got nothing at all to do with you, Bunny. It's all about me."

"All about me," she sneered with a weary shake of her head. "Where have I heard that before? Carson, husbands and wives are supposed to sleep together."

"I know," he said, touching her upper arm, a triangle of flesh exposed despite the fact that she was bundled up in the spread.

"I know, but there are times. Not often. But there are times when I need to do this."

"What is it you're doing?" The petulance has evaporated, her eyes narrow, tight, and wary.

"I know you think it's rejection, but it's not."

"Then why does it feel like that? I don't understand."

"I don't always understand myself."

"You're closing me out."

"I'm sleeping on the floor."

"I don't want to sleep alone," she insists, lying down beside Carson, burrowing into his side on the pallet of blankets and sheets.

"Sometimes you'll have to."

"So I've lost you already."

"You haven't. You never will."

"Can we talk about it?" Bunny's toes massaged his ankle; her breath, dank with sleep and night, smelled almost tropical grazing his nostrils.

"It?"

"Why you have to do this."

"There aren't words for everything."

"Yes, there are."

Once Carson had dared to ask Bunny *why* she loved him. *Were there words for that?* She had laughed in that rumbling-up-from-her-belly-button way and thrown back her head, that lovely head that he just cupped sometimes in his hands and massaged, her auburn hair like tendrils against his skin and his fingers, digging down to the roots, the tight curls, the nappy part, and his hands loving, feeding on both textures. She laughed as though the question was ridiculous, irrelevant. And when she answered she told Carson that she loved how serious he was, and she loved that he had never lied to her and she loved that he is wounded and sought her out as the cure. She loved him because she knew their children would be strong and indomitable, and she loved the manner in which he became his own father.

Carson tries to convince himself but is never really sure that he is the only one who suspects how little he has expected life to give him. His victories, The Job, Bunny, his children, even when they seem rock solid, belong, he sometimes suspects, to someone else. And for a while, for the first year or two of their marriage, the first couple of years, he felt redeemed just thinking of Bunny at home while he was on the streets.

One evening when in the middle of a slow night, unexpectedly partnerless for the shift, he drove home three hours before the shift ended. He knew that Bunny was working on a design or reading a novel in bed, waiting for him. Carson cruised back into the quiet, dark cul-de-sac where his house sat. For a while he sat in the car, looking at the house, grateful that it belonged to him. That what he wanted he actually had. The modest house, all brick with the wide picture window with a sill that Bunny had filled with tiny ceramics and photos. The house with three bedrooms, rooms for the children they would have. Before going inside, putting the key in the front door, Carson just sat and watched the house, going through every room in his mind. Not until he bought this house had he allowed himself to acknowledge just how orphaned he'd always felt.

Inside, he found Bunny at the kitchen table working on a logo for a mall and condominium complex planned for Crystal City.

"Hey, what are you doing here?" she asked, looking at her watch.

"It's a slow night."

"But what if . . . ?"

Carson put his fingers to his lips and whispered, "Our secret."

He removed his gun and radio and put them on the table. "My radio's on."

He stepped toward her. "I just came by to see if my wife is really home alone."

"She is."

Carson sat down and watched Bunny as she explained, "It's going to be in the city, but there'll be built-in parks, a small lake, and recreational facilities, so we want to get across the idea that in a way it's like being in the country while still being in the city. So that's why I chose yellow and green." She showed Carson several designs the firm was considering. After a while she yawned and rubbed her eyes, saying, "I'm bushed."

They stood up at the same moment, and his arms encircled her waist. He kissed her playfully, delicately, then Carson cupped Bunny's face in his hands and kissed her hard and deep and long. Bunny took his hand and led him out of the kitchen. Carson reached for his radio as he followed Bunny up the stairs.

When he unfastened her bra and her breasts spilled out onto his chest, she whispered, "You could get in trouble. Am I like an accessory to a crime?"

"This ain't no crime we're committing here, baby. No crime at all."

But there was much, so much that he did not ever tell her. Carson tried not to talk about seeing people so often at their worst. Didn't she know that's the *last* thing he wanted to talk about? How he'd learned *not* to think about it. *His death. The death of someone because of him.* The power he had. Just thinking of it sometimes chilled him. He'd be on the streets eight hours with a gun and the permission to use it when he felt threatened, when he felt the situation warranted it, and he didn't have to ask a soul. He was the first line of defense between the ordinary citizen and the state. Carson never told Bunny about Angelo Rodriguez, who shot a suicidal sixteen-year-old girl in a standoff outside her house, and three weeks later ate his own gun. He didn't tell her how it got out that Rodriguez was having visions and dreams about the girl and couldn't stop seeing her face. Bunny wanted to know everything. Kept saying, "I'm your wife." But *he* could hardly stand to know everything. Everything might *kill* Bunny. Or drive her away from him, make her wonder how she ever thought she could be a cop's wife. And there were times when he came in, got in the shower, and Bunny wanted to join him. But he would say no. In the shower he washed off the tension, the sweat, the blood that wasn't there but might be one day, the spit of some junkie he'd arrested, the grimy prints of a crack whore. Even the night he caught a rapist, chased and tackled him, running through a secluded walking path near Allen Pond, away from his victim, a woman huddled like a pile of leaves or a dead log on the ground; even when he spotted smoke coming from a bungalow and was the first to call the fire department, and he rushed into the house and led a teenage boy out, his pajamas on fire, even after shifts like that when Carson came home a hero, the hero he joined the force to be, he hesitated to tell Bunny too much, because it all cost, and even on nights like that he felt like he had one foot in heaven and the other in hell.

9

"*Tell me what happened* on the night of March third this year during the traffic stop of Paul Houston."

By now he should be certain about what happened. But for several moments he's confused. Stymied. Silenced. But he's thinking. *March, April, May, June, July, August*—six months. If he doesn't know now, when will he? He looks at Lester Stovall, the Internal Affairs detective that Matthew Frey wouldn't let him talk to the night of the shooting, his thin, angular face impassive, the eyes neutral, as though it's every day that he asks a man to tell him how he came to kill someone.

What happened? Carson is silent for so long that he feels Matthew Frey shift in the chair beside him, lean over, and ask him if he is okay. There it is again, the question that makes no sense. The question he hates. The question to which no one really wants an honest answer. And then finally he speaks. He speaks and he's hearing but not hearing his answers. As Carson recounts the events that led up to the stop and what took place during the stop, he wonders if it really happened to him. After six months the incident sounds, to his ears, unbelievable. But even if he won't claim the incident, its muddy paws have stained him for life. A video camera on the wall facing him films his statement and records every twitch, the shimmering glow of perspiration on his forehead, cheeks and chin, his refusal or inability to look too long at Lester Stovall, the slow, breathless recounting of each moment, as though the remembering and the telling are a physical assault. When he's finished telling as much as he can remember, telling it the way he's rehearsed, Carson looks at Matthew Frey, who nods approval.

"The IAD detective isn't a priest, he's an investigator, Carson, and you're to treat his questions as inquiries that require a brief factual response, not second-guessing or conjecture." That's what Frey has told him over and over. But in the minutes of the retelling he heard the events as an unexpected resurrection. He told the story the way he was supposed to. Sitting in this room in which the air crackles with the warmth of any possibility, palpable, alive, Carson wants to know and tell the story of that night, to know himself in a new way. There is no other story in his life. This is the story of his life. As the words poured through his lips, he was severed, rent, and simultaneously reformed. He told Lester Stovall what happened. What he did. And the words spoke back to him, under cover, muffled so only he could hear, and now he knows that he cannot leave this stifling small room unless he is in possession of another version of the story. He's willing to do anything for that version to take shape. He doesn't care what the new story costs.

"Now I have a couple of questions," Lester Stovall says, his face suddenly animated, no longer passive, as he leans back in his chair, then stands up and removes his jacket and sits down again. "If Corporal Jordan was on his way to provide backup for you, why didn't you wait for him to arrive before you proceeded with processing the stop? Why didn't you have Mr. Houston remain in his car until Corporal Jordan arrived?"

If he had waited. If he had waited. Everything would be different now. He knows that. He has relived the moment when he ordered Paul Houston out of the car so many times he wonders why the incident has not been altered just by his will to make it so.

"I . . . I've thought about that a lot, in fact," he says, "and I think"—he feels Frey beside him, shifting anxiously. "I had been following him for a while, and . . ."

"Carson, you don't want to do this," Frey whispers urgently.

"I was ready for the stop," he says anyway, plunging into the answer. "I got out of my cruiser, I guess, without thinking."

Although Frey's hand rests heavily on Carson's arm as if to hold him back from danger or tether him to earth, Carson feels the words he has just spoken have lifted him, curiously, out of harm's way.

"Without thinking?" Stovall looks at him through his thin, frameless designer glasses, his eyes sharp, blinking, and alert.

"Yes."

"You know the proper procedure for a traffic stop like this one?"

"Yes, I do."

"You thought the driver may have been eluding you?"

"I did."

"Yet you chose not to wait for backup before asking the subject to get out of his car?"

That decision made no sense. Was it a decision? Adrenaline? Instinct? Was I out of control? I wanted to show him I was in control. He feels himself sinking, liquefying before Stovall's bureaucratic gaze. "That's correct."

Stovall looks away from Carson and writes on a legal pad on the desk.

"Carson, what are you doing?" Frey asks in a loud whisper that Carson ignores.

"How did you approach the driver?"

"I approached the car with my weapon drawn and I told him to get out of the car."

"Why did you approach with your weapon drawn?"

"Because I thought he was eluding me and I wasn't sure what I would find." *Since I hadn't waited for Jordan, I needed my gun.*

"And because you didn't wait for backup?"

"Yes."

"Can I have a few words with him?" Frey asks.

The building is constructed like a bunker, a low, flat, sprawling series of small offices, all concrete walls and cheap, scarred linoleum and fluorescent lights. Outside the room, in the hallway, Frey says, "You're hanging yourself in there. Why are you doing this?"

"Something happened when I told the story. It just feels like the way I have to handle this. I don't want to hide anything anymore. I didn't plan what's happening."

"Do you know what you're doing?" he asks in exasperation.

"Not really. For the first time since this happened, Matthew, I don't care. I don't wanna save my ass. I want to get this off my back. Face myself. Face everything about what happened."

"This isn't the place for that."

"I've made it that place."

Back in the interrogation room, Lester Stovall asks Carson, moments after he and Matthew Frey are seated, "What commands did you give the driver?"

Carson folds his hands on the desk and looks at Lester Stovall full on for the first time. "I told him to drop what he was holding in his hand, but he didn't drop it, and he kept walking toward me and pointing the object at me." *But you had to be there. You had to be me. It was a blur. And it was the clearest moment of my life. I know there'll never be another moment that I know so well and remember as a slow-motion catastrophe, my own instant Hiroshima.*

"How many times did you give that command?"

I don't know. Did he even hear me? Maybe he was pissing his pants, scared and deaf and stupid and sure there was no way he was gonna die that night.

"Several."

"Why did you fire your weapon?" He hears the tremor of impatience in Stovall's voice, the judgments, and thinks, *I was afraid. I didn't know what else to do.*

"I was afraid for my life."

"How many shots did you fire?" *Seven? Eight? It felt like I unloaded my whole magazine. I'd never fired my weapon before. Never. That night was the first time. The first fuckin' time.*

"Three. I fired three shots."

"What did you do after you fired your gun?"

"I examined the driver for his condition. He was dead. And then I saw a cell phone a few feet away from his body." *And then I wanted to turn my weapon on myself. Then I crawled a few feet away and threw up. And then I lost everything and I still haven't got it back.* "I radioed in to the dispatcher that shots had been fired."

"*Where did you go* after you left Matthew Frey?" Bunny asks as they sit together on the bed. It's nine-thirty and she's been frantic, wondering where Carson went when he left IAD headquarters at three-thirty that afternoon.

"I drove around. Then I needed a drink. In fact, I needed a lot of drinks. So I could stand to look at myself in the mirror."

"I'm not gonna let you go back into that dark place, Carson. I don't care what you saw in yourself or think you saw today. I won't let you take us all back there again."

"When I heard the story this time, I was hearing a verdict. A judgment that I rendered on myself. And I asked myself the question I haven't wanted to ask all these months: Am I a bad cop? Have I become the kind of cop I swore I'd never be? If I'm not, how else could this have happened? I'd chalked it all up to a tragedy that couldn't be helped. I thought what I saw was a gun. It was a mistake. I wanted to believe it happened to me. That I didn't make it happen. I don't know what it was. What got into me. Everything Matthew and I had practiced, everything we'd rehearsed, the attitude, the correct type of answers . . . I lost it. Maybe I didn't lose it. It didn't feel like I lost it. It was more like it was lifted or stripped from me. Every question felt like a trial. I walked into that room with cataracts, or blinders. I came out and I'd caught sight of everything I did wrong that night. I caught sight, but it's a picture I still don't want to see. And I could tell Stovall was thinking what a fuckup I am. I'd never seen it clear like that in a fellow officer's eyes, on his face, with no bullshit offers of sympathy or support—how are you? Anything I can do for you? It was all there, staring back at me.

"Leave me alone, okay?" he orders, shrugging out of the grasp of Bunny's hands on his shoulders. "Leave me alone. That's the best thing you can do for me now."

When Carson sees Carrie Petersen again he tells her, "I don't know if I can go back. Not with what I know now. It doesn't matter if they sanction me or send me for retraining or what. I don't care about that now. There's nothing the department can do that'll come close to what I'm going through."

"Do you want to go back?" Carrie Petersen asks him. She's been on vacation, two weeks in Aruba, and she's returned with a bronze glow and highlights in her hair, now shortened to a pixie cut that has made her nearly unrecognizable, Carson thinks. She looks different, and she greeted Carson with a pronounced enthusiasm as she ushered him into her office that he knows is the after-glow of vacation, intense and sure to fade. But she's the same Carrie, he discovers, once he tells her about the IAD interview, quietly relentless and thoughtful in her performance of what he has come to consider a sixty-minute mental autopsy.

"Sure. I wanna go back."

"Why?" Her favorite question. No one has ever asked him why so many times. He never realized or imagined the depth of his motivations, how they lay camouflaged, ignored, denied, in the shadow of all his actions. *Why?* The one-word question sends him scurrying in his mind, looking for the hiding places where everything that makes him tick is buried.

"For vindication. To prove in some way that it matters to me that I managed to overcome what happened. That I didn't really lose everything. I don't want twelve years to be a waste."

"Twelve years is a long time, Carson, but not that long. You could start over in a new career."

"You sound like my wife."

"Is that a bad thing?" She laughs.

"No comment."

"What is it that you know now about yourself that you didn't before?"

"That if I'd done things differently that night, that young man would be alive."

"You didn't know that before?"

"I never let myself think about it."

"And this knowledge makes you feel what?" she asks, her eyes narrowed, lips pursed, forehead wrinkled in quizzical mockery of his pronouncement.

"Like a danger. To myself. To others. Maybe to everybody. There's something wrong with me. Otherwise it couldn't have happened. Not the way it did, anyhow."

"Does that conclusion give you any satisfaction? Does it make you feel in control?"

"At least now I know."

"Carson, you've decided to know; you've decided to conclude this about yourself."

"Maybe I have. And yeah, maybe I do feel like this is where I belong, this is who I am. Who I always was. And I'm a thief in a whole new way. I stole a son from another family. I don't dream about the shooting as much anymore, but now it's about that family and the son they no longer have. A thief. A killer, that's what I am."

"Do you think you can live in a meaningful way with such a conclusion?"

"I'm taking one day at a time."

"Tell me about the last couple of years. How've you felt about your job? You told me about Eric. When he was killed, what happened in your life?"

"I changed. The job changed. He was more than a friend."

"In what ways?"

Saying that he was a thief, that he is a killer, that was easier than what she wants him to say now. If he talks about Eric, which he realizes he's never done with anyone else like this, maybe the talking will bring him back. If for only a moment. "He was a lifeline. I didn't need the things some of the others on the force need—drugs, booze, other women. I had Eric. I always thought of him as my first real friend. My best friend. I mean, I love my wife and kids. But Eric was out there in the same situations I saw. He understood."

"What did he understand?"

"Me. The Job. And when I told him about the robberies I committed, nothing changed with us. He even gave me the courage to think about telling Bunny one day."

"Did you?"

"Naw."

"Why not?"

"I've got to keep some secrets."

"How did you grieve Eric's death?"

He's back now. Carson feels Eric not as a memory but as a presence, filling the room, inhabiting his own body. He hears his hoarse laughter, hears him telling him once again, "Slow down, brother, slow down." "I . . . I'm not sure. He had a full police funeral, you know the kind we give to a cop killed in the line of duty. But he had a reputation that everybody respected. We felt like he had died in the line of duty. Just being his friend made me a better man. They wanted me to talk about him at the funeral. Everybody knew how close we were. You know I couldn't get up there and talk about what he meant to me? It made his death too real. So I let him down. He'd never done that to me. And whenever it rains at night and I'm out, even now, I think how fucked up it was to be changing a stranger's tire in the dark, in the rain, and for death on four wheels to come barreling at you and snuff you out like a candle."

"How was your performance on the job after he died?"

"My evaluations started slipping. There were two brutality charges against me, but they were bogus. Nothing ever came of them. I was cleared. Sure, I was a little overzealous."

"Were you angry?"

"Damned right."

"Did you take it out on the people you had to interact with in performing your job?"

"I don't know. I don't know. But I stopped seeing their faces. I was on automatic. Yeah. I stopped seeing their faces. It was rough. A couple of months after Eric died, we had a spate of killings all over the county, seventy-two murders in six months. Do you know what that means? That's twelve a month. Three people a week. Coming to a scene and finding somebody shot in the head or the neck, slumped over the steering wheel of their car . . . Shit, we found bodies stuffed in trunks, in dumpsters, on the side of the road, as though they'd been tossed there from speeding cars." He shakes his head. "I'll never forget one week, there were three murders in my district and I was called to two of them. And when I looked at those bodies I saw Eric's face. Then after a while I had to stop seeing any faces in order to do what I had to do. I was on automatic."

"How'd you handle the pain?"

"I didn't want to take it home, so I'd hang out at The Blue Diamond with other officers after my shift. They weren't my friends, but they were my tribe. Being around them I didn't see the faces of the dead, Eric or some unknown, unidentified Jane or John Doe, or some mother's known son or daughter."

"Did it help?"

"Sure. Drinking and talking and talking and drinking, it helped . . . some."

"Were you in pain the night of the shooting?"

"I don't know."

"Did you see Paul Houston? Did you really see his face?"

"Either way I answer that question, I'm fucked."

Three weeks before Christmas, Carson is cleared by Internal Affairs, the shooting ruled *Justifiable*. That single word allows him back on the force. But it solves nothing. Lays nothing to rest. Does not make him feel vindicated, as Carson had long thought it would. Because if the shooting was justified, why did he feel so counterfeit when he received the formal letter, with that word one of many on the page, stating the outcome of the internal investigation? If the shooting was justified, why was he so surprisingly ambivalent about going back on the force when he got the call to report for duty? Why had the nightmares seemed to intensify in the days before he returned to work? Why is he afraid he could kill again?

Back on duty, Carson is assigned to evening desk duty, the assignment everyone hates. He answers phones, fielding calls about everything from barking dogs and busted water mains to shootings. He processes the release of impounded vehicles. The calls are ceaseless, as, it seems, is the flow of confused, haven't-got-a-clue citizens who appear before the front desk, asking for an answer to a mundane inquiry that the police department often can't answer.

"*You sure* you wanna do this?" Wyatt Jordan asks Carson. They are sitting in Wyatt's cruiser in the district headquarters parking lot.

"It's not about being sure—it's just something I feel I gotta do. I don't know why. But I feel like I gotta do it."

"Sure." Wyatt shrugs. "I'll run a check on the Houstons. Hell, we could do it right now," he says, pointing to the mobile data terminal stationed between them in the front seat.

"Maybe you shouldn't do it. Maybe you should ask one of the secretaries to pull the information. That way nobody can trace the request back to you or me," Carson tells him.

"That's a plan."

The lot is bordered by mounds of snow, icy, dirt-encrusted remnants of last week's storm.

"I ran a check on Monique before we got married. You see how much good that did," Wyatt says with a chuckle. "How you holding up on desk duty?"

"It sucks."

"They'll ease you back on patrol soon."

"Yeah, I know."

"When you get back out there, just remember not to second-guess yourself. It's too late for that, Carson. It won't do you or anybody any good. You did the only thing you could that night."

"That's what everybody tells me," Carson says wearily.

"They're not just telling you that. Whatever you got to go through to put this behind you, you better do it before you go back on patrol."

"How do you get over shooting somebody the way I did?"

"Look, I'm just saying . . ."

"I know. I know."

"What're you gonna do with the information, if you don't mind my asking?"

"I don't know. It's like the man I shot is a phantom, or a ghost. I want to know who he was, who his parents are."

"That's spooky shit, Blake."

"I don't just have the dream, Wyatt—I live with a picture of him in my mind that's half developed. Freeze framed, stopped at the moment I killed him. You talk about moving on, but I'm stuck, and I can't go on until the rest of that picture gets filled in. It's like there was a bond that was formed between us that night and it doesn't matter that he's dead. He's not dead for me. Fact is, he never will be."

Three days later Carson sits in a snug Jamaican café a block away from headquarters on his lunch break, reading through the printout from the National Crime Information Center. He pushes his half-finished jerk chicken aside and thumbs through the sheaf of papers a second time. The printout tells him that Temple Houston has gotten a couple of speeding tickets, where Temple and Natalie Houston live and work, the company that insures their home, their car, and more information than he knows what to do with.

It's all data. All facts. And yet the outline of the life that he can compose from these bits of information comforts Carson. He can guess their politics, what their house looks like and what's inside, what they talk about. He can speculate on how they raised their son, even what kinds of clothes he wore as a child.

Carson has read about the Stockholm syndrome, in which kidnap victims begin to identify with and form bonds with their captors, and as he folds the printout and stuffs it in his jacket pocket he realizes that he is held hostage to not just the memory but the lived and unlived life of the man he killed. He has even dared to think that one day he would meet the young man's family. To explain. To apologize. Just the other day he read a story in the newspaper that profiled a group of women in D.C., mothers who had forged bonds with the mothers of the incarcerated men and women who had killed their children. He'd begun collecting similar *Ripley's Believe It or Not*–type articles about what he viewed as incredible acts of forgiveness—like the young White college student in Corpus Christi, Texas, a born-again Christian, who testified in court, asking leniency for the Black woman who, while driving one night, high on a nearly lethal cocktail of hallucinogens, struck and killed his father, a homeless man crossing the street pushing a shopping cart stuffed with newspapers and clothes. Carson has collected dozens of stories like that, and he keeps them in a scrapbook only he's seen. These stories amaze him, and he is drawn to them for what they inform him about what men and women as ordinary as he are capable of. He doesn't even know how he'd initiate such a miracle in his own life. But he has to believe such a thing is possible. That belief, he knows, is the first step. Alone at home, he thumbs through the scrapbook, pores over the stories, has read them so many times he knows them word for word, by heart. These people found miracles, made them happen. He hasn't told anyone, not Bunny, not Carrie Petersen, but he's had other dreams too. Dreams in which he made a miracle out of all that now remains.

Carson reluctantly agrees to go out for a drink one night with Vince Proctor. When he walks through the door of the Blue Diamond and feels the dim, low-ceilinged bar bearing down on him, Carson trembles as memories flash through his mind like a wrenching prophetic vision. Memories of himself sitting at 1 a.m. in the corner where he had a clear view of the television elevated over the bar, nursing a beer or two, huddled at the table that had one too-short leg, with Davis, Quarles, and Jeeter, swapping complaints and *you won't believe what happened on my shift* stories that on some nights sounded like tall tales or outright lies. The man arrested for walking nude down 193 at 5:00 a.m., armed with a machete and quoting from the book of Revelation. The woman who called to report a robbery and came to the door in a sheer nightgown and tried to seduce Jeeter. The fifteen-year-old who blew her brains out on her front lawn before Davis could stop her. He sat there with the others, all of them bound by a desire to protect and serve, bravado, courage, and an addiction to risk as insatiable as any junkie's jones.

"Come on, I see a table." Proctor nudges Carson. It's 9:00 p.m. The place is half full. Raleigh Stevenson, the 350-pound owner, waves at Carson from behind the bar as he and Proctor walk past.

"It's about time, man, how you doing?" he calls out to Carson, who stops at the bar and extends his hand. Raleigh is a heart attack just waiting to happen, so large that he wobbles unsteadily, lumbering toward Carson.

Carson looks around, trying to delay sitting down with Proctor, who has found a booth, but he sees no one he recognizes.

"What're you having?" he calls over to Proctor.

"Gimme a Heineken."

Raleigh hands Carson two bottles and he walks slowly, reluctantly, over to Proctor. He sets the beers on the table and slides into the booth.

"You look like you held up okay," Proctor says.

"Yeah, well, looks can be deceiving."

"You know, I been on my share of administrative leaves. They call it leave but it's really punishment, the way they isolate you. It's really about breaking you," Proctor says moodily.

Proctor has shot five suspects in the last four years. Been disciplined for excessive force in three of those cases. Most cops never fire their weapons. Ever. Proctor can't stop unloading his. His pale skin is chalky white, a plaster cast shattering at the seams. Crow's-feet pinch the space around his eyes, pucker the skin above his lips. A crazy quilt of crinkled veins scars his craggy, aged face. Carson has seen the faces of cops who should have quit the force, who simply couldn't handle the streets, the stress, but the ruin that stares back at him is a decay that has spread from within.

The thought that one day he could look like that forces him to turn away from Proctor, to look at the nearby wall with the dartboard, the television set airing the news, at Raleigh pouring a shot of scotch for a U.S. marshal whose face Carson vaguely remembers. He turns away from Proctor just so he can breathe.

"So what'd you do all that time?" Proctor asks.

"Why you askin' now? You coulda called if you'd really wanted to know."

"Ouch." Proctor laughs. "C'mon, you know how it is. Life goes on."

"So they say."

"Know what I did when they'd put me on leave? Spent the day at a shooting range out in Prince William County. Worked out a couple of hours at the gym. You know, so I'd be mentally and physically sharp when I came back. You can't let them break you, Carson. Not the brass on the force or the punks we arrest."

"Can't remember what I did. How the hours, the days passed. I just remember feeling like shit. I still do."

"You gotta move on, man. I know being on desk duty is the last thing you want, but they'll ease you back on the streets."

"That's kinda what I'm afraid of."

"Whatcha mean?"

"They say if you shoot one person, you're likely to shoot somebody again. You feel more paranoid, you've got a different perception of danger."

"Hell, it's the same streets as far as I'm concerned."

"You ever dream about the guy you shot?"

"The one I paralyzed in that drug bust?"

"Yeah, the one you shot in the back."

"Come on, man, you make it sound so cold, make me sound like a hit man."

Proctor stares at Carson through hazel eyes turned wary and cold.

"No. I never dreamed about him. What the fuck would I wanna do that for? I don't have trouble sleeping. Never have."

It's a lie that he offers up without a hint of defensiveness or shame. The stilted tenor of his voice, the word *never*, inform Carson that Proctor's torture has indeed been immense.

"Well, I dreamed about the man I shot. I still do."

"Too bad."

"Yeah, it is."

"You know that sumbitch Griffin tried to get me transferred," Proctor says, steering the conversation onto rocky but less threatening shoals. "I been on the force eighteen years—shit, I can retire, get the hell outta Dodge in two. What you wanna bet I outlast him? I went straight to the union reps. Told them he was harassing me."

Before he realizes it, Carson has been sitting in the booth an hour and a half listening to Proctor, his complaints about the new recruits, the pay raise the legislature voted against, the civilian review board. The three beers Proctor drinks turn him loud and nasty, and when two detectives at a nearby table ask him to keep it down, Carson has to push him back in the booth to keep him from bolting across the small room to nail them.

When Proctor calms down he rises to go to the john, assuring Carson that he won't stop at the table of the two who told him to be quiet. His seat is empty, but Carson still feels the booth charged, crackling with the sound of Proctor's voice and his anger and fear. Carson wonders if he will burst into flames or, even worse, end up like Proctor. Imprisoned by The Job. A danger to civilians. A stranger to himself. These thoughts inspire Carson to throw a ten-dollar bill on the table and head for the door, and make him ignore Proctor calling out to him when he comes out of the john, "Hey, Blake, where you going?"

He is in the parking lot, opening the car door, and Proctor is all over him, pulling on his arm.

"Where you going?" he demands again.

"I gotta go."

"You were gonna leave just like that? What'd I do? What'd I say?"

"Why did you ask me to meet you? Just tell me that," Carson shouts, inching so close to Proctor that he steps back.

"I thought you could use a friend."

"I'm not like you, Proctor. I want you to know that. I'm not like you. So how could we be friends?"

"You're more like me than you know."

"Everything you said back there was a lie or a cover-up. I can drink alone. I can lie to myself without your help."

"What do you want from me? A confession? Yeah, I lied. I've thought about the perp I shot."

Carson shrugs and gets into his car. Proctor leans on the door, his face close to Carson's through the window. "I lied about another thing too. It was me who needed a friend. Come on, Blake, you know how that feels."

"Yeah, Proctor," Carson tells him, placing his key in the ignition, "I do."

1 0

She wanted to name him Prince. But Temple insisted on Paul. For the great Black athlete, actor, singer, and activist Paul Robeson. Temple was convinced their son would grow, like Robeson, into a man defying categorization. That he'd carry his own world with him. She too possessed grand dreams for the long-limbed, husky baby delivered after an agonizing eighteen-hour labor, a birthing that defeated Temple's promise to last at her side in the delivery room, to be the one to place their child in her arms.

Natalie had decided on Princess for a girl. Like Prince, it was an affirmation and an anointing. She yearned for a daughter radiant with a sense of her own worth, or a son of whom it would be said, "He has a good heart." As always, Temple wanted much more. His son (and Temple knew absolutely that Natalie carried a boy, even as they decided against the ultrasound exam that would have confirmed his intuition), *his* child, must roar through his life, not merely live it. And so Temple named their child for a man who beat all the odds. He named their child Paul.

But Paul had always been *her* prince. And because of that they had done everything right. Still, Temple warned her, back when

Paul was five and enrolled in a Montessori school, when he was eight and joined the Cub Scouts, when Temple and Paul accompanied Natalie to Senegal for a weeklong conference on African diaspora literature, with side trips to Ivory Coast and Ghana, "Doing everything right might still not be enough."

In the tremulous, secret-code-filled conversations instigated by Temple's admonition, they never completed the thought. Never said it out loud. *Doing everything right might not be enough to save him.* For if they lost Paul, then they too were doomed. Their construction of a psychic space beyond White folks' reach. Their massive love for their son. None of it, in the end, perhaps even at the beginning, was guaranteed to be enough.

Two pregnancies before Paul had ended in death. A cyst on the back of the baby's neck killed the first; a cord bunched around the neck of the second prevented the baby from breathing. Natalie might have had her Princess, for both babies were girls. So Paul bore the weight. He had lived most intensely in their imagination, suspended between what he was and what he was to become. Always, it seemed, Paul was most real in their dreams for him. Dreams that encompassed all the good they could imagine and some that they could not even name. A child is a whispered prophecy. Hope is the middle name of every child ever born.

Once, the instant the door closed after Paul's departure from the house, Natalie felt the fear. The turning of the lock, such a minute, momentary sound, summoned the demons. When Paul got his license and went with friends to weekend parties, Natalie lay in bed restless and fitful, until she heard the lock on the door once again and Paul ascending the stairs with a purposeful stealth designed not to wake them. On those nights, Temple slept beside her, his snores and stolid, heavy slumber signaling a trust of the night that she could never call forth. Her dread was mighty, the imagined calamities numerous—a traffic accident, a fight, a shooting at a club, a stop by the police, a robbery. She harbored the un-speakable, shameful thought that if the early-morning call must come, let the phone jar some other couple awake—God help her, she would pass this cup on to another.

Before he moved into his own apartment in D.C., some nights Natalie stood at the wide front window, pulled back the curtains, and watched Paul's Nissan coast down the driveway, turn the cor-ner, leaving Glory Road and turning onto Pleasant Prospect Lane, the taillights, the car, disappearing with that sharp left turn, as though the darkness, the night itself, had quickly and ravenously feasted on the vehicle and Paul. Gone. Out of her reach. Beyond the sound of her voice, her admonition, her protection. Her love.

But that night, Paul's last night, she had not felt the fear, deep, abiding, terrible. Even when she called out to Paul before he bounded out the door on his way to the supermarket at the nearby mall to get her a bottle of aspirin, Natalie brushed aside the eerie ache of doubt that shot through her like an echo of the old famil-iar fear. She had not felt the fear. Not at first, anyway. It was the headache, she told herself as she embraced Paul, her hands wet, her body arched backward to give herself up and over to his height. It was a headache that made her feel so odd, so uneasy. Nothing more.

When an hour and a half passed and Paul had not returned, Natalie thought to call him on his cell phone. It was a Tuesday night. How crowded could the supermarket be? Then she recalled the surprisingly long lines that greeted her sometimes at night when she dashed in to pick up an item or two. No, she wouldn't call him on his cell phone. It might not even be on. To suppress the distress bubbling inside her, she turned on the stereo in the liv-ing room, heard on the jazz station an early-fifties ballad by Miles Davis pouring through the speakers, the sounds unfurling as lazy as the shy, coiled petals of a rosebud, but not calming her, not for a second. She willed herself to think of something else. Anything else. Her mind drifted to Lisa, carrying Paul's baby. *Carrying.* How apt was the term. Wasn't she carrying Paul right now? Wasn't he at twenty-five still a blessed burden that she had wanted more than anything? Even more than Temple or his love. To be a mother. And soon she would have a grandchild.

The knock on the door was firm and Natalie would think in the aftermath of that night, *That's when I knew. I could hear it in the sound of their knuckles pounding my front door. A sound that was heavy, yet strangely hesitant, that would not be denied, yet that pushed me deeper into the chair in which I sat beside the front window (where I had sat down finally after pacing I don't know how long). Waiting to see the lights of Paul's car swing back onto Glory Road.*

In remembrance, and she sometimes heard it even now, the knocking seemed to go on forever. She would not respond to it. Because she knew. Maybe if she simply did not answer the door . . . Maybe if the lights were out. But the house, their stately three-story brick Georgian colonial with the wide white columns, was ablaze with light. So whoever was knocking, and she knew it was the police (who else knocked like that), knew someone was home.

Temple's voice broke the spell of her resistance. Her determined denial. He'd been in the basement practicing his golf swing and come upstairs, shouting, "For Christ's sake, Natalie, answer the front door." *No, don't answer it.* That's what she wanted to scream. But before her lips could part, lips raw and bleeding—she'd bitten into them so deeply, in her fear—the door was open. And now she could hear everything. The door was open. Open and evil, and disaster entered like a tidal wave in the form of the two policemen in plain clothes who stood on the porch and asked if Paul Houston lived here. Paul hadn't gotten a D.C. license yet, still carried his Maryland license with their address.

Temple's impatience gave way to wary anxiety, which Natalie heard throbbing in the simple "Yes." And after the yes, she was drowning and everything was swept away.

"Are you his parents?"

"Your son's been involved in a shooting. We need you to come to the hospital with us."

Natalie rose from the chair, sprang from its confines. Standing at the door beside Temple, she could not have said what the policemen looked like. Who really gazes deep, fearlessly, into the face of the angel of death?

"What happened? What happened?" Temple asked. "We can only tell you that your son is at the County Hospital and we've been told to take you there, one of the men said."

"Is he alive?" Temple asked.

"I'm sorry, Mr. Houston. I can't tell you anything more."

From that night she remembers few sounds, except the thud of Temple's fist breaking through the wall in the small family counseling room when the doctor told them that Paul was dead. And the chairs and tables he scattered as the security guard pulled him away from the wall and tried to calm him. She remembers her scream; it was a howl, really, a sound that echoes still behind every thought. It felt as if her lungs were on fire. How did the building withstand all that her voice unleashed? How did the hospital not crumble around her feet, shaken to the core by their grief? When she thinks of it now, she can't remember any of the faces, not the counselor who met them at the main entrance, the doctor who told them Paul was dead, the nurse who accompanied them to the room to look at Paul's body. But the face of her son she would never forget. The bleeding was massive. The bottoms of his feet and the palms of his hands were as white as chalk. The nurses had placed Paul's hands on top of the sheet. Natalie wanted to see with her own eyes how Paul had died. When she reached to pull the sheet back, just to see his body, she didn't care what she'd see. She almost longed for the blood, wanted to see the wounds. How else could she believe her child was dead? But she wasn't allowed to pull back the sheet. The trauma nurse pulled her arms away from Paul's body, saying, "This is a coroner's case now. Everything in this room, including your son's body, is evidence we can't tamper with."

The two policemen drove them back home, back through the gate that lifted when Temple entered the pass code, down Pleasant Prospect Lane and onto Glory Road. Natalie and Temple passed that night together encased in an ancient, primordial silence. Not until the first stirrings of dawn slid through the curtains did Natalie begin to weep, a fulsome, baptismal release that she had stalled all night.

It made no sense. Not then. Not now. The police explanation. Carson Blake's defense. A year has passed since that dreadful night, and she still doesn't understand. On too many nights Natalie has sat parked in the mall lot, outside the Chinese restaurant where it happened, staring at the spot as if to make Paul rise from the scrubby cement walkway that had been covered that night with his blood. According to the police, Paul was stopped for driving with no headlights and speeding. *"Be polite. Courteous. Remember Rodney King. Keep your hands where they can see them."*

"You have to let Paul go." That's what Temple keeps saying. He tells Natalie this even as his own memories of their son are for him an unremitting, nearly blinding light. "Let him go," he says, so they can give Paul what he was denied the night of his death, the only pursuit worth embarking on in his name—justice. No, Temple firmly has told Natalie, "I won't delay or reschedule any more appointments. If you don't go with me, I'll go see Quint Masterson alone."

Her husband has been patient, understanding, has given wide

berth to her grief while in the throes of his own. But he will hesitate no longer. For Temple, Natalie often thinks, unfairly she knows, that it is all so simple. He wants justice. She wants their son back. She wants him alive.

Natalie opens her eyes after twenty futile minutes spent trying to quell her thoughts. Sitting on a meditation cushion on the carpet in her study, Natalie recalls bitterly that she'd closed her eyes to find relief from everything that haunts her thoughts. The usual monkey mind she combats throughout her meditation sessions, the restless resistance to tranquillity, was heightened by the internal dialogue about the second meeting with Quint Masterson scheduled for this afternoon. How can she be still, quiet her breathing, slow down her heart, when she is so unsettled by the idea of the wrongful death suit Temple wants to file? The fact that Blake was neither indicted by the courts nor punished by the police force has added urgency to Temple's arguments that a civil suit is all the recourse that remains.

But for Natalie, a suit will make Paul's death real. Memory renders him unto her with a generosity that humbles her anew every day. Temple wants "the system" to pay. For what they have lost and will never have again. Yet how much would a jury conclude the life of her son was worth?

The first meeting with Masterson, just weeks after the funeral, sickened her. Considered one of the area's top civil lawyers, Masterson was high profile and frequently in the news. He met with Natalie and Temple in the high-ceilinged boardroom of his Bethesda office. The long, sweeping marble conference table, the softness of the high-backed leather chairs that enveloped them in a plush embrace, the thick carpeting that she felt herself sinking into as they were ushered into the room by the blond, model-thin receptionist, all of it held the scent of commerce. And that, Natalie felt, had nothing to do with Paul. But money is why Temple chose Masterson. Temple had researched the lawyer exhaustively on his Internet site and even managed to find and talk to former clients who rated him highly, called him "a bulldog" on a case. "This is our man," Temple had said, beaming when he told Natalie about the appointment for the first meeting.

Masterson was a small, tight, energetic man whose soft voice came as a surprise to Natalie even as she was charmed by the still thick Louisiana accent he made no attempt to alter and clearly used to enhance an image of regularity and down-home honesty. "I have to tell you that I'm not quite ready to consider a suit yet," she told Masterson that day, "but I am curious as to how a judgment would be determined."

"Well, we would not ask for a definite amount, although we certainly would have one in mind. The jury would consider your son's life expectancy, what his lifetime earnings would have been, his value to the community because of his work as a teacher, the emotional cost to you and your husband because you lost a son so tragically." Masterson took them through every laborious step in the process of filing the suit: discovery, which could require two years of research just to make the case against Carson Blake, appeals, continuances, delays, the possibility that the county would seek to have the suit dismissed, appeals.

Natalie was wearied just by the recitation of the process. That meeting was enough to convince Natalie that there could be no justice or fairness in a suit. Although Natalie let Temple ask most of the questions during this initial interview, she asked Masterson, "Tell me, how much do you think my son's life is worth?"

"Mrs. Houston," Masterson said, shaking his head in the motion of pity she had grown used to, "no one can put a price tag on a life, but I would try to get you fifty million dollars." The sum seemed paltry to Natalie.

"What would be likely?"

"I have had judgments in similar cases in the range of eight hundred thousand to three million dollars."

"Those figures are an insult. O.J. Simpson had to pay twelve million dollars for the life of Ron Goldman, even though he was found innocent of killing him. The best the system would give me for the life of my son is maybe one fourth of that if we were lucky? I don't like the way these figures are computed, and this is why I've told my husband this process will just prolong our grief and tarnish my son's memory."

"Natalie, come on," Temple said, gazing apologetically at Masterson.

"It's all right, Mr. Houston. People are often ambivalent about filing suits when they realize all that's involved and the likely outcomes. People surprise themselves. They think money will make them feel better. That's not always true, and I have to tell you, this is not going to be an easy case."

"My son was killed by mistake," Temple said indignantly.

"But we have to prove excessive force, and the situation we are dealing with, as tragic as it is, can be interpreted as justified force."

"Are you saying we can't sue?"

A tiny sardonic smile blossomed on Masterson's face, and he crossed his legs and placed his small manicured hands on his knees and told Temple, "You can sue a ham sandwich. We can always make a case, and if that is what you want me to do, I will."

That's exactly what Temple wanted. For Quint Masterson to make a case, for what seemed obvious to him and to Natalie— what happened that night was not justified use of force but murder.

But Natalie thinks, now standing up from the mat on the floor, *If we file the suit, go to court, that will be proof that my son is gone for good.* She knows her son is dead, but the knowing feels tentative, questionable, even negotiable. How can he be dead when he lives in her memory so radiantly, with an incandescence that is ablaze in her heart? How could so much love still fill her for one who is dead?

Resistance to the idea of filing the suit has become a habit, a way of life. Temple first mentioned a wrongful death suit the day after Paul's funeral. She still shudders at the memory of how calmly he broached the subject even as she was still mired in absolute disbelief, a ravaging hurt so deep, she felt as though a vital part of her—her legs, or arms—had been amputated while she slept.

"If I were any other kind of man, we wouldn't need a lawyer. I'd find out where that bastard lives and deal with this myself," he told her, sitting beside Natalie on their bed, his eyes red from weeping. "Revenge never made much sense to me until now. I understand why an eye for an eye could give you a way to go on."

She too was filled with rage, but it had morphed into a sorrow and longing that made it impossible then to think of suits, lawyers, courts, judgments. Returning from the hospital, knowing her son would never walk through their front door again. The perfect stillness of Paul's body in the casket, where he looked not at peace but like a mummified caricature of her son. The sound of the minister's voice at the cemetery as Paul was lowered into the ground, his voice sonorous and filled with faith, when she had never been more certain of the absence of God. She was numb and raw, suspended between yesterday, a definite place in time where she was a mother, and the thousands of days stretching before her, a hell where she had been cast and wandered like a motherless child, for her son had created her as surely as she had made him.

As Natalie sits down at her desk, massaging her jaws, her cheeks, her forehead, Temple's words reverberate in her thoughts. "If I were a different kind of man . . . an eye for an eye . . ." She wants revenge too, but the kind that promises resurrection, that could erase history, beam them into an alternate universe where they'd find Paul waiting for them.

She thinks of Temple's words often. Even as she has rejected the assertion that is also a plea, its vigor, strength, and honesty have swelled her with pride for their unbridled passion. If she could, she would move heaven and earth. For Temple, the civil suit will place the world back on a semblance of its axis—it has become his weapon of choice, his antidote to grief. Natalie has prevented him from using it, but she can't stop him any longer.

She looks for Paul everywhere. There was no bedroom to keep intact like a shrine. Paul lived in a Silver Spring, Maryland. But he'd come to have dinner with Natalie and Temple that night, his last night, like he did once a week. And Natalie can still find him in the 1993 Mansfield Day School yearbook on her desk. Mansfield, the prestigious prep school that sat on thirty lushly wooded acres behind an imposing iron gate in upper northwest Washington. Paul took physics with the sons of cabinet members; attended a birthday party for a classmate whose Democratic Party fundraiser mother spearheaded a capital campaign for the school that raised five million dollars. In his junior year he dated the biracial daughter of a popular local newscaster.

Everybody knew Paul. Everybody liked Paul. He seemed to fit easily into the snug, privileged world of the school. Paul entered Mansfield in first grade, scoring well on the entrance exam. But by ninth grade he complained of feeling insecure and inferior around his wealthy classmates, who had given him a bird's-eye view into the world of actual wealth. Even the most affluent Black families seemed like paupers compared to the White students at Mansfield. Over dinner Paul told Natalie and Temple that his classmates talked about nannies and maids from El Salvador, Christmas vacations spent in Aspen, and that the environment that had once fascinated him made him feel like an outsider. Everyone was friendly, White liberal politically correct, even though in the lower school the eight-year-old daughter of an assistant secretary of state had called one of her Black classmates, during a tussle over ownership of a ball, "a stupid nigger," sparking an indignant, tearful defense by the child's mother that the girl had never heard those words in their home (a two-million-dollar mansion tucked in the wooded, secluded upper reaches of North West, a stone's throw away from the home of the vice president). The Black parents, including Temple and Natalie, consistently complained about the need for recruitment of more Black students.

Temple and Natalie had made the proverbial post–civil rights era economic leap, Temple from Boston's Roxbury, where his father owned a small auto mechanic shop and his mother was a supermarket cashier. Roxbury ranged from middle class to piss poor, and Temple grew up in the largely Black neighborhood's most hardscrabble section. His younger brother, Johnny, returned from Vietnam in one piece but died of a heroin overdose in a Mattapan alley two years later, his body sprawled as carelessly as if he had been ambushed. Temple remembered Johnny's death every day, and was embittered by the sordid battlefield his brother had returned to Stateside to find and the death he had outsmarted in Vietnam.

Smart, bristling with drive, Temple won a scholarship to Boston University and did graduate work in political science at Harvard. Memories of Johnny, whom Temple had seen weaving high and unsteady on the streets of Roxbury, Johnny's dream of being a singer like his idol, Marvin Gaye, singed, gone up in smoke, and their father, who worked fourteen-hour days in the garage behind their rented house repairing long-past-glory Crown Vics, used Volkswagens, and the battered trucks of his small but loyal clientele drove Temple in his ascent. And he remembered his mother, who turned down a scholarship to Bennett, a small Black women's college in North Carolina, when she discovered she was pregnant and married his father in order to become, in her words, "an honest woman." His mother squirreled away enough money to buy Temple and Johnny a new set of encyclopedias every three years and forced Temple, against his will back then, to read the *Boston Globe* every day and make a list of new words and their definitions. Now Temple was Dean of Humanities at Washington College in Baltimore County, where Natalie taught African American literature. Everything he had, Temple felt—his degrees, his job, his home in Heaven's Gate, even the contentment he knew as husband and father—had somehow been bought and paid for with the dust of his family's ruined dreams.

Natalie grew up in D.C.'s Petworth neighborhood, an area of middle-class Black strivers. Her mother, Donna, who was widowed when Natalie was ten and her sister, Rosalind, fourteen, was a civil servant at the Justice Department who had not imagined Natalie a full professor with a Ph.D., the author of a book of essays on Black women writers that was a required text at scores of colleges. Natalie, who spent hours alone, reading in the attic of the small, close two-bedroom house on Shepherd Street, fantasizing about writing poetry like Gwendolyn Brooks, reading *Oliver Twist* and Jane Austen novels and *War and Peace* to escape the barrage of her mother's predictions that her sister Rosalind would go farther in the world because "she's got personality," never saw herself delivering lectures in Europe and Africa, or living in a home with walls filled with art and other mementos from travel in eighteen countries. Natalie and Temple had come far, and were members of the ACLU and the NAACP, had voted for Jesse Jackson when he ran for president although their friends chided them that it was a wasted vote. They knew their roots, were proud of their heritage, and wanted nothing less for Paul than that he should climb onto the next rung of the ladder they had climbed, they felt, with an invisible hand trying to pull them down.

There had been family vacations in Jamaica, Toronto, France. Paul was fluent in Spanish and had spent his junior year abroad, living in Mexico. And Natalie and Temple encouraged Paul to spend time with his cousins Jake and Antoine, her sister Rosalind's sons, who were star high school football players at Coolidge High in D.C. Paul partied with them and spent weekends with the two boys, not just because they were kin but because Paul wanted to know and speak the lingua franca of the inner city. Natalie and Temple wanted him to possess that particular expertise as well. Heaven's Gate and Mansfield Day School represented tiny slivers of the world, and Paul was never to forget that.

To their relief Natalie and Temple watched Paul move with apparent ease between the divergent zones of his life. He learned to turn aside his cousins' jests about attending a "preppy school," and he could jone and joke with his cousins' friends in the gruff ghetto slang that gave him a street seal of approval. Paul had told Natalie once, "Mom, Mansfield, Petworth, PG—they're all just different hoods, and I can talk the talk and walk the walk anywhere I find myself."

If anything was to ever happen, Natalie imagined Paul caught up in the unthinkable while out driving with his cousins on their way to or from a party in D.C., not shot down outside a Chinese restaurant at eleven o'clock on a Tuesday night a mile from their house because of a cell phone. Paul could talk his way out of anything. Where was his voice, Natalie wondered, that night?

The leather photo album devoted to Paul's graduation from Mansfield lies in her lap, open to her favorite picture. Of all the photos of Paul, this is the one she cherishes most, his wide, dark brown face, the thick, bushy brows that hid small, perceptive eyes.

The smile so broad, so bright. The face that Natalie always thought was a map of all that Paul was and could be.

In the weeks and months immediately after his death, Natalie sat for hours, staring at the photo obsessively, as though just looking at it would bring Paul back to life. She has spent other full days rummaging through boxes of mementos in the basement, for treasures and keepsakes neatly packed in cellophane, plastic, stored in boxes that she never thought she would need to look through for anything again. Paul's report cards from third grade, fifth grade, eighth grade, always filled with A's and B's; his first book report written in cursive, his handwriting at eight, large, loopy, big shouldered; a Little League uniform with grass and dirt stains; a letter Paul wrote to God asking why Temple's father had died from a stroke. There are days that she still spends in the basement, in a solitary, witnessing communion with her son, looking at pictures and remembering. Temple has come upon her in the basement while she was engaged in conversation with Paul, unawares, transported, laughing, arguing gently with him. This is how she grieves.

Temple has told her that it is time to release Paul. A year has passed since his death and she still spends hours alone like this. Grief counseling, which they attended together, did not quell the desire to look back. The counselor spoke of her grief for Paul as though it was an ailment that would subside with time. Natalie cannot imagine that happening. She is lost and found in the hours of this repetitive search for what cannot be. If she gazes away from Paul's face, she must look upon a world that exists now without him.

He'd been raised to give to and give back and was teaching at a D.C. school under a program that helped him pay back his student loans. He cared about and wanted to help others. Despite all that, Paul was shot in a strip mall parking lot by a cop who thought he had a gun. What might he have been? What could he have done? Those questions plague Natalie and disrupt her sleep, her peace of mind. But there was the darkness and the confusion too, which she has to remember, for to remember Paul she must remember all of him.

There was the summer Paul came home from his first year at Morehouse and was arrested one weekend in D.C. for selling marijuana to an undercover police officer. It was only then that they learned he'd been selling and smoking it for three years. Paul told Natalie and Temple, without a trace of remorse, when they interrogated him at home after paying his bail, "You wanna know how I got started? All the kids at Mansfield used it, sold it. That's where I got into it."

"I don't give a damn what those kids do. You aren't them. They can do drugs and still end up a CEO, a general, a senator. Boy, have you forgotten who the hell you are? Who we are?"

"That's not what you said when I was at Mansfield," Paul shouted bitterly. "You said I could do anything. Be anything. Which is it, Dad? Am I free, or just a nigger anyway?"

Temple grabbed Paul by the collar of his oversize shirt and through clenched teeth told his son, "If you choose to be a nigger, that's your call. Don't blame me or anybody else for your stupidity. I didn't raise a pothead, and if that's the best you can do, get out of my house."

Natalie felt bewildered and betrayed. An expensive attorney got Paul probation and his record expunged. Paul rebounded, returned to Morehouse toeing the line, calling Temple and Natalie during the middle of the fall semester to tell them by phone what he could not face-to-face: "I love you and thank you for saving my butt." He graduated cum laude and decided to teach, getting a master's degree in education from Columbia, then returning to D.C. and opting to teach in the D.C. public schools.

Natalie looks for Paul everywhere, because in the year before his death there were times she wondered if she had ever known him at all. He pushed his girlfriend, Lisa, when they argued, because she was pregnant. Natalie couldn't believe the call from Lisa one morning, the girl in tears, recounting the argument with Paul and how it had degenerated into a shoving match. Lisa wanted to have the child. Paul didn't.

Natalie stormed over to Paul's apartment and found him at home watching television. When he opened the door, Natalie strode past him furiously without a hello and shouted, "You never saw your father put his hands on me—where the hell is this coming from?"

"I didn't mean it," he told Natalie, slinking onto the twin bed he'd camouflaged to look like a sofa, pushing aside a stack of textbooks, a pizza box with a stale, half-eaten vegetarian pizza and several CDs.

"She's carrying your child. You could have caused a miscarriage. Is that what you wanted?" Natalie demanded, furious that the son she had raised to honor and respect women had shoved the woman carrying his child.

"No."

"Well, what, then?"

"She wants to get married," he said angrily, his face clouded by a confusion and near terror that made Natalie's heart tremble. "I'm not feeling that right now."

"What are you feeling, Paul? Tell me why my son struck the woman who is carrying his child? This isn't you."

"I didn't strike her," Paul insisted. Natalie felt like screaming, listening to the self-serving linguistic hair-splitting of her Ivy

League—educated son. "Lisa's cool. We been together a year, but I can't hardly take care of myself, and now a baby?"

"What's really going on?" she asked, softening her voice, mostly to calm her nerves as she sat down beside Paul.

"Everything's messed up. It's like school was easy compared to real life. You ever try to teach third-graders? I got a poor evaluation last week and got in trouble for touching a student while trying to break up a fight. I wanna get out of this gig, but I need it to pay off my student loans. I go in pumped up, enthusiastic, and spend three quarters of my time trying to get the kids to be quiet. All we do is teach them how to pass standardized tests. I feel like I'm in a holding facility, and damn, I didn't know there could be so many papers to grade."

"And that's why you hit Lisa?"

"I don't know. I'm not saying it is, but—"

"Do you ever think what she must feel, Paul? She's in her senior year at Howard. Wants to go to medical school, is in love with a young man who apparently isn't serious about her, finds herself pregnant and doesn't believe in abortion so she's gonna have the baby. And when we talked last night she said she's been accepted at Johns Hopkins Medical School and she's going to delay going until after she has the baby. She steps up to the plate. Can you? You don't have to get married, but you can't run her and your child out of your life. She won't stand for it and neither will I."

Natalie has looked for Paul in the face of Darren, his son, born three months after Paul's death. She sees Paul in the baby's face. Thank God, if not for the child. Darren is Paul; he is his father's child.

Paul asked her once how she could stand to teach African American literature at all: "It's so damn depressing." But she found bravery, eloquence, woven into the simple testimonies of the literature and especially the slave narratives. These men and women had chosen to speak. Were willing to speak and remember the unbearable. She often told her students to think of the slave narratives as a gift from those who had been told they were nothing. Their gift was to alchemize their suffering into a door, a gateway into the depth of the human experience and the human heart. Slave narratives, she told her students, were proof that the human heart could not be broken. For the stories always came, she told them, from the heart, hearts bleeding, tattered, that were repaired in some way by the telling of these stories. She had lied. The human heart could break.

Natalie has not read slave narratives as she has grieved for her son, not once during this long, endless year of mourning. Most of her life has been devoted to writing and reading; she spent hours holed up with books in her bedroom, shunning the company of others as a child, and the feel, the touch of a book that she wants to read can still send a thrill through her body. But she has not read much during this time of grief. Reading would crowd her memories of Paul. And writing? What is there to write now, except the single word, the only question that matters: *Why?*

"Our son died for no reason. His death was a mistake. If he had died of a disease, even in a train wreck, during a robbery, perhaps I would not feel so empty. But our son died because his cell phone was mistaken for a gun. Tell me why?" That is all she would write on the tableau of the heavens. In Natalie's dreams Carson Blake is a monster. She cannot know that he dreams, as does she, of her son.

"I think we should leave around one o'clock," Temple says, quietly entering the study without knocking, finding Natalie staring out the window at the overcast, sullen sky. Natalie turns around, her arms folded across her chest. She's been in this room the last two hours, Temple imagines just from the sight of her, those arms crossed, the face so serious and drawn, sharpening her argument against the necessary and the inevitable, which is how he thinks of the suit he wants to file.

"What good will it do? It won't bring Paul back," Natalie says. Temple sits in the chair at her desk. This room is where Natalie writes, prays, meditates, composes her class lectures, where she wrote her book, the room where she seeks and finds refuge from the world. Temple wonders how, in this room, his arguments have a chance.

"Natalie . . ."

"Temple, don't use that voice with me. That tiptoe-toward-the-crazy-woman voice, trying to tell me I don't know what I feel."

"All right. I'll talk to you the way you haven't let me since I first told you what we should do." Temple moves toward Natalie even as she, her arms still folded across her chest, turns away from him, as if the words to come will arrive like a blow.

"Yes, I do want revenge. I know nothing will bring Paul back. But I can't do nothing. He was my son. I spent my life trying to protect him from everything in the world that was out to get him, and when he needed me most . . . When he needed us both the most, there was nothing we could do. Now there is. We can remember Paul by standing up for his life and his dignity. Nobody should die the way he did. In some deserted parking lot, in the dark, facing down a cop who just sees you as another criminal, when you're unarmed, when your only crime is driving with no lights, and you get killed for no reason. No reason at all."

Natalie stands unmoving, bearing the onslaught of her husband's words. Temple sees her wipe tears from her cheek.

"It will take years," Natalie moans softly.

Temple dares a step closer to his wife.

"I don't care how long it takes. Paul is gone forever."

When she turns to face him, Temple sees the horror in Natalie's eyes, feels it stab him as he watches her crumble slowly onto her knees.

"No, don't say that. Don't say that," she whimpers.

Temple lifts Natalie from the surface of the small Turkish rug and shelters her in his arms. Her fists against Temple's chest keep time with the staccato of her sobs.

"We have to do this for Paul, honey. It's all for him."

"You want me to let him go, and I can't do that."

"I can't do it either. We have to live with his memory and without him."

"The suit won't bring him back and it confirms he's gone for good," Natalie says.

"Honey, you know he's here. You can feel him right now. Right here. So can I."

"We'll have to go through it all over again, Temple."

"I'll be with you. We'll get through this. We'll do it for Paul. For Paul."

BOOK
2

11

Carson pulls into the circular blacktop driveway in front of the two-story brick Greek revival and parks in front of the garage. The house rises preeminently against the even more commanding heights of the trees and foliage beyond the border of the neatly carved two-acre backyard that holds the woods at bay. Two broad white columns hold up the roof and stand as bold as if shouldering the world. This house is one of a dozen completed homes in a development just off narrow, winding Church Road. The residential community, Belair Mansions, has been carved out of four hundred acres of woodland sprawling on both sides of the two-lane road. New homes have joined the farms, churches, cornfields, the modest split-levels, the occasional weatherbeaten abandoned barn, the rolling hilly turf farms that give the area a secluded feel that pays homage to its once solidly rural past.

Half the houses in this still unfinished community stand like women caught naked, forced to be on display, their roofs consisting only of rafters, the drywall and plywood underbelly exposed. Hispanic immigrant workers, small brown men in blue jeans and plaid workshirts, their raven black hair covered by baseball caps, hammer shingles on the roof of a house fifty feet away and stand almost protectively over a concrete mixer near the entrance to the development. Carson has lived all his life in Prince George's County and never imagined that one day he would be a real estate agent who had sold a house for eight hundred thousand dollars. He pulled that one off last month. It's only June, but so far it's been a good year.

He has a good feeling about this house, but the Fullers haven't liked much of what he's shown them. Not the Georgian in Bowie, the rambler in Springdale, or the colonial in Laurel. Carl Fuller strode through the previous houses like General Patton inspecting the troops on D-Day. He's one of the few Black partners in any of the K Street power-broker D.C. law firms. Built like a linebacker, Fuller starts every sentence by clearing his throat, thrusting his hands behind his back, and entwining his fingers, as if to give himself more backbone. He told Carson during the initial meeting in the Century real estate office that he wanted a showcase home, something to "impress the members of the Old Boys' club at my firm when I invite them for a Christmas party." Carson figured that as a partner at McNeill, Covington, and Lowry, Carl Fuller had won all the battles that mattered.

His wife, Rose, is tiny, with a short, frizzy mass of curls framing her high-cheekboned face; a distant, harried look resides in her eyes. But it's Rose, not Carl, who grills Carson about the test scores in the local schools, the area's crime rate, median income, the possibility of flooding in the basement, the materials used in construction. Rose wants a house, as she told Carson, "That will make me feel like I'm living a life nobody else possibly could. And I want a big backyard where I can grow tomatoes, collards, and sweet potatoes."

Belair Mansions. Paradise Acres. Heaven's Gate. Now that he is selling homes, Carson understands why developments are named to prick the skin of people's fantasies, their yearnings and dreams. Buy the right house and you will have a perfect life, save your marriage, erase a nightmarish childhood, fill your friends with envy, feel once and for all like you are somebody. That's what people think. Every time Carson makes a sale he recalls the day he and Bunny chose their first house. And he relives all the reasons why. That's one thing he likes about what he does now. He makes people happy. For a while, at least.

Inside, the house is cool, even without the air conditioning. The tan parquet floors in the large living room shimmer with a hard polished glaze, the alternate diagonals of the wood turning the floor into a continuous mural beneath his feet. Carson stands beneath the three-tiered crystal chandelier in the formal dining room and reaches for the light switch, which floods the room in an ostentatious yet entirely serene display of warmth and radiance. The light is playfully brilliant and as confident as an edict from heaven.

He likes the empty houses best, rooms bare of pictures or mementos, unburdened by the past of former owners or the artificial present implied by model home decor—cherrywood credenzas filled with china and wineglasses, mantels lined with framed photos of ruddy-faced, freckled White toddlers or handsome Black families, all to stoke the imagination of whoever stands there, grafting their hopes onto the still life they have walked into.

The kitchen is the spiritual nexus of a home. It's the hub and the heart, where nourishment comes in many different forms. In the kitchen Carson leans on the cool black marble top of the island in the center of the room, a shower of sunlight bathing him through four slanting skylight windows above a plant ledge. The kitchen, so functional, so necessary, often sells the house. This kitchen is an atrium, a greenhouse, a canvas of sorts. Where the

Fullers will expect a wall, the designer of this house placed windows from just above the sink to the ceiling. This is the room that will sell Rose Fuller on the property. Through the expanse of glass she will have an unobscured view of the backyard, the massive oak and the tangle of foliage surrounding it. Carson hopes she will have visions of her garden.

He's dealing with different people now. That's what he thought in the beginning. But Carson now knows that if he sneaked into the homes of the people he's sold property to, he'd find illegal drugs, stolen property. If he were psychic, he'd read their minds and find them raging with criminal thought, malicious intent. These people aren't different. They're just luckier than the people he busted for drug deals at midnight on the playground of an elementary school or wrestled to the ground after they'd tried to hold up a pizza deliveryman with a BB gun. But he *does* make people happy. In his top desk drawer at home are letters of praise and thanks from his real estate clients. Some even send him Christmas and birthday cards.

An estate planner Carson settled into a luxury condo gave him a free consult about retirement plans, now that planning for retirement is on him. That beats free coffee and doughnuts any day. Bunny persuaded Carson to give real estate a try after asking her cousin in Baltimore, an associate broker, to talk to him. Sam didn't have to twist his arm. In the accelerated two-week course Carson took, his fellow students were ex-cops, former firefighters, retired teachers, housewives whose children were grown, laid-off white-collar corporate types, all of them, like him, starting over, getting a second chance. His hours spill over into family time, but he can also make his own schedule and he now has more time and sees more of his children than when he was on the force. And nobody hates real estate agents. When Carson tells people what he does they don't shut down, instead they ask his advice, eagerly take his card. Two years have passed since that night in March, and Carson is thirty-nine, nearing the age of burnout on the force. Thirty-nine, starting over.

The sound of the front door opening pierces the silence of the house, cuts through his thoughts. "I'm in the kitchen," he calls out, deciding to remain where he is. Carl and Rose Fuller are walking slowly through the hallway, the living room, and the family room. He can't see them, but their footsteps—leisurely, pronounced, halting—inform Carson that they are studying the spaciousness of the house. Finally he hears their voices, murmuring, soft but animated. He'd bet money they are standing beneath the chandelier. Carson isn't hard sell. He figures his job is simple—find a house his client will want. Houses are like clothing, books, the man or woman you want to sleep with or marry, personal and unpredictable. Everybody's got tastes they can't explain and would never change. There are hundreds of houses, and he can keep showing until the client walks into the place they want to live in.

"Damn, man, how'd you find *this*?" Carl asks, scanning the circumference of the kitchen. This is the first time he has addressed Carson, without his K Street lawyer persona strapped on like a shield. Rose stands in the entrance to the kitchen, staring at the roof windows as if to ascertain the source of the light. It's hard to tell if she's amazed or disappointed. But when she enters the kitchen Carson sees the look on her face that tells him the deal is done. It's not a look of happiness but rather a look of relief. Everything clients like about a house, everything they hate, gets mapped on their face, fills it with tension, fatigue, disappointment, anger because Carson hasn't found their dream house, impatience because they took a long lunch break to see a house they don't want and have to get back into traffic, hoping they aren't late . . . and when they're standing in the house they want, the house they would move in that day if they could, he gets to see a face he hasn't seen them display before.

Carl is opening the chrome and black refrigerator, twisting knobs on the stove. Rose walks to the sink and lets her hands rest on the sill, and she looks out the wall-wide windows into the backyard. Her pale blue linen pantsuit is slightly wrinkled. She stands with eyes closed, her hands on the windowsill, as though channeling the spirit of the house. This action stops Carl's busy inspection and he and Carson both stand watching Rose, her breathing an audible pulse. She opens her eyes, turns around, and hugs Carson, telling him, "Thank you for bringing us home."

For the next half hour Carson and the Fullers inspect every part of the house, the basement, unfinished but large enough to exist as a separate domicile within the house, the second-floor master bedroom with a built-in den and a tiny but functional kitchenette in the hallway. He hasn't had a sale in a while, and the Fullers should be a slam dunk. His commission on this house will be sweet, very sweet. There's qualifying, finding a lender, paperwork, and bureaucracy, but the Fullers will qualify easily.

As the Fullers drive away, Rose turns around and waves, the look on her face exultant. Driving out of Belair Mansions a few minutes later, Carson passes the Hispanic workers. They pause to watch him driving out of the complex, their gaze on Carson, unflinching and inscrutable. It wouldn't surprise him at all if in a couple of years he was selling houses to them. A good day. He and Bunny will have something to celebrate tonight.

Carson drives along Route 1 to his new house. When Carson resigned from the force, he and Bunny decided to put everything from the past behind them. The house swollen with memories they both wanted to forsake. The rooms Bunny called a crime scene because of what their walls had witnessed after that March night. They moved a mere fifteen miles away from Paradise Glen, the Bowie, Maryland, enclave where Carson and Bunny first sunk the roots of marriage and became parents. But it feels a world away.

This part of Hyattsville is a crazy quilt. The University of Maryland sprawls, a concrete behemoth, spawning bookstores, diners, boutiques, all strung like pearls on a necklace choking the area around the campus, infusing it with a perpetual frenzy of people, cars, and motion. The campus is bordered by stretches of gas stations and budget motels. Then there are the aging strip malls whose major draw are warehouses selling really cheap shoes, storefronts specializing in used CDs, basement walk downs with neon signs offer tarot card and palm readings by Madame Rosa. These commercial throwbacks give much of the Route 1 strip the feel of a main road that fell to earth from the twilight zone. Parts of Route 1 stretch a scarred arm along this part of Hyattsville into Mt. Rainier, the liquor stores spilling over the line onto D.C.'s Rhode Island Avenue.

He's half a mile from his house. His street. His new life. When Carson stops at a light, on his left is Franklin's, a renovated, jazzed-up former abandoned building that has been turned into a popular brewery. The restaurant and brewery occupy the corner of a block with gentrified stores that are the wave of the future—a gallery specializing in Black art, an upscale women's boutique, and a store that sells high-quality antiques.

Carson's house is a five-bedroom American foursquare surrounded by a large sloping lawn and braced by front and back porches. It sits solid and confident on a half acre, set back from the wide swath of street. He and Bunny know everyone in the eight houses on the block. A month after they moved in, Danielle

Robinson and her husband, Edgar, who had once lived in their three-story frame house with four other couples in a commune, and who own a nearby health food store, hosted a backyard barbecue welcoming them to the neighborhood. Danielle wears Birkenstock sandals and colorful thick socks year-round. Her brown hair flows to her hips and is threaded through with glints of silver. Her titanic laugh erupts often on the occasions when she and Edgar come for dinner, and he tells stories about his years in the Foreign Service as a cultural officer in Istabul, Madrid, Caracas. Whenever Carson is asked why he's no longer a cop, he just shrugs, the movement implying, falsely, that he has never given the question much thought, and says, "It's a tough job."

Bunny calls the street "U.N. Central." Their neighbors include an Indian physicist who teaches at the University of Maryland. Velu Arulsamy is a tall, stately man nearly the color of coal who at the barbecue told Carson that he was a Dalit, a member of the untouchable caste in India, and of his journey from Tamil in southern India to the United States. His wife, Reeta, gave Bunny a lavender-colored sari for her birthday last year. Their daughter, Sonia, is the same age as the twins, and Bunny and Reeta shop for school clothes for the girls at Potomac Mills and go to plays at Arena Stage. Juan Martinez is a Dominican who works for the county's office of outreach to its burgeoning Hispanic population. When Carson and Bunny spent ten days in the Dominican Republic last summer, Juan's cousin was their unofficial tour guide, showing them around the island.

Carson counts Alan Powell, who lives across the street in a Cape Cod, as a friend. He hadn't seen Alan since they graduated from high school together in 1983. Alan would solve seemingly inscrutable algebra problems on the board in front of the class and then pimp-walk back to his seat and slouch his gangly frame in its confines as though what he'd just done had no significance at all.

He was a track star, but he wasn't a jock. Carson didn't know him well back then, but Alan had a reputation as everybody's friend, from the dudes headed nowhere fast to those everybody figured would one day make the school proud.

"You're Carson Blake, right?" Alan asked the day they moved in, striding with that same offbeat pimp walk to where Carson stood outside the house, extending his hand and shaking Carson's, pumping it eagerly. He was still in good shape, trim, muscular, in a fleece jogging suit that early September day. As the movers streamed past, in five minutes Carson learned that Alan was a widower raising his son, who was a year older than Juwan, and that his wife had been killed by a speeding driver running a red light as she crossed Georgia Avenue in Washington.

Over beers on the second level of Franklin's Brewery a week later, Carson and Alan talked about Largo: Principal Jackson's "Mickey Mouse" ears, and how students joned on him behind his back; the suicide of Seymour Arliss, the chemistry teacher, when they were juniors; the big fight after school one afternoon between two Black guys on the football team over Holly Calhoun, the Swedish/Black cheerleader half the boys in school wanted to nail.

Alan told Carson about his wife, how they had met at Morgan State and got married because she was pregnant. "Nobody thought it would work. Hell, I didn't even think we would last. But we did," he said wistfully. "I didn't even know what I wanted or who I was when we got together. Olivia made it possible for me to be my *best* self. You get my drift?"

"I hear you, believe me I do," Carson told him. "Bunny and I, a few years back, we went through a bad patch. I don't know what I would have done if we hadn't worked it out."

"Life goes on," Alan said. "I got a son to raise. One of my sisters told me there'd come a time when Olivia would be such a deep part of me, I wouldn't feel like she was gone, I'd know she was still here, you know, like in a spiritual sense. Well, that day hasn't come yet. Hell, I don't even know how to get there—that place sounds like it's in another dimension." He laughed quietly.

"Maybe you don't have to know."

"Yeah, maybe."

Alan has a small but busy contracting company, and Carson hires him for renovation and repair jobs on the two rental properties he owns. He and Alan talk frequently, trading anecdotes about buying, selling, contracting, tenants, owners, contracts. For all this camaraderie, these binding rites of friendship, Carson has never told Alan about the shooting. He feels it is an unexpected blessing that Alan appears uninterested in Carson's years on the police force.

Carson walks past the profusion of brash, hardy sunflowers planted below the front porch, which hover protectively over the pale pink antique roses planted in their midst. The two flowers, one so sedate, the other a bolt of botanical lightning, stand tall in the heat. Below the other side of the porch, the coppery spikes of purple leaf fountain grass whisper into the ears of the white plumes of feathertop stems. On the porch beside the glider, several pots of begonias sparkle radiant and red.

Entering the house, the cool openness of the space envelops him. The air conditioning is on low and the windows are shuttered with bamboo shades. It's a big, spacious, sprawling house of high ceilings and windows. Juwan's pictures grace the living room walls. He now works mostly in pencil and charcoal, creating scrupulously detailed images, two of which won prizes in his arts class at the Y. The twelve-by-twelve framed drawings on the wall capture faces—light, dark, shadowed, the pencil and charcoal a veritable rainbow of feeling and color. Juwan turns black into a

color not mournful or despairing but filled with depth and surprise. There is the sketch of a Black clown from the UniverSoul
circus, his face distorted by layers of makeup yet the man beneath
the mask fully revealed; a toddler asleep on a mother's shoulder,
and his sister Roslyn, her hair a mass of twisted braids, her face lit
by a bodacious smile. Carson and Bunny's friends regularly offer to
purchase the prints. Juwan always tells them, "Right now it's still
fun. One day I'll make it a business. But not now." Carson changes
into a pair of cutoff jeans, a sleeveless T-shirt, and sandals, and
thinks that maybe he'll take Bunny out to dinner this weekend to
celebrate her pregnancy and today's sale. Last night Bunny told
him she was pregnant.

"It'll mean starting over again. Are you ready for that?" she
asked.

"I can't say no to a child of mine."

"I don't know how this happened. If I skipped a pill I can't
remember."

"How do you feel about it?" he asked.

"Scared. Unsure. Excited."

"I want what you want," he assured her.

"I want this baby."

"Then I do too."

Carson assured her of this despite the ambivalence he sat struggling not to reveal. Then he allowed himself to look for a long,
eternal moment at Bunny, and he saw all that she had been to him.
He saw the face that looked at him the day he showed up at her
house the first time, a face so calm, betraying just a flicker of surprise. The face primal and determined and afraid, giving birth to
Juwan. The face that challenged him when he was wrong. The
face that has shone a constellation of love on him in the midst of
a darkness he was sure would never yield. Bunny cut her hair and

now wears it short, curly, almost boyish. She rarely wears makeup anymore, just a practiced smear of color to highlight her lips. These changes have made of her face a declaration. Carson responded to what he saw in her eyes, "We'll have this baby. Everything will be fine."

Carson pours a glass of lemonade and goes into his office. Bunny is at work and the twins are at summer camp; Juwan, at fourteen, too young to work, is volunteering at a nearby animal shelter. Carson turns on the computer and begins work on the one-page newsletter he mails to prospective buyers and sellers in the county, then calls his contacts at several mortgage-lending institutions and checks on the progress of contracts for several clients. He's an agent with Century Realty and has had more success in real estate in a year than anyone could have predicted, working long hours, making hundreds of cold calls, networking. He's not just selling houses. He is selling himself.

As a police officer, he could let his uniform speak for him. Now he's had to learn to speak for himself, to convince clients that he is the agent above all others who can make them happy. On duty as a cop, he was prepared for anything to happen on his shift. As a cop he possessed unparalleled authority. Now when he ushers a client into a new home for a walk-through, he literally opens the door to the possibility for them to change their lives. The process of purchasing a home reveals not just the state of a person's bank account but the psychic terrain of their lives.

Carson had been off the force two months and taking real estate classes when he found out that he and the county were named in a wrongful death suit filed by the Houstons. Matthew Frey recommended a lawyer who handled the case for him, and it was dropped just six months ago, when the Fourth Circuit Court of Appeals ruled that as a police officer Carson had "qualified immunity" from prosecution. He was a police officer doing his job. The job was dangerous. He thought Paul Houston had a gun and he feared for his life. So he could not be sued. The judgment brought no relief from the wearying sense of dissatisfaction that seeps into his feelings about everything he holds dear. He felt no vindication then, feels none now, but only shameful relief for having been spared a judgment that he still feels he deserved.

Justifiable, qualified, immunity, the words that have shielded him from sanction, have taken permanent residence in his mind, are a silent, accumulated sentence he has to serve despite the judgments of the courts or Internal Affairs. The words that should have freed him merely incarcerate his spirit. He has so much. But everything he should feel confident of strikes him as counterfeit, unearned, stolen from the gods.

He has confounding parallel lives, one in which the past seems to be past and the other in which he knows it is not and never will be. He still dreams about the shooting and about Paul Houston. And he assumes that he always will. How to live with a dream of such malevolent, threatening proportions and prevent it from making everything that dares to follow in its wake a fraud? There have been no more attempts to take his own life, despite sinking without warning into days-long bouts of unflinching remorse and depression, a cycle that he has come to expect to be as reliable as his most basic bodily functions. No, he—foolishly, perhaps, with more stubbornness than wisdom—holds on to his life. Maybe he can't make the dreams stop, dissolve the dark hand of perennial, persistent despair. But he has to do something. The judgment of the appeals court informed Carson that he owed the Houstons nothing, but that verdict has ironically filled him with a sense of obligation to the Houstons that is a torment and a damnation and, Carson feels, the only possibility for salvation. He had secretly hoped the Houstons would win the case, for then the county would pay a monetary judgment that, while settling little, would at least fill the black hole that he imagines every day as an ocean between him and these people, this couple, these parents he does not know but to whom he is so terribly and intimately connected.

Carson opens the bottom drawer of his desk and retrieves the folder that contains the letter, takes it out of the now-wrinkled, almost grubby envelope, and reads it. It's only one paragraph and yet it's taken him all the months since the appeals court judgment to compose, in jittery fits and starts: on a flight to San Diego for a Century agents convention, after he'd downed two tiny bottles of scotch purchased from the flight attendant hawking drinks forty-five minutes after they left BWI; sitting at 3:00 a.m. at this desk, when he could not sleep and the house was quiet, and he was afraid, and the mere soundless presence of his sleeping wife and children buoyed him with momentary courage; in his head while jogging around Allen Pond, the stunted, shamefaced epistle overflowing like lava, singeing and embedding his resolve to actually do this amazing thing that he had shared with no one.

He has written to Natalie Houston, the mother of the young man he killed. If he is to be forgiven, Carson dares to imagine it springing from her heart. Whenever he thought of writing to the young man's father, or even to both parents, it is only the mother that he envisions crafting a space in her life for the miracle he wants to make. He wrote Natalie Houston, convincing himself that she is cut from the same cloth as those D.C. mothers who found and gave absolution and by that act made God and love more than a conjecture or a hope, made them real.

He'll mail it tomorrow, Carson decides. Mail it first and then tell Bunny. Another breach of trust, faith, love—that's how she will see it, he's sure. But if he doesn't mail it first, he fears he never will.

As he places the letter in a new clean envelope and addresses it, he allows himself to think gratefully of how humble his expectations are. He is asking for nothing. And yet his heart stops, stammers for a flickering second at the thought of what could rain down on him once the letter is mailed.

Carson hears the front door open and Juwan shouting, "It's me, Dad." Hearing a pair of footsteps, Carson goes downstairs and finds Juwan and his friend Will standing in the kitchen.

"Where've you two been?"

"Riding our bikes. We got thirsty and wanted to hang out here for a while."

At fourteen Juwan stands an inch taller than Carson. Tufts of hair darken the skin above his top lip. His voice has shed its light, bubbly lilt and is deep, nearly smoky. To Carson's relief, the boy's gangly growth spurt has muted and altered the too-feminine rhythmic gait.

Will's shoulder-length dreads are an almost reddish brown, pulled back from his face and held by a rubber band, revealing a high forehead that wrinkles when he flashes a smile that dazzles like a burst of sunlight. The boy's face is open and inviting, and he's the color of caramel; his oversize shirt and baggy jeans are neat and crisp. Reflexively, Carson measures and assesses Juwan and his friends, searching always for the telltale signs. Will attends Juwan's art class at the Y. They are friends, just friends, Carson tells himself, nothing more. Still, he has walked past Juwan's room late at night and heard the sweet groan of a muffled sex dream. Juwan is fourteen, so there's no surprise in that. But Carson finds himself wondering if Juwan dreams of Will. There is the way Will's hand lingers on Juwan's arm, rests on his shoulder, too long, too gently, Carson notices, and how Will's fingers absently caress Juwan's neck as the boys sit in the family room, huddled over their sketch pads, talking, laughing about their drawings as though they are alone. Are their feelings, he wonders, hidden in plain sight?

Of all the things she thought he might tell her, these words are the most unexpected, and once she hears them, dreaded. Dreaded because of their power to unsettle and disturb the hard-won veneer of normalcy she has worked so hard to impose over the thudding heartbeat of their lives—a hard, shiny glaze that tells the world that happy endings are possible after all. She sits beside his desk, on which lies a copy of the letter he wrote to Natalie Houston, and the computer printout he's had since before he left the police force, detailing the sterile, dry facts and figures of the life of this couple she had hoped to forget and that Carson now wants to invite into their lives. Carson showed her a photocopy of the letter almost proudly, holding it out for her to take, watching her sit passive, angry, resisting, until he reached into her lap, lifted her hand, and placed the letter in her palm. Bunny is less surprised by the letter than that Carson wrote it, and when she completes it she hands it back to him, wondering how he has come to be this brave, this foolhardy, and, she fears, this dangerous. In the letter he wrote, "There's been no immunity for me. I've suffered. My remorse is continuous and it's real." He tells Natalie Houston how the desire to make amends is now as strong as the guilt, how some days it overtakes the guilt and he sees it in his mind, like a tiny distant star.

Bunny is silent for several long minutes in which, rather than speaking, she spends the moments looking at Carson's hair, thick and a bit unruly on this day and in need of trimming, the fringe of gray hairs around his hairline as uniform and lovely as lace. There is the gray hair and the gaunt slimness of his face, because of the weight he's lost. His eyes are lit as they often are now by a resilient, starry glint that she has seen in cancer survivors, who, having danced with the angel of death and refused the summons, look upon life with a transformed gaze.

"Why are you doing this now, Carson? Why are you doing it at all?"

"I don't feel like they're strangers. I never have. I killed their son. I have to live with that. This is one of the things I'm doing to try to make that possible."

"So you've been planning to do this for a long time?"

"In the last couple of months the idea of the letter just came to me, and I couldn't shake it. I have my son. Because of me they don't have theirs."

"But what on earth do you want from them? They tried to sue you. Why not leave them, leave what happened, alone?"

"That's not a choice, Bunny. It's in my life; it's in our life. Do you think I ever forget that I killed a man? I was sentenced that night. The grand jury, the internal investigation—that was all legalities. My punishment started in that mall parking lot."

"I know, Carson, but—"

"I don't know exactly why I wrote Natalie Houston. I don't know what I want, but I've got to find some way to stumble into some meaning, a glimmer of hope, and this was the only thing I could think of."

"I don't want you to be hurt anymore. They could rebuff you. You don't know them."

"But I do know them, Bunny, I do," he says with a passion that startles her. "We've had the same dreams. We've mourned the same person and wondered, Why me? Don't tell me I don't know these people."

When Bunny walks out of Carson's office, she walks away from him, trembling. Walks past Roslyn and Roseanne playing Monopoly in the kitchen and Juwan barefoot and huddled on the living room sofa, watching music videos. Bunny walks through the house that she has felt as a haven since they moved here.

In her bedroom she closes the door and sinks into the rocking chair beside the bed. She's only six weeks' pregnant, but she clutches her stomach anyway. Carson had his secrets. She had hers. She stopped taking her birth control pills. She wanted this baby. If marriage is destiny, then parenthood is too. Another reason to live. Another reason to love. Another reason to put the past aside. For her the judgment of the appeals court set them free. They had put everything behind them, or tried to, anyway.

Now she wanted a baby, to symbolize their new life. She kept thinking of their life as before and after. Before and after. Before the shooting and after the shooting. Of course she knew that he could never forget what he'd done. But couldn't they try? Maybe he couldn't forget, but because she loved him she could make them a world in which on some days, anyway, amnesia was possible. She was the one who urged them to move, who'd suggested he try real estate; everything, it seemed to her, was possible once he decided to leave the force. He'd foundered, but Bunny would never forget how she felt the night he came home and told her, "I had drinks with Vince Proctor. I don't know what I'm gonna do, but I'll be damned if I end up like him." Carson was a brooder and decision making for him a slow, methodical, tinkering process, but Bunny knew that night that he would resign, that she did not have to say any more.

Carson told her more about The Job in his final months on the force than in the previous twelve years. How once he was relieved of the boring and demeaning desk duty and reassigned to a regular shift, patrolling his district, like before he was gripped by uncertainty and fear. "I don't trust myself. I'm letting too many things slide. I'll see a driver go through a red light, catch sight of a car speeding past me, and when I start to pursue them it all comes back, everything about that night. I see the Nissan speeding past me in the dark on Enterprise Road and I'm back there, two years ago, wondering what the hell is going on, why this guy doesn't pull over, feeling exactly the same things I felt that night." He didn't wear his gun when he was off duty, courting a reprimand if he was caught, and on three occasions when he was on duty, dressed in his uniform, left for headquarters and realized he'd left his weapon at home. When his commanding officer called him into his office one day for what he hoped would be a fatherly lecture offering support rather than sanctions, Carson surprised himself by resigning moments after he took his seat.

Now they had a new house, a new marriage, and a new life. After the months of private sessions with Carson, Carrie Petersen asked Bunny to join them in the counseling sessions. It was during those sessions that Bunny discovered and confronted Carson in unimaginable ways. Carrie Petersen helped them create a language to talk about their marriage and their love in ways that exploded every lie they had told each other and perfected in order to keep the peace between them or to make it through another married day. She told them over and over that Carson had to write a new story about his life, one that wove the night of the shooting into its chapters. He had to change, she told them. And he had tried, more and more, breaking the seal on his emotions and taking an interest in every aspect of the children's lives. Now they had a life worthy of bringing another child into.

Last month, to celebrate the end of the school year, they drove to Ocean City, Maryland, to spend the weekend. Carson and Bunny and the twins were relaxing at table a few feet from the hotel pool one afternoon when Bunny noticed the stricken gaze of Roseanne looking past her, her brown eyes bulging with panic as she pointed to the pool, where when she turned around she saw Juwan, arms flailing, bobbing unsteadily on the surface of the astringent chlorinated water and then sinking fast.

Carson dove into the pool, his turquoise trunks a quivering flash past Bunny's still-uncomprehending gaze, his lean, charged body treading a thick shower of water, his arms scattering other swimming children. Carson's left arm was a stabilizing caress around Juwan's neck as he sank beneath the surface of the water and he pulled him up and to the pool's edge, where he coughed up a spasm of fear and terror. Inside the twelfth-floor bedroom suite, Carson placed Juwan on his bed and watched him shiver beneath the sheets but soon fall into a heavy, restorative slumber. In bed that night Carson wondered aloud if what almost happened was some kind of retribution.

"That's not the kind of God I believe in, Carson, and you don't either," Bunny told him.

"It's just that, what if . . ."

"But we don't have to ask that, because you saved our son."

Bunny can imagine what Natalie Houston must feel, had known it long before she watched Juwan flailing for breath and life before her eyes, a crowd of stunned strangers hearing her son's cries for help.

She isn't blind, and she doesn't care if she's selfish. Carson thinks he knows the Houstons because he was the last one to see their son alive, because he knows the value of their house and the name of their insurance company, because they sued him and they both have surely wished for some cosmic exchange of his life for their son's. But he doesn't know them—he has only just recently begun to know himself . . . again. A self risen from the ashes of everything they don't want to remember but must because it's now their name. They have a good life now. Why spoil it? In bed some evenings while she's reading a novel, Carson to Bunny's amazement and satisfaction is thumbing through self-help books. And once or twice a month he joins Bunny and the children for services at a Unity church in Bowie.

And now he wants to offer himself up as a sacrifice to a family who might be praying for *his* death. Hadn't they sacrificed enough?

1 2

Natalie Houston hasn't answered the letter. But why should she, Carson wonders, now that months rather than days or weeks have passed since he drove to the post office, parked his car, and walked up to the mailbox as though approaching a cliff that had become in his mind his destiny, willing his mind into a blur, a blank, so he couldn't talk himself out of the act. *One hundred days.* And still no response.

Carson doesn't think of what he's doing as stalking. After all, these occasional reconnaissance missions grew out a stroke of happenstance. *Luck* doesn't sound or feel quite right as an explanation for how he came to be sitting this day in the bleachers around the outdoor track of the Sports and Learning Center, watching Natalie Houston take her morning walk. His navy blue fleece running suit and athletic shoes feel like camouflage, although he wears them when he takes his own run around Allen Pond.

She's rounding the middle ring of the circular track for the third time, her strides moderately paced, matching the rhythm of her arms. The other walkers are fit, prosperous-looking middle-aged retirees, walking leisurely, waving to one another in recognition. Carson knows Natalie Houston's routine well by now. She

walks three days a week for half an hour, then goes to her bur-
gundy Avalon, reclines her seat, turns on her car radio, and closes
her eyes and cools down. She sits like this for five or ten minutes
and then leaves the track. He doesn't follow her wherever she's
headed next; it's enough that he's seen her.

For a while he felt redeemed by the small acts he had performed. He wrote the letter (and quickly forgot that it required six
agonizing months to compose the paragraph of a hundred and
thirty-two words). After he wrote the letter he mailed it. Small,
simple acts that cost him everything to perform.

After Labor Day when there was still no response, the panic set
in. Was the letter lost? If not lost, why not even a response that
damned him, that took offense at his invasion of the Houstons'
grief? This utter silence was a rebuttal and a crucible. And then he
got a listing in Heaven's Gate. Few residents of the exclusive community once ensconced in its embrace chose to leave. But Brad
and Mary Beverly were moving to Los Angeles to be near their
grown daughters and grandchildren. The Beverlys, it turned out,
lived two streets over from the Houstons.

When Carson left the Beverlys' house he drove on to Glory
Road, and as he turned onto the street, saw a woman that he knew
must be Natalie Houston coasting toward him down the driveway
of 11304 Glory Road, the address to which he'd mailed the letter.
Carson pulled in front of the Tudor next door and caught a
glimpse of her behind the wheel—it was more mirage than an image he could hold on to—the handsome, serious face a blur of the
colors she wore: mauve and navy blue. In the seconds it took her
to drive past, a momentary, precise flashback to the shooting rose
like spewing volcanic ash, littering and singeing his mind, and
continued unfolding even when he closed his eyes. He shook his
head to loosen its grip, wiped his face suddenly flush with sweat.
Yet as awful as he felt, Carson roused himself and followed Natalie

Houston out of Heaven's Gate. Carson followed Natalie Houston along the smooth blacktop roadway past one-of-a-kind houses, many of them occupying an acre or more of land. Past three couples teeing off on the golf course despite the overcast October sky and the frost-tinged chill in the air. Carson trailed her up Route 202 to Landover Road, then turned left onto Sheriff Road and followed her into the parking lot of the Sports and Learning Center. The modern glass and chrome facility was conspicuous in the neighborhood, a mixed bag of well-tended but older houses and apartments and scruffy, weathered domiciles. Like the football stadium behind it, the Sports and Learning Center, which featured state-of-the-art pools, gymnasiums, and exercise equipment, was an architectural taunt to its modest surroundings.

Parking that first day several rows over from the spot where Natalie Houston parked, Carson watched as a short, plump, silver-haired woman exiting the sports center, a small canvas bag over her shoulder, waved and called "Natalie" as Natalie Houston retrieved a bag from the trunk of her car.

The next day he returned to the outdoor track, hoping to see her again. Two days later she returned. It turned out that Natalie Houston came to the track three days a week, Monday, Wednesday, and Friday at eleven o'clock, and walked for half an hour. In the month since he's been watching her from the bleachers, Carson has been content to look, to watch her as he would a monument. Sitting in the bleachers this day, he wonders if maybe this will be enough. If he watches her long enough, whatever it is that he seeks could pass between them by osmosis. Is this the answer to his letter? He's imagined leaving the bleachers and walking behind her, but he can't stand a reprise of the awful muteness that overwhelmed him the day he caught sight of her coming out of her driveway, his choking on unspoken, impossible-to-speak words.

The NCS printout told him she's a professor. When are her

classes at the university? Carson wonders. What subjects does she
teach? She walks, he thinks, like a teacher, surefooted and focused,
faster than the amblers around her, but as though she's not just
walking in circles but gaining ground only she can see. Natalie
Houston has been walking for eighteen minutes, and Carson sees
her slow down as the woman who approached her the first day he
followed her comes onto the track. They begin to talk as they walk
and suddenly Natalie Houston laughs. How long was it, he wonders, before she could do that? She stops in her tracks, halts mid-
stride, throws back her head, and her laughter rains upward, its
echo the sound cracking open the sky around him. Carson smiles,
the movement of his lips a tiny, momentous reflex.

He's so much like Paul. How many times has she thought
this about some young man who reminds her of her son at his
best—ambitious, certain he could take on the world, *be* anything,
do anything? This has been the only hard part of advising Ian Har-
rington on his senior thesis about the novelist Ann Petry.

"Petry was really amazing," Ian says solemnly. "The same
woman who wrote *The Street* then writes *The Narrows*, and the
novels couldn't be more different. The sweep and scale of the later
book, and the almost claustrophobic quality of the first. To tackle
interracial sex and love, class, wealth, and murder and race in the
soul of a small New England town that symbolizes America, and
to do that in the early fifties?" Ian's tight, narrow eyes gleam with
a seductive intelligence as he poses the question in a breathless gust
of adulation. Natalie sits evaluating the reading list Ian's submitted
for her approval.

"I finished *Miss Muriel and Other Stories* last night, Professor
Houston," Ian continues as Natalie writes in the margins of the list
several other essays Ian can reference. "It's one of those gems like

Hughes's collection *The Ways of White Folks*," Ian effuses. "She kept transcending her patrician background and gave more dignity and complexity to her characters trapped in ghetto experiences I think than Richard Wright did. Don't you?"

"Very thorough, Ian," Natalie says, reaching across her desk to hand him the list. "I agree, but remember, Wright remained a naturalist and Petry's dramatization of the forces influencing her characters was always pretty subtle. Unfortunately that may be why Petry's oeuvre had to be virtually unearthed, and Wright remained a reference point. He was a brilliant sledgehammer who validated the need to name so much in our experience that was raw and ugly and disturbing." She hands him the list. "I wish more of my students got high on literature like you, Ian. You make me remember why I teach—to try to infect others with the passion I feel about these stories."

"You do, Professor Houston," he tells Natalie earnestly, a spasm of alarm quivering in the rich baritone voice that Natalie imagines lecturing before a class. "Your seminar is the high point of my week." From anyone but Ian, Natalie would hear those words as no more than unabashed brownnosing. But Ian's been taking her classes since his sophomore year. She's been his adviser since he entered Washington College. At a private college of generally bright students with solid writing skills, reading Ian's essays has been for Natalie a special pleasure.

Ian is a young Black male who wants to teach. Just like Paul. When Paul was killed, Ian left a book of sermons by Howard Thurman in her English Department mailbox with a note that read, "These have helped me." Helped him, Natalie later found out, when his father committed suicide in his senior year of high school.

"I'll get that recommendation letter off to Yale in the next week, Ian. I have a good feeling about your chances of being accepted."

"What do you think my backup schools should be?"

"Let me think on that and I'll send you an e-mail."

Ian stands up, and from the commanding heights of his six-foot-three frame asks Natalie, "Will you be at the Friday-night poetry slam? I'm on the mike," he announces proudly. Ian's got a "Thinking While Black" button on his corduroy jacket. His neat old-school Afro haircut and sideburns frame his rather large face and head.

"Ah, poetry slams and literary criticism. I like that, Ian."

"We're clean. In fact, we pride ourselves on not relying on profanity."

"Is the profane a concept that means anything to your generation?"

"Aw, Professor Houston, that hurts." Ian laughs and clutches his chest as though wounded.

"Listen to me. I swore I'd never turn into a midlife head-shaking naysayer yearning for the good old days. And that's exactly what I sound like."

"You and Dean Houston could come. Not too many faculty come out. If we did use gangsta rap lingo, there'd be letters to the editor of the school newspaper from all the faculty who heard an account thirdhand. Come on, Professor Houston, y'all got to represent."

"I'll be there, Ian. I'm eager to hear the rhymes of the next Alain Locke."

"I'll look for you. Seven o'clock, Tigner Hall."

When Ian walked into Natalie's office as a freshman for his first advising session, Natalie assumed he was on the basketball team. "Sorry to disappoint you and everybody else, but I spent more time reaching for books off the library shelf than dunkin'," he said apologetically. The young man has inspired a maternal affection in Natalie that, now that he's a senior, haunts her with fears of losing him.

After Ian leaves, Natalie spends another hour reading essays from her Topics class, then makes notes for her brown bag presentation tomorrow to the English Department faculty on new African writers. At four-thirty, while tossing out old files, she feels the prickly stab of hunger and pauses to envision the sumptuous architectural culinary creations she and Shirley will be sharing over dinner at the Cheesecake Factory at six o'clock. This pleasant thought is hijacked by images of the rush-hour Beltway traffic she will have to navigate to get from Washington College to upper-northwest D.C.

Finally ready to depart, Natalie opens her black leather briefcase, given to her as a gift by Temple when she received her doctorate. The stitching on the shoulder strap is frayed, and scratches and marks have been worn deep into the aged, thinning skin of the leather, which is soft and pliable. Natalie rarely cleans the briefcase, preferring the scent of perspiration and fingerprints and embedded, invisible dirt to the caustic, acrid clean of the leather polishes. She stuffs the briefcase with a folder of résumés for a junior position the department has to fill and the galleys of a novel by one of her students who graduated five years ago for which she has promised a blurb.

Opening her purse, Natalie catches sight of the tip of the envelope stuffed in a side compartment. Over and over she's read Carson Blake's letter. Her tears have burned the page. Her fingers more than once almost tore the letter to shreds. On one especially bad day, when she had dreamed the night before not of Paul but of his last moments, her palms balled and crushed the letter, and her hands tossed it into the wastebasket beside her desk, only to retrieve it moments later. The single-paragraph letter has made her a captive of the man who killed her son. She and Temple owe him nothing: not forgiveness, not recognition, not anything. Yet she hasn't thrown the letter away, and in the four months that the letter has been in her possession, she's failed to show it to Temple.

The court's ruling that Carson Blake had qualified immunity left Temple embittered and made him literally sick in the months immediately following the judgment. He developed hypertension, diabetes, had a prostate cancer scare. The biopsy was negative. He spent hours on the Internet looking up cases like Paul's, calling Quint Masterson every few weeks and asking if there wasn't some other way the case could still go forward.

Masterson patiently took the calls and only once called Natalie to express concern about Temple, telling her, "I've dealt with these kinds of cases before. It's a setback for you, I know. But I am concerned. Temple needs to put the idea of the civil suit behind him. He's still a young man, and he has many years ahead of him. You seem to have—"

"Quint, I'm as angry as Temple," Natalie said quickly. "But it's different with me. I never looked to the suit to make any real difference. I thought whatever judgment we got would be my son's blood money. Temple saw it as reparations. He feels cheated. I feel nothing at all."

"I've seen clients so invested in these cases that they got stuck living in the past. Even when there was a judgment in their favor. I don't want that to happen to Temple."

"You mean living in a past with a loved one who's dead?"

"That's not quite what I meant."

"What else could you have possibly meant, Quint?" Natalie asked icily. "How can my husband think about a future without our son?"

When Masterson failed to reply, Natalie told him, "Quint, I appreciate your concern. We'll get through this. I don't know how, but we will."

While Temple refused to accept the ruling, Natalie wrestled with thoughts that she rarely shared with him. Paul's death was an injustice they would have to live with. There was little justice on earth, even less in the courts. There was no cosmic answer, only the terrible thing that happened.

Natalie moved to this place of acceptance during retreats spent in silence at a former monastery in Germantown, Maryland. The twenty-six acres were rustic and elegant. Six elderly nuns, pale, sturdy, white-haired women, feisty and chaste as a flock of aged birds, who still wore old-fashioned habits, lived on the grounds. Natalie's room in the monastery was as spare as a cell, with a small single bed, a chest, a desk and a small lamp with a forty-watt bulb. The silence was a respite from Temple's anger and the pressing need to respond to it. Over time, the days she spent walking the grounds, huddled in the monastery library reading, picking a book at random from the library shelf, tamping down her energies, fear, and anger, overhauled her soul. She exhumed Paul in the confines of this quietude, experienced anew his spirit, absolutely present and vivid, as a cool drink quenching the thirst of her love for him. And it was in that place that she most often found herself filled with thoughts of one day meeting Carson Blake. So stunned was she by the initial invasion of the thought that she tried to resist it, convincing herself that it was merely another example of God's strange sense of humor. But the idea haunted her, tough and re-silient. She refused to stoke its life by speaking of it aloud, and yet she was soon radiant with belief that one day the meeting she dreaded, but that was now clearly ordained, would take place. Her spirit grew quietly vigilant. She was exhausted by the demands of hatred, the requirements of grief. She'd been paddling her boat steadily toward that shore day after day, and now the waters had shifted in another direction. The waves were pulling her leaky craft inexorably toward the deep end of the ocean. She did not know how, she did not know why, but she threw her paddle into the murky, enlightened depths and gave up and gave in.

Natalie had searched for words to say to describe the inexplicable. When she stopped talking, the tyranny and significance of words expired. She'd spent much of her adult life working with words, ferreting out the meanings of language, depending on her ability to summon the power of words and speech for her livelihood. But it was silence that whispered unto her all she needed to know. Natalie eased back gradually into the awesome, weighty arms of her husband's love and need. Her heart wept and bound itself into an instrument that they both could count on. There were days when she was awash in emotion too tender for expression, as potent as prayer, as normal as the gift of love and her husband's unabashed hopes.

Out of those days of silence came the idea to establish a scholarship in Paul's name in the master's of education program at Columbia. The school was receptive to the idea, and Natalie and Temple stipulated that the scholarship would go to a worthy African American student accepted into the program.

Temple had accepted Washington College's offer of early retirement and the chance to continue as a part-time administrator, which with his pension left his income nearly unchanged. Now on campus only two days a week, Temple spends time with their grandson, Darren, who lives with Lisa's mother while Lisa attends medical school at Johns Hopkins. At a year and a half, the boy's mere existence seems to them both a miracle.

Babysitting Darren one weekend, as the child lay asleep between them in bed, Natalie wondered aloud, "What will Paul possibly mean to Darren? My Lord, he's just a picture in an album, some man Lisa will tell him that she once loved long ago."

"That's where you're wrong, Nat—Paul's all over this boy, inside and out. He's gonna be tall like his father, I can tell that already. And when he smiles, I swear, Paul is in the room. Paul wasn't just some nameless, faceless seed-bearer. His imprint will shape Darren. And we're not just grandparents, Nat, we're Paul's representatives. This is the assignment he left us."

"You mean our assignment from God?" Natalie asked, grateful beyond expression for the tranquillity she heard in Temple's voice.

"I'll let you call it that," Temple said, stroking the perspiration on Darren's forehead. "But by the time I get through telling him about Paul playing Frederick Douglass in his sixth-grade Black History Month play, about how hardheaded he could be, showing him pictures of Paul with us on Goree Island, taking him over to Burroughs Elementary where Paul taught, he'll know who his daddy was."

"Is that all we tell him?"

"When he's old enough, you and me and Lisa together, we tell him about how Paul died. Ain't nothing to hide, no reason to feel ashamed."

After she read the letter the first time, Natalie wept for her smallness and the hardness of her heart. The brief, clearly tortured epistle, so inarticulate and yet so eloquent, has filled her mind with thoughts of writing Carson Blake, of one day even meeting him. This still-nascent but outrageous yearning is more than she often allows herself to think about, much less reveal to her husband. The letter pricked the skin of Natalie's desire to live in the world whole again, informed her that her work is not yet done. There's more to the rest of her life than muted perpetual grief, love of her son's child; there is also this cursed bond with Carson Blake, which he out of desperation to calm and perhaps save his own soul had acknowledged. Was this letter, this summons, and the response to it, that she and Temple had to shape, their assignment too?

Shirley is seated in a corner table beside a wide window through which she looks down upon now-dark Wisconsin Avenue when Natalie arrives. When the two women hug, Natalie takes in a whiff of cigarette smoke embedded in the weave of Shirley's pink cashmere halter-top sweater. She's a health-care professional who has tried repeatedly and unsuccessfully to kick the habit. With her big clip-on gold earrings that look to Natalie as heavy as small trees, the thick slash of black eyeliner and gray shadow, burnt red lipstick, and thin veneer of matte makeup on her high-cheekboned face, Shirley is, as she likes to tell Natalie, "prepared for anything."

"Well, you look like Christmas," Natalie tells Shirley as she removes her jacket.

"You never know where or when I might meet Mr. Wonderful."

"Love that sweater."

"Randall gave it to me for my birthday."

"The brother's got good taste."

"In clothes and women."

"Does he know how lucky he is?" Natalie teases.

"Honey, I remind him constantly." As the two women's girlish giggles peak, the waiter approaches their table. Shirley tells the cherub-faced White boy that she wants a glass of house white wine, and Natalie orders a cosmopolitan.

"You have another one of those faculty meetings, that why you need something pretty and strong?"

"No, not today. In fact, I had a very satisfying meeting with one of my best students, a young brother who's got 'save the race' written all over him."

"How young?"

"Shirley!"

"This is a new day. You've been happily married so long you'd need a passport to enter my world."

"What about Randall?"

"Oh, his days are numbered."

"I'm not gonna ask why."

"I hope he'll be as generous. But come on now, what's going on? You sounded in need of handholding when you suggested dinner in the middle of the week."

The waiter places the drinks on the table and they place their orders, then Natalie reaches into her purse and retrieves the letter, hands it to Shirley.

"What's this?"

"Just read it."

Shirley gasps as she quickly scans the letter, then takes a sip from her glass of wine and reads the letter again more slowly.

"Well, I'll be damned. What did Temple say?"

"I haven't shown it to him."

"And why not?" Shirley asks, turning as stern as Natalie imagines she is in the triage unit at Washington Hospital Center, where she's a head nurse.

"I don't know how he'd handle it." Squirming under the disbelieving gaze of her friend, Natalie looks out the window at the street below, the slow-moving snarl of traffic and the lights studding the breast of the city.

"I'd say you're crazy if you answered it."

"At first I agreed with you, but I want to."

"This is too much," Shirley moans. "If you answer the letter, that'll open the door for more contact."

"I know."

"And . . ."

"I'm going to answer the letter. I don't know what I'm going to say. I won't know until I say it." Natalie practiced this three-sentence mantra through the zoo of Beltway traffic and as she parked in a nearby lot, anticipating Shirley's reaction.

"Natalie, I've known you too long to believe that. You'll know what to say."

"Shirley, for all my hatred of Carson Blake, he was never real until the letter. It was like Paul had been killed by some anonymous force in the world. He was a bad cop. A dangerous man. A murderer. A thief who stole my child's life. But Shirley, he was never real. And as long as he wasn't real, my bitterness was a balm. When I saw his handwriting, when he told me what he's gone through, hating him made no more sense than Paul's death."

"But doesn't the letter make it hurt more?"

"I thought it would. You don't know how many times I've imagined and dreamed about confronting him, trying to make him feel everything I've felt. I counted on seeing him during the trial for the civil suit, looking him in the face, but I was denied that. I lost my son because he killed him. How do you tally whose personal hell is worse?"

"You almost sound like you feel sorry for him. You know you've got to tell Temple."

"Answering the letter seems easier for me at this point than telling Temple, not only that I got the letter but that I've held on to it for months without telling him about it."

"Well, you better figure out something to say. You owe him that."

"This could be a setback for him."

"Stop the bull, Natalie—it's had the opposite effect on you."

"But we've dealt with all this in different ways. I can't see us finding common ground on this."

"If you two didn't live in the same world, you wouldn't have come this far."

"I've known you had something to tell me for a while now." That's all Temple says after reading the letter and letting it fall onto the bed between them. He picks up the remote and turns on the

television. She looks at his profile, his receding hairline and bushy brows, his lips pursed and angry, the only sign he allows as a hint of what he must feel. Natalie rests her hand on the sleeve of his pajamas. Temple's skin bristles at her touch, a reflex that scorns her.

"I'm sorry I didn't show it to you when I first got it, but—"

"That's one thing you don't have to apologize for," he says, not turning away from the screen.

"How do you feel?" she asks.

"That I don't give a damn how guilty he feels. But what I don't understand is why you still have the letter. What on earth are you keeping it for? If he'd been anybody but a cop, he'd be in jail, where he'd have plenty of time to do nothing but write letters." For this blast he looks at Natalie, and she wishes that he hadn't.

"I'm as confused, as surprised as you are that I've held on to the letter so long. I didn't tell you because I didn't want to upset you." The words are inept, weak, an insult.

"You think this letter upsets me? Losing my son upsets me. A letter from a coward means nothing to me at all. I know you, Nat, and if you're holding on to that letter it's because you want to write him back."

"Look, Temple—"

"Whatever is happening to you, you have to go there and be with it on your own. Don't involve me. I won't answer the letter and I want nothing from the man." Temple turns off the television and orchestrates a brusque yank on the comforter and huddles beneath it, reaching out to turn off the lamp on his bed stand.

Natalie slides beneath the comforter and burrows on her side. There are nights when Paul comes to her untouched by life or death, pure essence washing up on the outer shores of her sleep. Maybe she can will him to come to her like that tonight, Natalie thinks as she closes her eyes and allows herself a shallow whimper at the thought of what she wants to do. She hears Temple snoring beside her. But no tears, she promises herself and her son. *No tears. Not tonight.*

The next morning Natalie writes:

Mr. Blake:

    Writing you this letter is an amazement to me. I could never have imagined myself communicating with you. Initially, your letter resurrected the intense feelings of rage and violation I've lived with for so long. The senselessness of my son's death haunts me every day, and every year that passes I wonder what he would be doing now if he were alive. When I received your letter that act seemed as arrogant as the way in which I assumed you had so easily taken my son's life. I wanted to destroy the letter, but I didn't. Your honesty frightens and humbles me. You were the last person to see my son alive. I am the woman who brought him into this world. I don't know what I would say to you if we ever met, but I believe that whatever you want or need to say to me should be said to me rather than written. I promise you nothing, Mr. Blake, neither forgiveness nor closure of a wound that for neither of us can ever really heal. You are asking more of me than anyone has ever asked before. More, I think, than you have a right to ask. I'm certain that I can't give you what you ask in between the lines of your cryptic yet painfully revealing letter. I find myself now wanting to see the face of the man who took my son from me. Are you willing to see the face that your actions made? The greatest discomfort that your letter has provoked in me is that I now know that you are more human than I wanted with my shattered heart to believe.

                                                Natalie Houston

1 3

The boy watches rap videos by young Black men with names like Nelly, 50 Cent (is that what he thinks he's worth?), Ludacris (is that a sly judgment on his existence?), Black men in braids and baggy jeans, sleeveless undershirts, and gold chains, bristling with attitude and anger, sublime behind the wheel of Benzes and Land Rovers, driving through ghetto streets, rhyming out loud about casual, incidental murder, death, and destruction of other Black men who look just like them. He loves school and is always prepared in his classes, and he feels deep in his heart the quiet, brave soul of Emily Dickinson and her poems that Miss Cole has them read aloud in her American literature class. He loves the way French rolls off his tongue, how the vowels play like happy children in his mouth, the alphabet, *a, be, de; je ne sais pas*, a concoction of melody and meaning that set his spine tingling. *Je ne sais pas*—how could those words, that *song*, mean "I don't know"? In algebra the hard, substantial resilience of the equations energizes him.

Art is the only elective he's got this year. When he opened the door to the classroom on the first day he saw a wall filled with prints and reproductions—Picasso's *Guernica*, the Mona Lisa, photographs of the pyramid at Giza, an African sculpture of mother and child, a mural by Diego Rivera, a collage by Romare Bearden, a darkly haunting photograph of a man sitting in a bar in Harlem by Roy DeCarava.

His classes are a respite from the raw, unfettered push and pull and tug-of-war to find a place, to become anonymous yet known, invisible yet designated by a group—ghetto fabulous, rock-and-rollers, nerds, preppies, the Whites, the Blacks, the cliques all offering shelter and status. This is high school. Ninth grade. This is what Juwan has told them.

All this, the profane and the beautiful, makes up his son's world. Negotiable, all relative, Carson thinks, a world without borders, built on quicksand. Carson feels he has been granted a passport into the headquarters of that universe on the day he goes to school for a meeting with the principal, Mr. Mitchell, not about Juwan but to discuss the house he wants to list with Carson. After the meeting Carson decides to walk the wide corridors of the modern school, its wall-high solid glass windows lit with streams of light. He passes "smart rooms" lined with desks with built-in computers. On the second floor he passes the in-progress Black history mural that fills one long wall, protected by scaffolding. Although only a freshman, Juwan has a coveted spot on the project. Carson hears a bell ring, sharp, jarring, the only nostalgic moment in his survey of the school, and there is the cacophony of classroom doors opening, youngsters spilling into the halls.

The fierce, almost strained silence of the moment before is shattered as the sound of bawdy, raucous laughter and conversation surrounds him. There is a blur of backpacks, jeans, braided hair (he can hardly tell the girls from the boys), energetic bodies. Lockers open and slam shut. Teachers stand in the doorways of classrooms, herding the students down the hall from a safe distance. A young blond teacher who looks no older than the kids he passes asks if she can help him.

"I'm looking for my son, Juwan Blake."

"Sorry, I don't know him," she says with a smile. "If you check in the office they can tell you where his next class is."

"Thanks," Carson says. He's not really looking for Juwan, has no desire to surprise and embarrass him by showing up in one of his classes. But since he's here, it would be nice to see him. Carson checks his watch and sees it's a quarter to twelve. Juwan told him he has his lunch around this time. Maybe he'll check the cafeteria, ask one of the kids where it is.

Back on the first floor, Carson is struggling to remember what Juwan wore to school. Just as suddenly as the corridors seemed to overflow with students, they are now emptying. But farther down the hall, near the end of the wall-length line of lockers, he sees two boys walking, arms around each other's waists. They walk slowly down the hall away from him, dreamily oblivious to the sound of his footsteps behind them. Their hands are fondling their shoulders, grazing their backsides. The sight of this display clenches Carson's heart in a vise of disgust. These are the last kids on earth he wants to direct him to the cafeteria, but the main office is at the other end of the hall, a hike he figures is unnecessary.

Carson quickens his stride, walking faster to catch the boys. As he nears them, a flood of recognition halts him. He knows the boys, is sure now who they are, he thinks, as at the sound of his encroaching footsteps the boys both turn to look over their shoulders. Juwan moves his arm from Will's waist, furtive, quick, but too late. "Dad, what are you doing here?" he asks in a husky whisper, his eyes bright with fear.

"What're you two doing? Why aren't you in class? What's going on?" Each question brings Carson closer to the boys, but not close enough to stop Juwan's sudden desperate bolt down the hallway, dropping his books as he runs out of Carson's sight.

Will stands his ground, stooping to retrieve Juwan's books.

When he stands up, Carson is at his side. "Keep your hands off my son." He issues the words slow and harsh, his voice a brutal warning.

Will stares at him, unflinching. "I don't mean no disrespect, Mr. Blake, but I'm not ashamed of anything. You can't make me feel that way."

"Maybe I can't, but I can keep you out of my house. I can put my boy in another school, one where you won't be," Carson says, grabbing Will by the front of his T-shirt. The boy's light brown eyes are tense and unapologetic as he breaks free of Carson's grip, pushing Carson away with a strength that reminds Carson of the boy's youth and vigor, and that he might not prevail in a showdown.

"You don't know nuthin' about Juwan. Nuthin' at all if you think we won't always be friends," Will says, his voice smug and hard, the mere sound of it implying an understanding of Juwan that Carson has never dared. "If you think you can tell him what to do, or who to be, you don't know him at all." The boy casts a withering look of dismissal at Carson, rolling his eyes, turning away from Carson in a silver-quick shift of shoulders and legs that sets in motion a studied, precise, yet dallying retreat. Carson stands in the hall beaten and bloodied by the boy's retort and the memory of Juwan's slender arm around Will's waist, his fingers dug into the back pocket of the boy's jeans.

He wants the house and the boy to himself, and takes Roslyn and Roseanne to his mother's home after school and tells her he'll pick them up later in the evening. Bunny is in Chicago for three days attending a graphic design firm conference. Sitting in the kitchen waiting for Juwan to come home, he keeps seeing the look of terror on his face when he recognized Carson, and remembers the sound of his books thudding to the floor, and the sight of him running away. *Where is he?* Carson wonders, looking again at the kitchen clock. It's seven-thirty. He'll be damned if he'll call that boy's house. If he went there . . . if Juwan actually runs away . . . how will he tell Bunny what he saw? Where did all Will's anger come from, the disrespect? He'd never seen that side of him. He'll have to tell Bunny. Maybe now she'll understand his concern. He's sitting in the kitchen, waiting for Juwan. The way Jimmy Blake waited for him. *No, not like that,* he thinks. He loves Juwan. He hasn't been the perfect father, but Juwan knows he loves him. He's not like Jimmy Blake at all. And what he wants is what's best. The boy is fourteen. There's still time.

He's at the kitchen table, mulling over, practicing a thousand approaches to his son, and yet when Juwan walks into the kitchen after entering the house, Carson can only shout, "I don't want that boy over here again."

"Were you spying on me, Dad?" Juwan asks solemnly, letting his book bag drop to the floor at his feet. He stands against the kitchen counter, looking at his father through eyes reddened from tears.

"If I spied on you, believe me, you would know it," Carson shoots back, encouraged by the charge to stand up. "That boy's arm around your waist, you fawning all over him, leaning on him. No son of mine . . ."

"No son of yours *what*, Dad?"

"Acts like that. Lets another boy touch him that way."

"We weren't doing anything wrong."

"You don't call that wrong?" Carson explodes, moving closer to the boy, striding up to him, longing to be face-to-face now, to make and win his point.

"No, it's not wrong. It can't be."

"Is that what they tell you at school?"

"Dad, I like Will. I like him a lot. He likes me."

"You don't know nuthin' about Juwan," that's what Will told him. He said it once, then said it again.

Carson grabs Juwan, who flinches and shouts, "What're you gonna do, beat it out of me? Like those people you used to arrest? Put me in handcuffs? Throw me in jail? *Kill me?"*

It is the last two words that stop Carson's heart, that when he has regained his breath pump him full of so much anger that he shoves Juwan onto the floor beside his book bag, where he lies, his face a mask of stunned outrage.

"You can say anything you want to me, but I don't want that boy in this house again, you hear? You've got a choice to make. You better make the right one."

Carson can barely find his way to the bedroom, where he sinks onto the bed. Before tonight, he didn't know anything at all about his son. What he feels. What he thinks. Whom he loves. Or what his son really thinks of him.

"I can accept what he told me, Carson, about him and Will, whether you do or not. I can't accept what he told me about your banning the boy from our house. He wants you to love him and he wants you to show it," Bunny says when Carson tells her what he saw.

"I do love him."

"Not so that he can tell."

"Did he tell you that?"

"He didn't need to."

"Look, I can't handle all this right now."

"You've got to handle it. What's more important to you, Carson, meeting Natalie Houston or saving your relationship with your son? Meeting her won't give her son back to her. It won't do anything to repair the damage between you and Juwan."

"Bunny, I've got to do this."

"Why?"

"To find some peace, maybe an answer to a question that won't go away."

"You're looking in the wrong place. How can you meet that woman, how can you talk to her, when you can't even talk to Juwan?"

"I will, Bunny, I promise I will." Carson throws up his hands defensively against the onslaught of Bunny's charges and the specter of his son's unfulfilled need of him.

"He deserves more from you." Carson hears the pinched sob, looks at Bunny and sees the tears, a sculpted scar staining her cheeks.

"When I've done just this one thing."

"It's always one more thing, Carson. First you write her. Then she writes you and wants to meet. All the time you give to her, your son needs." Now she's crying audibly, her face plump from the pregnancy, a twisted, anguished mask.

"There's enough of me for Juwan," Carson insists, hoping this edict will halt Bunny's display.

"He doesn't know that."

"What you're asking isn't easy."

Bunny wipes her eyes with a tissue that dissolves into a snowflake-like flurry of white on her chest. "Why is meeting Natalie Houston easy? Because she's a stranger? Is telling her you're sorry you killed her son easier than talking to your own? If you can't look at Juwan with acceptance, how will you love this baby? How can you love any of us, really?"

"You're going too far now, Bunny. If you have to question that after all this time, then what can I say?" Carson's last-ditch retreat into nonchalance is unconvincing even to him.

"Say that *your* son means more to you than *hers*," Bunny shouts.

"Did he also tell you he asked me if I was going to kill him?"

"Only because he was afraid of you. Can you imagine how deeply he must've been hurt to dare say that to you?"

"Paul Houston is here with us, Bunny, has been since that night. I never meant for him to get between me and Juwan."

"You turned away from our boy a long time ago. And I blame myself. I should've stood up for him before now. But nothing's been as important as what happened to you and to us the night of the shooting. That's how we've been living."

"How else could we live, Bunny? You know so much. Just answer that. How else could we have lived?"

The letter from Natalie Houston arrived the day after he dreamed about her. In his dream she was a woman of enormous stature, her face hidden behind a veil as she loomed over a minuscule version of Carson huddled like a stowaway or contraband at her feet. In the dream his greatest fear was that she would lift her veil and reveal not just her face but the history of his world and her universe. This time he told Bunny about the letter the day it came, told her matter-of-factly after he read it and said, "She's willing to meet me. I'm going to call her," leaving the room before Bunny could say a word.

It took Carson six months to write his letter, but he called Natalie Houston the day her response arrived. The waiting, and the watching, mostly the watching her, had given Carson a sense that she was no stranger, had never been, could never be.

He couldn't read her emotions on the phone. She was calm. Said nothing about his letter or hers. But when he asked if they could meet soon, she demurred, telling him that she had a number of commitments and that a meeting in several weeks would be better.

Even when Carson accepts Juwan's shamefaced apology, offered, he suspects, at Bunny's urging, he still feels bereft, stripped of all the skills and instincts that had informed his sense of who he is as a father. The transgression with Will pales beside his fear that for his son he will always be guilty, a man who got away with murder. Carson carries Juwan's damning words not in his memory but in his flesh. He and the boy have exchanged few words since that night, Carson locked behind a steely, stony, silent anger, Juwan so stunned by his outburst that he feels he deserves the punishment of his father's silence.

And yet a month after the argument between father and son, Juwan approaches Carson in his office one night after dinner. The knock on the door is hesitant and quick.

"Who is it?" Carson calls out, gruff and short, aware that it's Juwan.

"It's me, Dad. Can I come in?"

Carson tosses aside the Real Estate section of the *Washington Post* and asks, "Whad'you want?"

"Can I come in? Please?"

"Yeah."

"What is it?" Carson asks before Juwan has even fully entered the room.

Juwan stands before him like a penitent, his hands folded in front of him, his head downcast.

"If you're going to talk to me, put your head up and look at me," Carson orders him.

He's always thought Juwan resembled Bunny more than him, but when Juwan raises his face Carson sees in the boy *his* eyes and chin, and more than any mere physical trait he sees the determined, strong curve of his lips and the resolute glance with which

he now looks at Carson. Carson looks at the boy's hands, so delicate and expressive, hands that create the pictures filling the walls
of this house. Hands that find sanctuary on the page the way his
own hands find meaning in the touch and feel of wood. The sight
of his son transports him suddenly to the night he straddled Jimmy
Blake, his fingers clenched around his stepfather's neck. He'd
imagined hurting Jimmy Blake that night, hurting him bad. Only
a heart famished and river deep could contain such massive longing. Did the words Juwan hurled at him spring from a similarly
starved heart, one that he himself had denied?

"I know you said you didn't want Will here, Dad. But can I at
least visit him?"

"If I don't want the boy here, why would I allow you to visit
him? Are you being willful or just plain stupid, Juwan? We've talked
about this enough. I'm not changing my mind. And Friday night at
the Art Works program at the Y, I don't want you all up under him.
That will be a big night for you, and I don't want it spoiled."

"I'm not going."

"Oh, really? And when did you decide that?"

"I don't have to go and I won't," he whispers spitefully through
clenched teeth.

"But you've won first place. You've worked all year for this
kind of recognition. You aren't hurting anybody but yourself."

"I don't care," Juwan says petulantly.

"Well, I do."

"Yeah, about my pictures, not me."

"Why shouldn't I be proud of you? You've got a gift. If you
won't be present, then that's okay with me. Your mother or I will
accept the award for you."

"I don't want it, and I won't take it, not from you or anybody,"
Juwan shouts, storming out of the room.

14

The atmosphere in the car is as frigid as the cold November night as Bunny and Carson drive to the Art Works ceremony. Juwan and Carson have been in a standoff since his promise a week ago that he would not accept his award. Unsure whether this act is petulance, hurt pride, or a strategic move to gain the psychological upper hand, Carson has ruminated over the meaning of Juwan's decision, and sees it ushering in a shift in his world and that of his son, a shift he should have seen coming.

"I was sure he'd give in at the last minute," he says to Bunny, his words soft and humble, a gentle attempt to prod her out of the silence she has maintained since they left the house.

"Why would you think that? He's as stubborn as you. You're his father. He's your son." Bunny's voice quakes with exasperation and fatigue.

"Look, I didn't plan this, okay? I figured this would be a crowning event for him, a night we could all celebrate and enjoy instead of leaving him at home to do homework and watch the girls."

"Maybe you didn't plan it, but you've got to deal with it. Fix it. Before it's too late. Before we lose him completely."

" 'We'? He's got no beef with you. You're always on his side."

"Don't you understand, Carson? If you lose him, then I lose him too. We're in this together. It's called a family."

Driving into the parking lot of the Y, Carson chooses to ignore Bunny's verbal jab and parks on the gravel-filled area on the side of the building. As Carson and Bunny close their car doors, Carson recognizes Will walking toward them with his mother. They have parked in the same row three cars over. Carson hopes that the clusters of parents and children walking past them will hide him from the boy's view. He dreads a reprise of all the emotions the boy sets off in him. But Bunny, standing close to Carson, clutching his arm and hunching her shoulders for warmth, says, "There's Will and Sahara," as she waves to them.

Sahara, draped in a heavy wool caftan, her blond curly Afro-cut hair glowing platinum in the dark, smiles as she and Will near Bunny and Carson. Bunny drops Carson's arm and hugs Sahara. Carson mutely nods hello to Sahara, refusing to look at Will. Bunny and Sahara trail Carson and Will as they head toward the building.

Carson hears Bunny say, "He's coming down with a cold and felt awful—I thought he should stay home."

"That's too bad," Sahara says. "He hasn't visited Will in a while. I've missed seeing him."

"I'm sorry for what I said to you that day at school, Mr. Blake," Will mumbles in a barely coherent whisper, his hands dug deep into the pockets of his jacket. "It's just that . . ."

"Forget it," Carson tells the boy, speeding up his stride in order to open the door and hold it for Bunny and Sahara.

Inside the gymnasium thirty paintings and drawings hang from the walls. The canvases of the winner and two finalists are draped in cloth and lean on easels near the elevated stage. Juwan has won first prize for a drawing neither Carson nor Bunny has yet seen. Bunny will accept the plaque for Juwan that will join the other awards and certificates on his bedroom wall.

Bunny and Sahara have been chatting nonstop and sit in the second row of aluminum folding chairs. Carson sits beside Bunny, and Will settles into a chair next to his mother. All over the gymnasium parents snap photos of their children standing before their drawings and paintings. Carson waves to parents he recognizes from two years of shuttling Juwan to the Art Works Saturday program. Youngsters drift toward the table in a corner laden with bowls of peanuts, trays of cookies, and a sheet cake with green and white icing, gazing hungrily at the spread.

When the program begins, Gina Rosen, the program coordinator, walks onto the stage, taps the microphone on the podium to test it, and then thanks the parents in the audience for their support of their children in the program and asks for a round of applause for all the youngsters involved in Art Works. She's a broad-shouldered, tall woman with gray-blond hair cascading around her wide face and down her back, so much of it, the hair appears to be a separate appendage. There are brief speeches given by the director of the Y, the head of the county arts commission that helped fund the initiative, and a high school senior who attended the program years earlier and praised it for giving him a sense that art could be a career, not just a pastime.

Carson only vaguely hears the speakers. He sits thinking about Juwan. That it was the boy's decision not to accept his award does little to absolve Carson of regret and the feeling that it is he who has hijacked his son's moment of glory.

The second- and first-place finalists are called to the stage to accept their certificates. One is a poised teenage Black girl who strides triumphantly across the stage, posing with practiced perfection and a huge smile as she accepts the certificate and gazes at the audience and her parents in the fourth row, who snap picture after picture; the other a chunky, freckle-faced White boy no more,

Carson guesses, than ten, who bashfully reaches for the certificate and nearly runs off the stage. As the runners-up accept their certificates, their canvases are unveiled.

When Juwan is announced as the winner, Bunny goes to the stage to accept his plaque and a one-hundred-dollar savings bond. "My son has worked very hard for this kind of recognition, but it was only possible because of the wonderful teachers in the Art Works program. He couldn't be here tonight, but he is very grateful," Bunny says, and then turns to look at the canvas that Gina Rosen uncovers behind her.

All the mystery, the weeks of not knowing the subject of Juwan's winning picture had prepared Carson for anything. The picture, he'd felt waiting for it to be revealed, would be a reprieve from the bitterness between them. He could always trust Juwan's drawings to soothe and restore him. But the pencil drawing of Will stabs him, a direct hit to the heart. The audience begins to applaud, but Carson sits drinking in the sensuality and precision of the portrait, which blasts open his shuttered eyes. There is sadness, defiance, and wariness in the broad lips and full-on gaze of the boy who sits two seats away from him in the flesh. This is no child's drawing but a reverent meditation.

"Oh my God," Sahara gasps.

"Did you know?" she asks Will.

"He did it back in the summer, but he didn't tell me he was entering it in the competition," Will says, gushing with surprise and leaning forward in his seat to look more deeply at the picture.

"Your son has an amazing talent," Sahara tells Carson, leaning over Bunny's empty chair to touch Carson on the arm.

"Yes, yes, he does" is all Carson can manage to say.

During the drive back home, Carson asks Bunny, "Did you know about the drawing?"

"I had no idea. He kept it a secret, even from me. Carson, that picture is a confession. What more does he have to say? What more can he?"

When Carson and Bunny arrive home, the portrait of Will in the trunk of the car, Carson pushes the remote to open the garage door. As it slowly rises, as Carson backs slowly up the sloping driveway, through the rearview mirror he sees a figure crouched over a pile of objects on the garage floor and the flickering of a sputtering flame.

"What the hell is he doing?" Carson asks as he stops the car and bounds toward the garage.

"Juwan, are you trying to burn down the house?" Carson yells, catching sight of the pile of papers, crinkling as they are devoured by the flame, which leaves an icing of black soot as fragile as lace. Carson pushes Juwan away from the smouldering mass and stamps out the small yet still threatening fire.

"What is this?" he yells.

"It's the only thing you care about, Dad—it's what means more to you than I do," Juwan announces with a sinister, bemused calm as he watches his father look in puzzlement at the papers, which in their disintegration fill the garage with an acrid, smoky scent.

Bunny is on her knees, searching in her leather-gloved hands through the pile. From the heap she lifts a singed drawing of Roslyn that, when she and Carson left home two hours ago, was framed and hanging on the living room wall. Juwan's pencil drawings from all the walls in the house lie in the pile, several burned beyond recognition, the others scorched around the edges.

"Not your drawings," Bunny cries, unbelieving. "Juwan, why?"

It is only as she looks at Juwan now, still holding the picture of

Roslyn in her hands, that Bunny sees the tear stains streaking his cheeks and the pursed-lip pout that is his attempt to hold back an onslaught of more tears. The boy's eyes are as brittle as glass, narrowed and angry, lancing Carson with a fury she never dared imagine he could feel or express.

Bunny rises from the floor and reaches out to Juwan, who shrugs off her touch and walks away from them into the house, slamming the door behind him so violently the frame shakes.

"You go after him, Carson. You make this right," Bunny shouts, as Carson helps her up from the floor. "*That's* the son that matters most."

Alone in the garage, Carson turns to salvaging what's left of the drawings, lifting the smoky, smouldering pictures from the floor, dousing them with a spray of water from a bottle on the garage shelf. He grabs a broom from the corner and begins sweeping up the ashes that remain. When he is done, he stands on the spot where Juwan set the fire and looks into the cold November sky, clouds bulbous and dark, every star, it seems, vanquished.

Rocked by thoughts of the son whose spiteful actions are a plea he has finally heard, the child whose birth he awaits, and the young man whose life he took, Carson sinks to his knees. In the midst of the tremors this trinity imposes, he sees the face of Jimmy Blake, a ghostly flash riddling his brain. In the seconds of this hallucination he imagines himself on his knees before this face, not begging this time but with hands stretched wide open and revealed. Carson issues a hoarse, guttural, heaving sigh, a cleansing, terrible ache that he has borne, he feels, all his life. Tears wash over the banks of his heart yet refuse to fill his eyes. Dues must be paid, a down payment made on the future that could swallow him whole or thrust him into the ever-shifting terrain of grace. The garage surrounds him like a womb, but he knows he must stand,

and he does, with suddenly wobbly, ancient knees, walking to the car and backing it into the garage. Sitting behind the steering wheel, after he's turned off the ignition he sheds tears for himself, for his son, for the shock, surprise, and gift of second chances. When he enters the house he walks through the laundry room and into the living room, where he finds Juwan sitting on the sofa. Carson sees the walls stripped of the boy's artwork, a sight that breaks his heart, and sits down beside his Juwan.

"Thank you," he says, reaching for the boy's hand.

"For what?" Juwan asks testily, refusing to look at Carson.

"For saying what I needed to hear."

Juwan roughly pulls his hand from his father's, turns, and asks him, "Do you love me anyway, no matter what?" the words as un-flinching as an interrogation.

Everything about the question, that the boy has dared to ask it, the steely precision of the inquiry, Juwan's willingness to stare Carson down inspires Carson to hug Juwan, this act so unfamiliar and new and in this moment precious, he doesn't know how he has lived without the sensation of the boy's skin against his, the sound of his breathing, raw and waiting, filling his ears. The silence that binds them is replenishing and complete, and it takes several long minutes before Carson says to him, turning to look at Juwan as he speaks, needing to see his son's face, "You're the son I want, Juwan. You're the son I need. Any way. No matter what."

He wakes at 4:00 a.m. Sleep of course was impossible. But his sleep was not disrupted by the familiar nightmares, the face of the son, the hidden, shrouded face of the mother; rather, what little sleep he was able to find was an electrified dance on the edge of his brain. At 4:00 a.m. he lay beside Bunny, awake and wonder-ing. The letter provided camouflage even as the form encouraged confession. Confession, it's good for the soul. He's never believed that. If it's so good, why is it always a last resort?

Hours later he's alone in the house and imagines himself sitting across from Natalie Houston at twelve-thirty in the coffeehouse in the rear of an antiques shop in Old Bowie. He's never heard of the place, but she gave him directions. He sits trying desperately not to think about what he will say. About what she will say to him. Whose journey has been longer? Harder? He and this woman are explorers who've surveyed and mapped the same virgin terrain within each other's shadow, inhabited the same forest of experience only miles apart. He's dressed except for his shoes, and he looks at his bare feet. The shoes that will carry him out of the house are willing soldiers beside the closet door. It's a thirty-eight-degree morning and a chill infects the bones of his house, yet he refuses to put on his shoes. A wave of fear comes over him and he remembers everything—the fateful encounter, the confusion of the aftermath, which lasted forever, the dreams, the nightmares, pushing Bunny away, Carrie Petersen, resigning the job he thought he had to have, the civil suit. Bathed in a baptism of sweat, rankled by old and new fears, Carson considers not putting his shoes on at all.

He won't go. He can't. The phone rings, but he refuses to allow an interruption of this bout of self-pity. When the answering machine comes on, Carson hears Bunny's voice. "Carson, I don't know if you're still there. I've dropped off the kids, heading into Safeway, and I'm on my cell. I just wanted to tell you you're the bravest man I know. I love you."

A bell rings when Carson opens the door to the antiques shop. A pale woman, her red hair streaked with a startling patch of white at the top, lifts her glasses from her chest and inspects Carson when he enters. A friendly, organized clutter surrounds him—bookcases, armoires, end tables, lamps, a table full of china tea sets, stacks of old magazines.

"Can I help you?" she asks, her voice winsome, chirping.

"I'm meeting someone in the coffeehouse?"

"She's already here. I'll take you back to her."

Carson follows the woman through several other rooms, where every item, no matter how large or small, is polished, positioned to catch the eye—an old-fashioned washboard, a music box, a 1950s Formica table with matching linoleum-covered chairs, stacks of jazz albums. He's going back and forward in time with each step.

The walls of the coffeehouse are plastered with posters from movies of the thirties and forties: Bogart, Cagney, Stewart, Bette Davis, Lana Turner, it's their faces he sees first, and then he sees Natalie Houston, the only person in the small coffee shop, sitting at a table in the corner beneath a poster advertising Paul Robeson in *The Emperor Jones*.

"I'll be right back to take your order," the owner tells him when she points to the corner table.

Unsure of the etiquette for a meeting like this, Carson doesn't extend his hand when he stands before the table but merely sits down and says, "Mrs. Houston, I'm Carson Blake."

Up close, face-to-face, he sees her beauty. The short haircut that emphasizes and endorses her face, her skin taut and soft, her visage possessed of a regal repose. Watching her, haunting her every move on the outdoor track, stealing a glimpse as she drove past in her car, revealed none of this. Natalie Houston watches Carson sink into the wide-backed wicker armchair across from her, saying nothing at first, only nodding a greeting.

She stirs her cup of coffee, Carson is sure, as a way to not look at him.

"I don't know what's going to come of this, Mr. Blake," she says, addressing not him but the coffee. "If this meeting will ensure a place for you and for me in heaven. Why don't we just talk and see where we land? You led me here. Let's pretend we're strangers and that we can't imagine what we've been through—maybe that's the best way to begin."

"Sure, sure." Carson expels the agreement, allowing himself to take a breath.

Natalie Houston takes a sip from her coffee and looks at Carson over her mug's rim as she asks, "Are you married?"

"Yes. I am," he says hesitantly.

"Do you have children?"

"Two girls, who're twins, and a boy."

"How old is your son?" She asks this with a wistful smile. Should he answer the question? he wonders.

"You don't have to tell me anything you don't want to, Mr. Blake."

"He . . . he just turned fifteen."

"Would you mind telling me about him? What does he like? Who do you want him to be? Who does he want to be? What's his name?"

1. In what ways does the unfolding plot of *After* defy readers' typical expectations?

2. What stereotypes about the work and life of police officers does the book shatter?

3. How is Carson Blake repeating the cycle of abuse he suffered as a child, in his relationship with his son?

4. What role does Bunny play as a catalyst for Carson's transformation?

5. Does Carson ever "get over" the shooting?

6. How does the author handle and dramatize the book's larger themes of guilt, redemption, and forgiveness?

7. Why did the author leave the conclusion open ended?

8. Why was Paul Houston portrayed as a young man who had his own past transgressions?

9. What is the moment in the novel that makes it possible for Carson to imagine changing his life?

10. What is Carson seeking from Natalie Houston?

A NOTE ABOUT THE AUTHOR

MARITA GOLDEN is the author of twelve works of fiction and nonfiction. Her books are read widely and have been used in college courses throughout the country. For Golden, the primary purposes of her writing are self-expression and deepening and correcting the often one-dimensional and stereotyped images of African American life. As a memoirist, Golden is best known for her debut book, *Migrations of the Heart*, which detailed her coming-of-age during the political change of the 1960s and her subsequent marriage to a Nigerian. The book is an intimate look at both a cross-cultural marriage and a woman's journey to find a larger sense of identity, an artistic voice, and a place in the world. The migration of Blacks from the South to the North (*Long Distance Life*), the legacy of the Civil Rights Movement (*And Do Remember Me*), and the meaning and role of friendship in the lives of Black women (*A Woman's Place*) are among the topics Golden has explored in her fiction. In her recent memoirs (*Saving Our Sons* and *A Miracle Every Day*), Golden has used her life as a metaphor to explore topics as varied as the challenges of raising a Black male child, single parenthood, and the color complex (*Don't Play in the Sun*). In these narratives, Golden creates a kind of "communal biography," a text that creates a vibrant dialogue between her life and the life of the Black community. As a literary institution builder, Marita Golden founded the Washington, D.C.–based African American Writers Guild and is President and CEO of the Zora Neale Hurston/Richard Wright Foundation, which presents a variety of programs in support of Black writers. Marita Golden is a respected teacher of literature and writing and is a popular speaker. The Authors Guild, Poets & Writers, and the Black Caucus of the American Library Association are among the many organizations that have recognized Marita Golden for her writing and cultural work. For more information on Marita Golden, visit www.maritagolden.com. For information on the Hurston/Wright Foundation, visit www.hurstonwright.org.